DEAD MAN'S WATCH

Kay DiBianca

Wordstar Publishing

Published by Wordstar Publishing, LLC. Memphis, Tennessee

Books may be purchased in quantity and/or special sales by emailing the publisher at wordstar@wordstarpublishing.com.

Cover design by Kristie Koontz.

Dead Man's Watch / DiBianca —1st ed.
ISBN 978-1-7357888-0-7
Library of Congress Control Number: 2020918291
10 9 8 7 6 5 4 3 2 1
1. Fiction 2. Mystery
First Edition printed in the United States of America.

Scripture quotations are from the ESV® Bible (The Holy Bible, English Standard Version®), copyright © 2001 by Crossway, a publishing ministry of Good News Publishers. Used by permission. All rights reserved.

In recognition of God's greatest gifts to me:

My husband, Frank

Our son, Arthur

My parents, Arthur and Virginia Carpenter

I dedicate this novel to them and to Him.

"And whoever saves a life,
it is considered as if he saved an entire world."

– Jerusalem Talmud

ACKNOWLEDGMENTS

The more I write, the more I understand that a novel is not the product of just one person. That is certainly true of this book, and I am deeply grateful to the people who have poured in their guidance, counsel, love, and ideas to help me bring this story to publication.

I owe a special debt of gratitude to my talented editor, Mel Hughes, who adamantly refused to let me take the easy way out on any part of the book and consistently pushed me to deliver my best work. Her advice is evident throughout. In addition, Rachel Hills provided her usual outstanding plot review early on, Barbara Curtis supplied her meticulous proofreading talents, and Kathy Ide continues to offer guidance through her mentorship. Nancy Roe formatted the manuscript for print, and Kristie Koontz created the most beautiful cover ever.

There were friends and acquaintances who provided their expertise on various aspects of the book. I think especially of Rabbi Binyamin Lehrfield, Larry Siler, Mike Jorgensen, Linda and Bob Serino, Joel Johnson, Annette Cartwright, and Matthew Raich.

Some very special people read the entire manuscript, and many of their suggestions are included in the final version: Jan and Gary Keyes, Lisa Simonds, Judy Karge, Angela Mutzi, Claudio Tombazzi, Glenda Higgins, Larry and Julia Siler, Lori Altebaumer, Sylvia Duke, Teresa Haugh, and Leslie Griffin.

Finally, I thank my wonderful husband, Frank, whose ideas are sprinkled throughout the book, and whose faithful love and encouragement have given me the confidence to reach beyond my grasp.

"The LORD is my strength and my shield; in him my heart trusts, and I am helped; my heart exults, and with my song I give thanks to him." — Psalm 28:7

CONTENTS

CHAPTER ONE

Sunday Afternoon in the Park

"**A**re you sure you're up for this?" Kathryn Frasier stopped her car in the field next to the trailhead and looked over at her half-sister.

Cece Goldman gave her curly blonde hair a shake. "You know I'm not an athlete, but you won the coin toss, so I'm doing my part." She shrugged. "Besides, what can go wrong with a little jog in the park?"

"Great." Kathryn took off her seatbelt and opened the car door. "It's just one mile. Half mile out, half mile back." She gave Cece a big smile of encouragement.

"A whole mile?" Cece wrinkled her nose. "You'll probably have to carry me back to the car."

"I know you'll enjoy this. We'll take it nice and slow. C'mon, let's do a few warm-up exercises." Kate swung out of the car and stood stretching her arms overhead, gulping in the chilly afternoon air.

The western foothills of the Rockies had finally thrown off their snowy blankets, and bright green shafts of spring pushed up through the brown stubble in the field, an earthy promise of warmer days to come.

Cece hopped out of the passenger side. "Ah, spring!" She whirled around with her arms spread like helicopter blades. "My favorite time of year."

The ground was still spongy from the rain the day before, and their shoes made little indentations in the dirt as they walked to the trailhead. But the rain had drained down the steep slope on the east side to the plain below, and the upper trail was dry enough.

"I like your shoes." Kathryn nodded toward Cece's feet as she leaned down to touch her toes. "Nice color."

Cece laughed. "I know what you're thinking. I shouldn't buy a pair of running shoes because of the way they look." She stopped her jumping jacks and held one foot out. "But the salesgirl said these are good jogging shoes for beginners, so I picked out the brightest ones I could find." She wiggled her foot. "I like fuchsia, don't you?"

Kate tilted her head to one side, pretending to consider the beauty of her sister's Nikes. "No doubt you'll be the most fashionable jogger on the trail." She twisted her body from side to side. "Maybe you'll start a trend."

"Now there's an idea I could get behind. A line of runners' clothes for non-runners. I think we're onto something!" She struck a pose to show off her pink T-shirt and running shorts.

"I'll let *Runner's World* know you're available for consultation. In the meantime, are you ready to jog?"

"After you, Wonder Woman. I'll try not to slow you down."

After a leisurely hundred yards, Cece picked up her pace. "Hey, this isn't as bad as I thought it would be. There're even some wildflowers alongside the trail. I didn't realize it could be so beautiful this time of year."

"Wait until summer. The hillsides will erupt with heather. It's magnificent."

"Do you run on this trail often?"

"No. I usually run at Campbell Park, but they're holding a half-marathon here in a couple of weeks, and I want to run it as part of my training for the marathon. I thought it would be a good idea to come out here and get a look at the course."

"Can you translate a half-marathon into miles for me?"

"It's a little over thirteen miles." Kate pointed to the ground in front of Cece. "Hey, be careful. This trail is level, but I see a few tree roots sticking out. Don't trip."

"Don't worry about me. I'm very observant." Cece quickened her pace again. "I think I'm getting the hang of this. Look, I'm becoming an athlete!" As she threw her head back and her hands up in the air in a gesture of triumph, her foot caught on an exposed tree root. "Arrrrrrrrgghh," she screamed as she tumbled over the side of the slope next to the trail and skidded down the hillside. She stopped about ten feet below the trail and grabbed onto the branch of a spirea bush. "Help!"

"Cece, are you all right?" Kate started to ease down the dirt embankment.

"I turned my ankle. Can you give me a hand?"

"Hang on. It'll just take a sec for me to get to you." Kate shimmied down the slope and wedged her foot against a rock. She reached out to Cece.

"A hand! A hand!" Cece screeched.

"Don't get nervous," Kate said. "I'm right here. Take my hand."

"Not *your* hand!" Cece screamed and pointed to the ravine below. "*That* hand!"

CHAPTER TWO

What's Hidden in Hyde Park?

"There's her car." Phil Warren leaned forward in the passenger seat of Ben Mullins's truck and pointed to Kathryn's old Maxima parked in the lot next to the trail head. "Take a left on that dirt road."

He spotted her as soon as the truck rounded the turn. She was standing alone in the shadows in the middle of the trail, wearing a loose-fitting gray shirt over her running shorts, her long brown hair pulled back in a ponytail.

She was looking down at her cell phone and, although he couldn't see her face clearly from a hundred yards away, he knew the expression she was wearing. It was what he called her "Kathryn zone." Her mind had locked onto a single thought and was pursuing it to the exclusion of all others. You couldn't break into that room—she had to open the door and let you in.

Ben ignored the "No Vehicles Beyond This Point" sign, but the trail narrowed so quickly he couldn't go far. Phil jumped out of the truck even before Ben brought it to a complete stop.

She looked up, and her face transformed into the I'm-so-glad-you're-here smile she shared only with him.

He sprinted the fifty yards to her. "Are you all right?" He held her by the shoulders and asked the question even though the answer was obvious.

"I'm fine." Kate put her arms around his waist, and he pulled her close and kissed her hair as she sighed into his embrace. She looked up into his face. "How did you and Ben get here so fast?"

"We were over at Ben's place repairing fence posts. It's only a couple of miles from here. Did you call the police?"

"They're on the way."

Ben trotted up. "Sorry to hear the bad news," he said as he nodded at Kate. "Are you two okay?"

"Yes. We were never in any danger. Cece tripped and fell over the edge of the hill. While I was climbing down to help her, she spotted it down below in the valley." She pointed toward the ravine and shuddered. Then she tilted her head toward Cece, who was sitting on a log by the side of the trail with her left leg extended in front of her. "But Cece hurt her ankle."

Cece smiled a little and shrugged. "You can always depend on me to shake things up."

Phil put his finger under Kate's chin and tilted it up toward his face. "As long as you're both okay." He smiled for the first time and felt the tension drain away from his chest. "Now show us what you found."

Kate took his hand and led him to the other side of the trail. "We're not even sure it's a body."

CHAPTER THREE

Campaign Headquarters

T he first thing Mike Strickland heard when he pushed open the door to Hodges Campaign Headquarters was Jeremy Dodd's voice. *Touting the latest version of his impeccable campaign management, no doubt. Again.*

Jeremy was holding court in front of a small group of campaign volunteers. "Ah, look who's here. The Strict Man." He looked down at his watch. "You're late." A couple of young women giggled nervously.

Ignoring Jeremy, Mike nodded at the receptionist and walked into the staff meeting room.

Liz Howley sat on one side of the small conference table while Representative Hodges leaned over her shoulder, looking at something on her laptop.

"Hi, folks." Mike eased himself down into a chair on the opposite side of the table. "Checking your latest Facebook posts?"

Hodges straightened up and squared his body to face him. "Coming from you, that's a little cynical, isn't it, Mike?"

Mike knew Hodges was right. He had been in a terrible mood since the shooting at ArcTron Labs a month earlier. He couldn't escape the feeling he had stepped over a line trying to help his candidate in the campaign. He had tried to contact Kathryn several times since the tragedy, but she wouldn't answer his calls or return his text messages. After five years of being Representative Robert Hodges's chief of staff, he felt dull and wasted.

Jeremy strutted into the room, his coarse black hair in a state of rebellion against recently acquired styling gel. "Bob, I've got more great news." He held up a spreadsheet as if he were hailing a cab.

"Good, Jeremy." Hodges moved to the head of the table. "We'll get to it in a second. But Liz has been tracking a breaking story we need to pay attention to first. Liz, fill everybody in."

Liz frowned at the screen in front of her. "It's this real estate business," she said. "It looks like it's becoming an issue. We need to consider our position carefully."

Jeremy installed himself in a chair and yawned. "We don't have anything to worry about. We have the election in the bag. Have you seen the latest polls?"

Liz shot him a withering look. "Polls can change in a heartbeat, as you well know. I've been at this a lot longer than you, Jeremy, and I'm telling you this story about Alexander Hadecker has legs. It can blow up in our faces if we're not careful."

Jeremy shrugged. "Alexander Hadecker gave the campaign some money. What's wrong with that?"

Mike's jaw tightened. *Doesn't this guy know anything?* "Alexander Hadecker is trying to buy the Barringer farm so he can subdivide it into nice little plots and make a fortune. That's what's wrong with it."

"So? It's a free country. If Barringer wants to sell his farm, what's the problem?"

Hodges used his pay-attention voice. "Alexander Hadecker is known to be a cheap developer. He buys property and subdivides it into small parcels for bargain-basement houses. The problem is the people of Bellevue are dead set against anything that would tarnish their perfect utopia. The newspapers are sniffing a headline here, and if they tie Hadecker to me, we'll have a problem with our constituency. Bellevue is essential to our success. This could cost us the election."

Mike shifted in his chair. "Plus, Hadecker is from out of state. People don't like it when an outsider tries to influence an election."

Jeremy clicked his ballpoint pen several times. "Listen, we all know money talks in elections. Hadecker's money will help us fund our voter registration drive." He clicked the pen again.

Hodges shook his head. "Councilman Grayson is a formidable opponent, and he'll make an issue of our relationship with Hadecker. Mike, what do you think?"

"I think the voters in Bellevue are smart. They'll want to know where you stand on the Barringer farm issue. If we're taking money from Hadecker and you come out in favor of his buying up the Barringer farm, it'll be a major problem. We can't afford to lose Bellevue."

Hodges ran a hand through his hair. "Jeremy, didn't you tell me you were going to meet with Hadecker?"

Jeremy looked down at his hands. "We were supposed to have lunch on Friday, but it didn't happen."

Mike noted the color rising in Jeremy's cheeks and took a guess. "He didn't show?"

Jeremy glared. "Something probably came up. He's a busy man, ya know."

Liz closed her laptop. "We need to get out in front of this. Mike's the expert at solving these kinds of problems."

Jeremy's face continued its race to dark red. "But Hadecker is my contact."

Hodges held up his hand. "I appreciate your position, Jeremy, but this is a special case. Mike, why don't you set up the meeting with Hadecker and see if we can come up with a way to smooth over any rough edges."

"Sorry, Bob. I can't do that."

Hodges took his reading glasses off and let them drop on the cord around his neck as he stared at Mike. "Why can't you meet with him?"

Mike crossed his arms over his chest. "It could be a conflict of interest for me."

CHAPTER FOUR

Dead Man

Cece sat on the log and watched Ben Mullins as he followed Kate and Phil over to the other side of the trail. She recalled the last time she had been at Phil's car repair shop with Kathryn when she had noticed Ben gazing at her as she was leaving. When their eyes met, he had nodded and grinned. Something about his smile had made her feel like they were alone in the big car repair shop, like he had wanted them to be alone. She had quickly turned and followed Kathryn outside.

But this afternoon he'd hardly glanced her way before walking to the other side of the trail with Kathryn and Phil. She could make out his profile as he turned back from looking down the hill, pushing his Stetson back on his head and leaning forward to say something to Phil. From this angle, he might even be considered handsome with his straight nose and strong jawline.

But it was the comfortable way he stood, hands on hips with his fingers spread apart, that pulled her attention. There was something genuine about him. Unaffected. His hands were large and muscular, those of a man who made his living with them. And yet the fingers were long, like those of a pianist. Quite a combination. Power and finesse.

As if he could feel her studying him, Ben turned toward her, and Cece felt that same sense of being alone with him. She looked down and brushed at the dirt on her leg.

* * *

Sirens sounded close by. Within a minute, an unmarked car followed by two police cruisers pulled up. Police Commissioner Blake got out of the first car, and a small group of uniformed officers trotted behind him. "Kathryn," he said and tipped his fedora to her. He shook hands with the men. "What's all this about a body?"

Kate pointed over to the hillside. "We don't know if it's a dead person, but we thought we should call you before we did anything."

"Wise decision." Commissioner Blake was not a big man, but there was a quiet authority about him. He followed Kathryn over to the side of the trail and squinted to see what she was pointing at. "Simon, take a look, but be careful. This could be a crime scene."

The policeman scrambled down the hill into the ravine and lifted the branches of a bush from which a man's hand protruded. He looked back at Blake and made a thumbs-down sign.

"Secure this area, Charlie." Blake turned to the officer standing beside him and made a sweeping gesture with his hand. Then he spoke to a third officer. "Dev, call for the ambulance. Make sure they alert the medical examiner."

As two of the officers wrapped yellow tape around the trees to block the trail, Kate followed the commissioner to the other side of the path where Cece was still sitting. Blake put his left foot up on the log and took a small notebook out of his shirt pocket. "Tell me everything, Cece, just like it happened."

"There's not much to tell." She looked up at Blake and shrugged. "Kathryn and I were jogging along the trail. I guess I wasn't paying much attention, and I tripped over a tree root and fell down the side of the slope. While Kathryn was coming down to help me, I spotted the hand."

Blake looked at Kate. "That's about it," she said. "I helped Cece back up to the path and called the police. Then I called Phil."

* * *

As Blake, Phil, and Kathryn walked to the other side of the trail to watch the operation in the ravine below, Ben stayed next to Cece. He towered over her. "You okay?" he asked, his dark gray-blue eyes intent on her face.

"I'm fine," she said.

He reached down and untangled something from her hair and held up the tiny green sprig with a blue flower. "Looks like you picked up a little souvenir from your fall." He twirled it around between his fingers. "It's a forget-me-not." He held it out to her. "Want to keep it?"

"Heck no. I don't want any reminders about today," she said and shivered.

Ben put the flower in his pants pocket. "Are you cold?"

"No. I'm okay."

"You're shaking. Here." He took off his hat and began to tug his sweatshirt off over his head. As he pulled it up, it lifted his T-shirt that was underneath exposing his midriff of ripped abs on a tight body.

Goodness. He could be on the cover of a fitness magazine. Cece felt her cheeks warming. She turned her head and pretended to pull at the seedlings growing out of the log.

"Here you go. Put this on. It's not great—we've been working outside all day. But it'll keep you warm until we can get you out of here."

"No. You keep it. I'm okay. You'll be cold without your shirt."

"Don't be silly. You need this more than I do." He handed it to her in a wad.

Cece pulled the dark brown sweatshirt over her head and lifted her hair out of the neck hole. The shirt smelled of earth and pine and sweat. And something else. Leather? "Thanks."

Ben looked down at her with a bemused expression. "I'd say it's a few sizes too large." He knelt beside her, straightened the sleeves that were twice as long as her arms, and rolled them up. "That's better. Now let's have a look at that injury." He cradled her foot in his hands. "Looks like you sprained your ankle. It's beginning to swell. I can tape it for you. I've got some sports tape in the truck."

When he returned, Cece was wiggling her foot.

"Don't move it," he said. "Keep it stationary."

"Are you a medical professional?" Cece asked and immediately regretted her tone. She had meant it to be funny, but it came out snarky.

Ben stopped unwinding the tape and looked at her. Even in the fading light she could see his lips turn up at the edges. "No," he drawled, "but I know enough to take care of you."

Cece opened her mouth for a quick comeback, but nothing came out.

"Sorry," he said as he knelt beside her again. "That didn't sound right." He continued to unroll the tape. "What I meant to say was, I know enough to take care of your foot." The lines around his eyes crinkled as he grinned at her again, and Cece wondered what he really did mean.

Ben gently removed her shoe and wrapped her foot with the tape. Then he put the shoe back on and laced it up tight.

An EMT truck pulled in and they all turned toward the men and women piling out of it.

"I want to see what they're saying." Cece swayed when she tried to stand. Ben put his arm around her waist and helped her as she hobbled to Kathryn's side.

Blake quickly filled the emergency workers in on the situation. "It'll be dark in an hour or so. You should be able to remove the body as soon as my men finish conducting their search. We'll put guards on the scene to prevent anybody from fouling it."

Blake stared toward the body as the EMT crew made their way down the slope. "We don't normally see this kind of thing in Bellevue. I wonder who the poor guy was."

Phil followed his gaze. "I think I know who he was."

CHAPTER FIVE

Flat Tire

"**Y**ou know him?" Commissioner Blake looked in surprise at Phil.

"Not exactly. But I think he was the guy who came into the shop a few days ago with a flat tire and asked us to replace it. I recognize the jacket." He pointed down to the loud blue and yellow plaid sports jacket that had become visible on the body. "Nobody in Bellevue would wear a jacket like that."

"Good eye," Blake said. "What's his name?"

Phil rubbed his chin. "Sorry, I don't remember. But we should have the paperwork at the shop and his name would be on the invoice. You want to drive over there with me and have a look?"

Blake nodded and called down to his officers. "I'm going to accompany Phil to his auto repair shop to see if we can get some information on the victim. You guys know what to do here. Call me if you find anything I need to know about." He turned back to Phil. "Let's go. I'll take the squad car and follow you."

Kate put her hand on Phil's arm. "I'm coming too. Phil can ride with me."

Cece limped closer. "Me too," she said.

"No way, little one." Ben took her arm. "You shouldn't be on that ankle. I'll take you to the twenty-four-hour minor med to have your foot X-rayed, then we'll go over to my place and put ice on your ankle. Kathryn and Phil can come by when they finish at the car shop."

* * *

"Let's see. I think it was Thursday when he stopped in." Phil flipped through the files on his receptionist's desk. "And I'm pretty sure he was driving an expensive ... ah, here it is." He pulled a file out of the stack and opened it. "Yep. It was a 2009 black Jaguar XJ—last year's model." He handed the paper to Blake.

Blake pointed to the customer's name on the form. "Alexander Hadecker. I got a call from one of my officers at the scene when I was on my way over here. They recovered the wallet and that's the name on the driver's license. Can I get a copy of this?"

"Sure." Phil took the paper and walked to the copy machine.

"Do they know what happened?" Kate frowned. "How he died?"

"The medical examiner was there and said it looks like a gunshot to the chest."

"He was murdered?"

"That's a preliminary conclusion and off the record. He'll have to do an autopsy."

Kate leaned against the side of the desk. "If there was no car, does that mean somebody killed him and stole his car?"

Blake nodded. "I'm guessing it was a robbery. My officers told me the victim didn't have any belongings on him. There was no cash or credit cards in the wallet, just the driver's license. Picked him clean as a turkey before Thanksgiving dinner. They even took his watch."

Kate frowned. "How do they know he was wearing a watch?"

"The medical examiner said there was a pale strip around his left wrist that implies he had a watch, but it's not there now."

"Maybe he just wasn't wearing it when the robbers stopped him," she said.

"Could be. Most people wear their watches all the time, though."

Phil handed the commissioner the copy of the invoice. "Why would somebody steal the cash and credit cards but leave the wallet?"

"I've heard of this before. Probably a young, inexperienced thief looking for money to buy drugs. Holds up a victim, demands money. He grabs the cash and credit cards and anything else he can put his hands on, but then gets scared, kills the victim, and runs. In this case, drove off."

Phil put his elbow up on the filing cabinet. "So if you find the car, you have a lead on the murderer?"

"Yes." Blake took a package of Life Savers out of his pocket and popped one in his mouth. "We'll put out an APB on the car. If we're lucky, we'll find it and enough evidence to track down the murderer. But the medical examiner said time of death was a day or two ago. It's hard to tell because of the rain, but that's time enough for the murderer to be long gone by now. He could be anywhere."

"And if you don't find the car?" Phil knitted his brows together.

"That makes it a lot harder. Especially since Hadecker isn't from around here. My guys told me the license listed Curtisville as his home. That's in another state." Blake sighed. "I have a bad feeling about this one."

Phil looked at the copy of the invoice he was holding. "Did they find his cell phone?"

"No. Nothing but the wallet."

Phil held the invoice up. "We have his cell number. It's on the invoice." He pointed to a line. "We called him when we finished the work."

Blake slapped his hands together and rubbed them. "Good for you, Phil. You just made our job a lot easier." He pulled his phone out of his pocket and hit a few keys. "Simon, I got the victim's phone number from Phil Warren." He read the number off the invoice. "See what you can find out about what calls he made or received in the last few days. Check the hotels in Bellevue to see if he was staying in one of them." Blake clicked off his phone.

"Would it help to see a video of him?" Phil asked. "We have a security loop on the outside of the building that should still be available, and it might show him when he left the shop to get a cup of coffee."

"It sure would help!" Blake's face brightened, and he rubbed his hands together again.

Phil led Kate and the commissioner into his office and turned on his desktop. "It'll take me a minute to get set up." He handed the folder to Kate. "Kathryn, take a look at the invoice and find the date and time stamp when he arrived. It'll make it easier for me to locate the video."

Kate scanned down the paper. "Here it is. Thursday, 3:20 p.m."

"Perfect. I'll start the video at about 3:25. Let's see if we pick him up."

While Phil tapped on his keyboard, Kate and Blake bent over his shoulder to get a better look at the screen. Phil fast-forwarded the video until they saw a man wearing a plaid jacket and walking away from the building. He stopped the recording and backed it up. "There's your man."

The three watched the man's back as he walked away from the camera. He pulled at the cuffs of his shirt and readjusted his lapels as he walked. He took a pair of sunglasses out of his pocket and put them on. Then he turned to the left, out of sight of the camera.

Phil backed the recording up again. "Not much to go on there. You can't even see his face."

"At least it's something." Blake crossed his arms over his chest. "You don't happen to have a video of him returning to pick up his car, do you?"

Phil rubbed the back of his neck. "No. I remember he asked if somebody could bring his car over to the coffee shop since he'd already paid for the tire. It's just a couple of blocks from here, and one of my guys was keen to drive that Jaguar, so we delivered it to him. He didn't come back. This is the only video we have."

CHAPTER SIX

Ben's Ranch

"Thanks for taking me to the minor med place." Cece smiled at Ben as he turned his truck onto a long narrow road lined on either side with burr oaks that laced their limbs together overhead. "It's good to know I don't have any broken bones."

"Glad it wasn't anything serious." They drove in silence for a few minutes until the road broadened to a large open area. "Here we are." He parked and turned off the ignition.

Cece craned her neck to see. Exterior lights illuminated a long, low ranch house constructed of Colorado stone. A front porch extended the entire length of the house, and Cece could make out rocking chairs and a swing on it. A red barn stood to the right side of the house and several corrals fanned out around it. "This is your place? It's beautiful!"

"Thanks. I like it."

Cece leaned toward the dashboard to get a better view. "That's an awfully big house for one person though, isn't it?"

"Well, I'm a big person." He grinned and walked around to the passenger side of his truck, lifted Cece out, and set her gently on the ground. "Don't put any weight on your bad ankle. Lean on me."

Cece held onto his arm as he led her slowly toward the front of the house. When she tried to put her foot on the first step leading to the porch, she backed off. "Ouch. It hurts more than I thought it would. I'm not sure I can make it up the stairs."

"Here, take this." Ben handed her a key. "Hang on tight," he said as he scooped her up in his arms and carried her up the steps and across the wide porch to the front door. She could feel his heart beating as he held her close to his chest.

"You'll have to unlock it." He nodded toward the door. "I'm fresh out of hands."

Cece managed to get the key into the lock and turn it. They pushed the door open and entered the house.

Despite being enormous, the front room had an intimate, inviting atmosphere. Dark paneling on the walls reflected the flames from the fire in a stone fireplace that gave the room a romantic, mysterious look. The right side of the room was open to a dining area and the left side was walled with bookshelves. There was a brown leather sofa in front of the fireplace and books stacked on the end tables.

"Benjamin, is that you?" a female voice called from another room.

"Yes, Mattie. It's me," he answered.

Cece's blue eyes opened wide. "Who is that?"

"It's Mattie. The woman who lives here with me."

He's carrying me around while his girlfriend is here? Cece tried to wiggle out of his arms. "I think I can walk now," she said as she pushed against him.

"Whoa. Take it easy." He took a few quick steps across the room and deposited her on the sofa. Then he stood with his hands on his hips and frowned at her. "You shouldn't squirm like that. I could've dropped you. Then you'd have another sprained ankle to worry about."

CHAPTER SEVEN

Mattie

Cece tugged at the bottom of Ben's sweatshirt she was still wearing and sat stiff and upright on the couch, waiting for the girlfriend to appear.

Instead, a short, wide woman waddled in from the back room. She wore a bright blue apron over her shift, and her face was flushed as if she'd been cooking in a hot kitchen. Her gray hair was tied back in a bun.

"Well, who is this?" she asked in an Irish brogue. She stared at Cece while wiping her hands on her apron.

Self-satisfaction etched itself into Ben's face as he leaned against the mantel over the fireplace. "Mattie, this is Cece Goldman. She sprained her ankle and I brought her here while we wait for Phil and Kathryn. Cece, this is Matilda O'Shaughnessy, my housekeeper, who keeps the house in good shape and tries to straighten me out too."

Mattie gave him a dismissive wave of her hand. "That's an impossible task." Then she smiled at Cece and offered her hand. "I'm proud to meet you, Cece. Please call me Mattie." She stooped down in front of the couch. "Let's see your ankle." She leaned in and gently touched Cece's foot. "Does it hurt much?"

"No, it's just a little sore to walk on."

"I'll get a bag of ice." She stood and gestured toward the couch. "You sit still and put your leg up there. We want to keep your foot elevated." She pointed at Ben. "Now you make sure Cece takes care of that foot."

"Yes, ma'am." Ben gave a mock salute before Mattie turned and toddled back the way she had come.

Cece looked up at Ben. He had a playful expression on his face. Did he mean to throw her off guard by telling her the voice belonged to the woman who lived with him? Was he one of those men who liked to tease women but never got serious?

Ben stood in front of the couch with his hands stuffed in the pockets of his blue jeans and smiled down at her. "I guess we'll have to get married," he drawled. "I've already carried you over the threshold."

Cece smiled back. *I can play this game too.* "Thanks for the ride," she said, "but I can't marry you. You're not my type."

Ben didn't so much sit, but rather sprawled on the other end of the couch, his left foot on the floor, right knee resting on the edge of the cushion "How do you know I'm not your type?"

"It's the cowboy boots." She pointed to his feet. "Cowboy boots mean you're an outside person. You probably like sports and stuff like that. I'm an inside person. I like books and movies and plays. And besides, I saw horses outside in your corral. I hate horses."

Ben took his cowboy hat off and carefully laid it on the table in front of the couch. "I can be an inside person." He pointed to the bookcases at the end of the room. "I love to read."

Cece tilted her head and looked in admiration at the bookcases. "You have a lot of books, that's for sure." She turned back to him. "But I didn't know cowboys could read."

"Ouch." Ben's smile disappeared. "I didn't know pretty blonde-haired ladies could be rude."

Cece felt her face grow hot and she hiccuped. "I'm sorry. That was disrespectful of me. Sometimes I get carried away trying to be clever and it comes out all wrong. I didn't mean it." She pressed her lips together and then blurted out, "I don't hate horses either.

I'm just scared of them." *And I can't believe I'm falling all over myself apologizing to this guy. How did that happen?*

"I'll accept your apology on one condition." Ben stretched his arm over the back of the couch and gave her a crooked grin. "As long as you agree to come for a ride with me one day. I have a beautiful little mare, as sweet and calm as a newborn kitten. You'll love her."

Cece wrinkled her brow. "I'm not sure I can promise that, but I promise I'll think about it."

Mattie returned with a bag of ice wrapped in a dish towel. "Here you are. Let's take your shoe off and put this on. It'll keep the swelling down and help it heal." She laid a bath towel on the couch, gently removed Cece's shoe and wrapped her ankle with the ice. "Is it too cold?"

"No. It's fine. But I'm sorry to put you to so much trouble."

"Oh, it's no trouble at all." Mattie fussed with an elastic bandage to secure the ice in place. "It's nice to have company in this big house. I don't get to meet a lot of Ben's friends." She shot a disapproving look at Ben as she stood.

Ben reached out and caught her hand. "Now, Matilda Claire, I bet you have a kitchen full of wonderful chow we can dig into." He turned to Cece. "You're in for a real treat. Mattie is the best cook this side of the Atlantic Ocean. Maybe both sides. When Phil and Kathryn come, we'll all have dinner."

"That's very kind of you, but I don't want to impose. Besides, you weren't expecting to have to feed an entire group."

Mattie waved her hand at Cece. "Pshaw. It's no trouble at all. And I want you to stay. I have a big shepherd's pie casserole in the oven and it would be a real pleasure to have some female company for a change. The only women I ever get to talk to around here are the Rutterman sisters who live on the next ranch down the road. They're spinsters. In their eighties. Nice enough, but I sure could use some younger company now and then."

Ben put his arm around Mattie. "Great. It's settled. I'll call Phil and let him know we'll all have dinner here." He turned back to Cece. "In the meantime, would you like something to drink? Soft drink or glass of wine?"

"I'd love a glass of wine."

Ben and Mattie disappeared into the kitchen while Cece looked around the room. The picture over the fireplace caught her attention. It showed a small boy astride a dapple-gray horse. A young girl stood in the foreground, holding the horse's bridle.

Ben returned with two glasses of white wine and Mattie was right behind him with a plate of homemade biscuits and spread. "Sustenance," she said and disappeared into the kitchen again.

Ben offered the plate to Cece. "Be careful," he said. "Part of Mattie's nature is to provide more food than anyone could possibly eat. She'll chase you around the room with a spoon of Irish stew if you're not careful."

"She seems wonderful." Cece took a bite of biscuit. "Umm. This is fabulous. Sweet and savory at the same time. Now, Ben Mullins, I want to know what books are on those shelves."

CHAPTER EIGHT

Shakespeare at the Ranch

"**H**ere ya go." Ben dropped an armful of books onto the couch next to Cece. "Tell me what your preference is."

Cece took the top book and held it in front of her. "*Persuasion.* Now you're talking my language."

Ben sat on the other end of the couch and held up one of Mattie's biscuits. "Ah yes, Jane Austen. All about baking misconceptions into the perfect Irish biscuit. Sweet and tart at the same time."

Cece shook her head, put the book in her lap, and picked up the next one. "*The Complete Works of William Shakespeare, Volume One.*" She looked up in surprise. "You like Shakespeare?"

"Is that another of your misguided opinions about cowboys? We can't like Shakespeare?"

Cece bit her lower lip and tried not to smile. "No. I didn't mean it like that. You just don't look like the Shakespeare type, that's all."

"Okay, so what's a Shakespeare type look like? Do I have to wear those funny balloon pants and tights?"

Cece couldn't help herself. She laughed out loud. "No, but I sure would like to see you in costume with the cowboy boots."

"'The apparel oft proclaims the man.'"

Cece put the book down and nodded in appreciation. "That's from *Hamlet*."

"'Tis true."

"So you do know something about Shakespeare." She leaned back against a throw pillow. "You're pretty smart. But then, 'Ignorance is the curse of God.'"

"*Henry the Sixth*." Ben shook his head. "If we're going to play this game, you'll have to give me something harder than that." He took a bite of his cookie. "Kathryn tells me you're an actress. Have you performed Shakespeare?"

Kathryn has talked to him about me? "Last year I played Helena in *All's Well That Ends Well* in Denver and received good reviews." She fingered the lettering on the book. "One of the directors of the Atlanta Shakespeare Festival saw the play and asked me for my credits. He said he could see me as Katherina in *The Taming of the Shrew*." She looked up and hugged the Shakespeare volume. "It would be a dream part for me. I hope I'll hear from him soon."

A crafty grin slid across Ben's face. "I can see you as Katherina. Maybe I could play ..."

The doorbell rang.

"Come on in," Ben called out.

Phil and Kathryn pushed the big oak door open and entered.

Ben stood. "Hey. It's about time. Mattie's been loading up the table with food, and we were waiting for you."

"Oh, boy." Phil rubbed his hands together. "One of Mattie's meals. I'm about starved."

Kathryn walked to the front of the couch and looked down at her sister. "You okay? How's the foot?"

Cece picked her foot up off the couch. "No broken bones, just a sprained ankle. The folks at the med center said I should take it easy for a day or two."

"C'mon, pretty one." Ben held his hand out for Cece to take. "I'll help you over to the table."

Mattie came in from the kitchen with a basket of fresh bread and added it to the array of food laid out.

Ben sat Cece down in a chair and put his arm around Mattie's shoulders. "Kathryn, I don't think you've met Mattie. Matilda O'Shaughnessy, meet Kathryn Frasier. Kathryn, Mattie is the best cook on the planet."

Mattie's eyes sparkled. "You stop that nonsense, Benjamin." She turned to Kate. "Kathryn, I've heard a lot about you from Phil." She giggled. "He seems to think pretty highly of you."

Kathryn smiled back at her. "I think pretty highly of him too."

"Well, I'm real happy all my favorite people are here in one place and I can give you some good food to eat. Now sit down and enjoy."

"Aren't you joining us?" Phil asked.

"No. I ate my dinner hours ago. I can't wait around for dinner like you young folks."

* * *

"This is the best food I've ever tasted." Kate took a last bite of shepherd's pie.

"Me too," Cece said. "Makes me forget all about my sore foot."

"I told you she's the best." Ben sat back in his chair and pushed his plate away. "So, Phil, tell us what you found out from Commissioner Blake."

Phil gulped down a swallow of water. "They identified the man. His name is Alexander Hadecker. You probably heard of him. He was the real estate developer who wanted to buy the Barringer farm and subdivide it into lots for cheap housing."

"There was an article in the paper about him a few days ago." Ben walked over to a basket by the fireplace, took out a newspaper, and shuffled through it. "Here it is. Listen to this." He cleared his throat and read from the paper. "The citizens of Bellevue are up in arms about the proposed development of a major tract of land that could result in changes to the nature of the town. Bellevue resident Jonathan Katz, president of a new organization dubbed Keep Bellevue Beautiful, has indicated he will challenge the move in court. After meeting with the Bellevue town council recently, Katz stated, 'I won't allow Mr. Hadecker to ruin the charm of our beautiful city.'"

"Wow," Cece said. "That sounds like a threat."

Ben handed her the paper. "I don't think so. Sounds more like a bantam rooster ruffling up his feathers to scare the chickens." He turned back to Phil. "What else did Blake have to say?"

"The commissioner said it looks like Hadecker was murdered—shot in the chest. He thinks it was a robbery gone wrong."

Cece looked up from the paper. "Murdered? How awful. What do you think, Kathryn?"

"I'm not sure. The robbery thing makes sense. It would explain why they didn't find his car. But then, Alexander Hadecker had a lot of opposition in Bellevue. Somebody could have decided to take matters into their own hands. I wonder why they didn't get rid of the body."

"That supports the robber theory," Phil said. "The robber dumped the body under a bush and took off, trusting he could get away before the body was found. Blake thinks the murderer could be far away by now."

Cece put the paper back on the table. "Okay," she said, "let's take a vote. Robber or non-robber. Ben, what do you think?"

"Definitely robber. What about you?"

Cece considered for a few seconds, then said, "Non-robber."

Ben chuckled. "I had a feeling you'd take an opposite point-of-view to me. What about you, Phil? Robber or non-robber?"

Phil rubbed his chin. "Robber. Kathryn, what do you think?"

"The robber explanation makes sense, but maybe it's too neat. Everything fits together perfectly. And it would make it easy for the police to throw up their hands and say it can't be solved. I vote for non-robber."

CHAPTER NINE

Police Headquarters

"**M**ornin', boys." Commissioner Blake balanced a cup of coffee as he pushed open the door to the office of Detectives Carlioni and MacMillan. He put his cup on Carlioni's desk and took a seat. "Any news for me today?"

"You bet we've got some news, boss." Carlioni picked up a folder from his desk and handed it to Blake.

Blake opened the file and flipped through the pages. "Real estate developer. Fifty-two years old, married, no children." He looked up. "Did you contact his wife?"

Carlioni shook his head. "We tried. I called the phone number you gave Simon. It just rolled over to a generic message, but we found another number that was his home phone. I called it and talked to his housekeeper. She said his wife is in Paris."

"Paris? As in Paris, France?"

"Yeah. She has her phone with her. I got the number. I figured you'd want to call her."

"Did the housekeeper have any information about Hadecker?"

"She said he left home early last Thursday morning to drive to Bellevue. She remembers him saying he was meeting with some folks about the Barringer farm issue, but she didn't know anything else about his trip or when he planned to return home."

"Did you talk to the Barringers?"

"We followed up with Mr. Barringer. He said they were supposed to meet with Hadecker on Saturday, but he never showed."

"I guess we know why." Blake shuffled through the papers in the file. "Did the housekeeper have any other information that could help us?"

"She gave me Hadecker's cell phone number. It's there on the sheet. It's not the same one you gave Simon. We called the one she gave us, but it rolled over to a voice message."

Blake squinted at the number. "Hmm." He took a sheet of paper out of his pocket and unfolded it. "Here's the repair order from Phil's shop. So he had two cell phones. Mac, can you get records for these phones?"

"Already done, boss." MacMillan handed Blake a list. "Here's the list of calls made to and from the cell phones and his home phone for the last four days. We also found out he had checked into the Bellevue Hotel Thursday and there were a couple of calls to his room. The list shows the numbers and owners of the other phones."

Blake scanned the list and read the names out loud. "Warren Repair Shop. That's Phil's place. We know about that one. Hodges Campaign Headquarters."

"We're going to pay them a visit this morning," MacMillan said.

Blake continued down the list. "Stan Palmerton? Who's he?"

"Private detective. He's one of the calls to the hotel."

"I'd like to be in on that visit," Blake said. "Last one is Brad Lassiter. Any information on him?"

"He works for the phone company. We called their offices this morning and they said he's out on a job, but he usually goes home for lunch, so we figured we'd drop by his place around noon today."

Blake eyed the paper. "He lives on Oak Leaf Lane. That's in my part of town. I'll go over with you guys, then I'll go on home for lunch with the wife afterward."

"Thanks, boss." Carlioni took the folder Blake held out to him. "But you've got your own work to do. Me and Mac can handle this."

"I know you can, but I want to be involved in this thing every step of the way. The mayor has already called me three times." He paused and rubbed his eyes. "If I can show him I'm personally working the case, maybe he'll give me a break."

"Okay. We'll run over to the Hodges Campaign Office now, and we'll meet you at Lassiter's house at noon." Carlioni slapped the folder down on his desk. "Don't worry, boss. We'll get this thing figured out fast."

"I sure hope so." Blake stood and stretched. "But first I have to call Hadecker's wife. This is part of the job I really hate."

"You want us to leave the room while you call?" Carlioni asked.

"No, I'll make the call from my office. Carli, ask Officer Fioni to meet me in my office in five minutes. I'd like a female to be present when I talk to his wife. Maybe she can help me find a delicate way to let her know her husband is dead."

CHAPTER TEN

Who Is Brad Lassiter?

"C'mon, Barkley." Kate got out of her car, and her sable-colored border collie bounded out behind her. "Let's check on our roomie." She opened the door to her house, and Barkley trotted over to the couch and put his head on Cece's arm.

Cece dropped her book in her lap and patted the cute dog's head while he thumped his tail on the floor. "Welcome back, buddy." She looked up at Kate. "How was your run?"

"Very good. It was my last ten-miler before the half-marathon in a couple of weeks. How're you feeling?"

"Better. I tried out your kinestatic treadmill, and I could walk without limping. But I thought I'd lie around for a few days to get as much sympathy as possible." She put the back of her wrist on her forehead in mock distress.

"Ha! Good luck on that one, sister." Kate sat on the edge of the couch and began taking off her running shoes. "Anything interesting happen around here while I was gone?"

"The mail came. That's always exciting." Cece pointed to a small stack of papers on the coffee table. "Just some ads."

"No letter from Atlanta?"

"No. They must be getting close to casting for the Shakespeare Festival, though. I hope I'll hear something soon."

"I know it would be great for you, but I'd hate to see you go to Atlanta. Even if it's just for a season." She stopped tugging at her socks and looked at Cece. "It's been wonderful having my own sister as a roommate."

"I know. I feel the same way." Cece ruffled Barkley's ears again and then suddenly sat up straight. "Oh, I almost forgot. I learned something about the murder."

"Really? What?"

"One of the girls from the Bellevue play I was in last month works in the police department. She called to talk to me about the next theater production, and I told her about how we found the body in Hyde Park when I hurt my foot. Anyway, she told me the police have the phone records of the man we found. You won't believe this. One of the numbers was to Hodges Campaign Headquarters!"

"You're kidding."

"No. The police were following up."

"Did she tell you anything else?"

"Yeah. There were a few calls. One was Phil's shop when the guy's car was being worked on. One was to a private detective. And one of the others was to somebody named Brad Langley or Lassley or something like that."

"Not Brad Lassiter?"

"Yes! That's it. Brad Lassiter. Why, do you know him?"

Kate felt heat rising in her face, and she stood and turned away from Cece. *Should I tell her? No. There's no need to bring that up.* She forced her voice to sound nonchalant. "Yes. I knew Brad. I went to school with him." She unzipped her hoodie and slowly pulled it off. "He was two years ahead of me."

"Do you have your high school yearbooks? Can you show me?"

Kate took an album off the shelf and handed it to Cece. "This was my sophomore yearbook, so he would have been a senior."

Cece opened the book and flipped the pages. "Wow. What a gorgeous hunk. Did you date him?"

Kate smiled. "Hardly. Remember, I told you I was a skinny, nerdy girl. Not exactly the type to date the captain of the football team. I knew him because he went to my church and we were in the same youth group, but different ages." She pulled off her fleece headband and shook her hair. "Also, I tutored him in math his senior year."

"You were a sophomore and you were tutoring a senior in math? Okay, genius, what was it like to tutor the captain of the football team?"

"He was having trouble in geometry. That was my best subject." Kate disappeared into the kitchen and returned with a bottle of Gatorade. She sat on the other end of the couch. "He had a beautiful girlfriend named Ellie. Ellie Weatherspoon."

Cece quickly turned some more pages. "Here she is. Oh my gosh. Beauty queen material. The perfect high school couple."

"Definitely a match made in heaven. I heard they got married not long after graduation."

"Well, the police are interested in your friend."

"And I'm interested in a shower." Kate picked up her socks and shoes and disappeared into the bathroom.

"I'll check on your friend Brad while you're cleaning up," Cece called after her.

After her shower, Kate pulled on a pair of blue jeans and a green turtleneck sweater. "Getting anywhere, Sherlock?" she asked as she walked back into the living room, drying her hair with a towel.

"Yeah." Cece looked up, but she wasn't smiling. "You need to look at this. It's about Brad Lassiter's wife Ellie. And it's not good news."

CHAPTER ELEVEN

Police Visit Campaign Headquarters

*P*olice? *Will this campaign never end?* Mike Strickland walked from the staff room to Representative Hodges's office.

Hodges had called to let him know two police detectives were in his office, and Mike knew from his tone of voice it was an unwelcome visit.

"This is Detective Carlioni." Hodges nodded to the shorter of two men standing by his desk.

Mike looked them over. Carlioni was the older one. Dark, balding, squat, but not fat. His eyelids drooped slightly over brown eyes that stared unblinking at Mike.

Carlioni motioned toward the young man beside him. "This is my partner, Detective MacMillan."

MacMillan was all long arms and legs so loosely attached to his skinny frame it seemed like one of them might break loose and fly across the room if he moved too fast. He had a full head of sandy brown hair and a genial expression. He smiled and nodded. "Nice to meet you."

"Good to meet both of you." Mike smiled and shook hands.

Hodges motioned the two detectives to have a seat. Mike leaned against a side table while MacMillan folded his angular limbs into one of the chairs.

Hodges took a seat behind his desk. "Is this in regard to the shooting last month? I thought that was all over and the police in

California had caught the guy who confessed." He raised his hands in mock pleading. "Please don't tell me I'm going to have to testify at some trial."

Carlioni slumped down onto a chair facing Hodges. "No, sir. That's all taken care of. We're here to ask you about something that happened recently. About some calls that were made to and from your office here."

"I'm sure our staff can assist you, detective. You can ask the receptionist. She handles all those sorts of things." Hodges stood. "I don't believe I can help you with telephone calls."

"Actually, sir, we hope you can be of help. This is a serious matter. It concerns a murder."

Hodges sank back into his chair, and Mike took over. "Murder? What murder? And what does that have to do with us?" *These guys need to know they can't come in here and start throwing their weight around.* He put on the darkest face he could manage and crossed his arms over his chest.

Carlioni looked unimpressed, but MacMillan leaned forward with an amiable smile. "Do you mind if we record this conversation?" He took a small device out of his pocket and laid it on the table in front of Hodges's desk.

Hodges started to speak, but Mike held up his hand. "Yes, we do mind. Representative Hodges is in the middle of an important gubernatorial campaign, and we can't have him distracted by some police business that doesn't concern him."

MacMillan's expression didn't change. He ran his hand through his thick mane, but his clear blue eyes radiated sincerity. "We don't mean to upset the apple cart, Mr. Strickland, but we have an investigation to conduct, and we need to get some information from this campaign. If you'll bear with us for a few questions, we'll be on our way."

Hodges looked over at Mike and gave a slight nod. "All right, gentlemen. Let's hear what this is all about."

Carlioni continued to address Mike while he answered Hodges. "The murdered man was staying at the Bellevue Hotel, and one of the calls came from Hodges Campaign Headquarters to his room at the hotel last Thursday."

Mike pushed himself off the table and stood straight. "Who is this murdered man?"

"His name was Alexander Hadecker."

Hodges's mouth dropped open. "Alexander Hadecker, the realtor?" he asked.

"That's the victim." Carlioni turned his attention back to Hodges. "Did you know him?"

"No." Hodges brushed at an imaginary stain on his tie. "We never met, but I heard about his offer to buy the Barringer farm."

"Any idea who called him at his hotel?" Carlioni squinted at Hodges.

"No idea at all."

"We'll have to question your staff." Carlioni jotted a note on his pad. "If you'll arrange to have everyone present tomorrow at noon, one of us will be back to question them then."

Hodges nodded. "I'll get the word out to my staff. Of course, you understand we have a lot of volunteers working with us. Anyone can pick up the phone here and make a call."

Carlioni looked up from his note-taking and twirled his mechanical pencil. "We'll need to talk to them all as a group." He looked down at his notepad. "There was another call. This one was made from the dead man's cell phone to the main number here on Friday afternoon. Do you know anything about that one?"

Hodges shook his head. "No. I ..."

Mike squared his body to Carlioni. "I know who he called."

Three pairs of eyes turned toward him. Carlioni lifted one eyebrow. "Who?"

"He called me."

CHAPTER TWELVE

Police Visit Brad Lassiter

C ommissioner Blake pulled in behind the detectives' car outside the Lassiter home. He nodded to Carlioni and MacMillan as they walked over to meet him. "I hear you fellas had an interesting visit to campaign headquarters."

"Yep. We'll write up the report and have it on your desk later today." Carlioni shook his head. "But one of us is gonna have to go back to question the whole group tomorrow about who made the call to Hadecker's hotel room. Don't hold your breath that one of them will fess up to that. There's no way we can identify the caller unless they're willing to admit to it."

"At least we're beginning to know the players. Let's hope Lassiter is around so we can put another piece in the puzzle today."

They approached the front door of the small, Masonite-sided house. Commissioner Blake rang the doorbell while Carlioni and MacMillan stood behind and to the side of him. Although Blake didn't carry a firearm, his detectives did, and they all knew to be especially vigilant when knocking on the door of an unknown house belonging to a person of interest in a homicide.

Blake was familiar with this neighborhood. It was filled with young married couples. Mostly law-abiding, blue-collar, dyed-in-the-wool Americans. Unlikely to find anything here to do with the Hadecker investigation. He listened carefully and heard a child's voice. Lots of kids in this neighborhood. After a few seconds, he heard a heavy tread inside. *Must be a man.*

Instead, the door was opened by a tall, heavyset woman who looked like she was in her fifties or sixties. She wore an apron over her dress and had a dish towel in her hands. Her face registered surprise at seeing the group of men standing on the front porch. She raised her eyebrows. "Yes?"

Blake held up his badge. "I'm Police Commissioner Blake, ma'am. These are detectives Carlioni and MacMillan."

Her eyes widened. "Police? What do you want?"

Blake caught an inflection in her voice. Maybe not surprised after all.

"We're looking for Brad Lassiter." Blake watched her face closely. "Are you Mrs. Lassiter?"

"I'm Thelma Weatherspoon, Brad's mother-in-law." Her eyes flickered as she looked from one to the other of the three men. "What do you want with Brad?"

"We're investigating a death, and we think Mr. Lassiter may have some information to help us."

The woman put her hand up to her throat. "A death? What death?"

"Can we come in, ma'am? I'll explain everything to you."

A small child appeared next to the woman and latched onto her leg. "What's wrong, Telly?"

The woman reached down and patted the young girl on her head. "It's nothing, pumpkin. These men just want to talk for a minute. You go back to your room and I'll bring you a chocolate chip cookie in a little while." She leaned down and kissed the child on top of her head.

The youngster looked skeptically at the men standing outside the door, but she turned and disappeared into the house.

Blake felt the thick grip of remorse at having to question this woman. The way her expression had softened when she talked to the child. The tender way she had touched the little girl's head.

She seemed like a decent sort. He silently prayed there was nothing to this, but something didn't feel right.

The woman straightened up, but she didn't open the door. She obviously wasn't going to. "Brad isn't here."

"Do you know when he'll be back?"

She paused as if trying to decide the best way to answer the question when a blue Toyota Corolla pulled into the driveway.

Based on the frown spreading across the woman's face, Blake guessed this was Brad.

The man who got out of the car looked like a weight lifter. He was average height with strong upper body musculature under his blue working shirt. He didn't hesitate as he approached the men.

Blake could see from the tight shirt and jeans that he didn't have a weapon on him. "Mr. Lassiter? Brad Lassiter?"

The man's face turned sour as he stopped a few feet from Blake with his arms at his sides. "I'm Brad Lassiter. What do you want?"

Blake had seen this before. Lassiter's reaction could mean a lot of different things. He could know something, or he could simply be a suspicious type. But he wasn't likely to offer any information on his own. Blake showed him his badge.

"I'm Commissioner Blake of the Bellevue Police Department. We're investigating the death of a man, and phone records indicate he may have sent a text message to you recently." Blake took a small notebook out of his shirt pocket and flipped it open. "Can you confirm this is your cell phone number?"

Lassiter glanced at the paper. "That's not my phone," he said gruffly. "It's my wife's."

"Is your wife at home?"

Lassiter's voice went flat, and his face turned to granite. "My wife is dead."

CHAPTER THIRTEEN

At the Cemetery

Earlene Weatherspoon Lassiter
1981–2010
Rest in Peace

Kathryn laid a bouquet of flowers delicately at the base of the tombstone. "It's hard to think someone I went to high school with could be dead. Especially somebody like Ellie. I remember envying her because she was so beautiful, and all the guys wanted to date her."

"Funny how things work out, isn't it?" Cece brushed dead leaves from the top of the tombstone.

"Yeah. I thought she had it all. Like the world was hers. But I guess things went bad for her in a big way." She shook her head. "I just can't imagine Ellie being addicted to narcotics."

"Did you ever do drugs?" Cece asked.

"No. I never really thought much about it. I was into math club and cross country. Geek girl. Not the kind of person anybody thought to ask to a party or to try to have a good time with." She tucked a lock of hair behind her ear. "Sometimes I think it was God's way of protecting me from myself. What about you?"

"When I was seventeen, this friend of mine was experimenting with stuff and wanted me to try it. I told her I wasn't sure if I wanted to, but I'd think about it. When I got home that afternoon,

I asked my father what he thought about illegal drugs. You should have seen the expression on his face."

"Was he angry?"

"No. But he looked at me like he was examining my soul." She chuckled. "It's a look he's perfected over the years."

Kate remembered the way Harry and Sylvia Goldman had talked about their love for their adopted daughter. They had said Cece was the greatest gift God had given them. She could envision the shock on Harry's kind face when he learned Cece would even consider doing drugs.

Cece shook her head. "It took him a couple of minutes to recover, but then he went full-bore at the issue. He quietly asked if I would throw away thousands of years of wisdom and do an experiment with my own body when I didn't know how it would turn out." Cece tilted her head and gestured with her hands, palms up. "That made a lot of sense to me. Why would I take a chance on my own health just because a friend of mine was doing it?"

"So did you ever talk to him about it again?"

"Oh, yeah. Big time. The next day he came home with around twenty library books about the evils of illegal drugs. We sat at the kitchen table while he went through page after page of the effects on your body. There were lots of pictures. Awful things. There was this one photo showing a woman with a horrible pock-marked face. Most of her teeth had fallen out and her hair was thin and wispy from heroin use. That's when I told Dad he could stop. There was no way I'd ever do that to myself."

"Your father is a very smart guy."

"Yep. The truth is a pretty good convincer, and he's extremely good at finding the truth and pointing it out to you. In spades." Cece picked up a vase of artificial flowers that had fallen over and set it upright.

"I wish your folks were here now. We could use their wisdom."

"I know. But they're going to stay in Denver until the sale of Dad's jewelry shop goes through. Then they'll be back in Bellevue. This time they'll be here to stay."

"In the meantime, maybe we should take a covered dish to Brad to show our sympathy. What do you think?"

"I think it's the right thing to do. Why don't you give him a call later today?"

CHAPTER FOURTEEN

My Wife Is Dead

"Your wife is dead?" Blake winced. "I'm sorry to hear that, Mr. Lassiter." He tried to keep his voice under control, but the investigation had taken an unexpected turn. He cleared his throat. "We're still going to have to ask you a few questions."

Lassiter pushed by the men on the doorstep and entered the house. He dropped his keys on the table by the door. "Make this fast. I'm on lunch break and I need to be back in an hour."

Blake and his men followed him into the house. "We'll make it as fast as we can."

Thelma closed the door behind them. "Can I get you something? Coffee maybe?" She looked worried.

"They're not staying long enough to have coffee, Thelma. Why don't you go back and check on Sara?" As Thelma headed down the hall, Brad turned to face the officers. "Let's get this over with."

Blake cleared his throat. "Mr. Lassiter, a murder was committed in Bellevue a few days ago. The dead man has been identified as Alexander Hadecker. Do you recognize the name?"

"No."

"Did your wife ever mention that name to you?"

"No." Lassiter stood with his legs apart, hands planted firmly on his hips. In the world of "fight or flight" he was definitely in the "fight" category.

Blake prided himself on never prejudging a suspect. Leave that to the jury. But this was obviously an angry, aggressive man. Good candidate for a murderer. "Mr. Lassiter, how long has your wife been dead?"

"What does that have to do with anything? She obviously couldn't communicate with anyone who was trying to contact her."

"Mr. Lassiter, I'm sorry to ask this question, but was your wife using illegal narcotics?"

Lassiter's hands balled into fists. "Why would you ask that?"

"Al Hadecker sent a text message to your wife's phone last Friday. I have the message here." Blake flipped a page in the notebook. "It says, 'Drop tonight 8:00. Where?' That's the kind of text a drug dealer would send."

Lassiter frowned. Long seconds ticked by. He seemed to be considering his answer. He wiped the palms of his hands on his blue jeans. "My wife was addicted to narcotics. She died of an overdose. That was three months ago. She obviously couldn't have arranged to buy drugs a few days ago."

"Then somebody else used your wife's phone to send a text message back to Hadecker." He looked again at the small notebook. "It said, 'RR Terminal back lot.'" He refocused on Lassiter. "Do you have any idea who could have sent that message?"

Brad Lassiter walked slowly, almost robotically, into the small kitchen that adjoined the living room. He moved around behind the island, put his hands on the edge of the counter, and lowered his head.

Thinking? Or getting ready to bolt? Does he have a gun behind that island? Blake glanced at Carlioni and MacMillan. They were laser focused on the man in the kitchen. MacMillan had moved so he had a clear line of fire. His hand was inside his jacket, ready to pull the Glock 19.

Blake held his breath.

CHAPTER FIFTEEN

Herman Is Dead

"He's dead! He's dead!"
    Blake heard the child's panicked voice as it preceded her down the hallway before she burst into the room and ran to Brad Lassiter.

"Herman is dead! Oh, Daddy. Help!"

Thelma Weatherspoon followed, holding a small goldfish bowl. "I'm so sorry, Brad. Sara noticed her goldfish lying on the bottom of the bowl. I don't think he's dead, but he doesn't look good."

Brad took the goldfish bowl, set it on the island, and shook it gently. The fish made a slow swimming motion, then stopped.

Sara clenched chubby fists around Brad's pant leg and sobbed. "Herman's dead."

"No, honey. He isn't dead. But he looks sick." Brad shook the bowl again. "Have you been feeding him every day like you promised?"

Thelma answered. "I change the water once a week, and I remind Sara to feed him every morning."

Brad picked Sara up and sat her gently on the island. "Do you always feed him, Sara? Every day, like we agreed?"

Sara locked her fingers together in her lap and looked down at her tiny hands. "Yes." But it was more of a question than a statement.

"Sara." Brad put his hand under her chin and lifted it so she looked at him. "Remember what we talked about. Being honest is the most important thing. Even if we do something wrong, we should always tell the truth about it." He paused. "Did you forget to feed Herman?"

Her lips quivered. "I'm sorry, Daddy." She held her arms up and he picked her up and hugged her.

"It's all right, honey. We all forget things." He set her down on the floor and handed her the goldfish bowl. "Now take Herman back to your room and feed him. He'll be okay."

She took the goldfish bowl and walked back toward the other end of the house. Blake heard her say, "You'll be fine, Herman. Things will be better soon. Just wait and see."

Thelma turned to leave, but Brad stopped her. "Thelma, I'd like you to stay for a minute. You need to hear this." He faced the men in the room. "Commissioner Blake, you asked me a question."

Blake swallowed hard. The child had stolen his professional demeanor. He took a deep breath. "Mr. Lassiter, do you have any idea who sent the text message from your wife's phone?"

Lassiter spoke quietly. "I sent the message."

"Why did you send it?"

Lassiter's jaw tightened. "I wanted to meet the man who had sold drugs to my wife."

"Did you meet him last Friday night?"

"Yes."

"Do you own a gun, Mr. Lassiter?"

It took Lassiter a few seconds to answer. "I own several guns."

"Do you have any small handguns? On the order of a .38 caliber?"

"Yes. I have a .38."

Blake felt the sour taste of pity in his mouth. "Mr. Lassiter, we're going to have to take you into the station for questioning. I suggest you contact your lawyer. Mac, read him his rights."

CHAPTER SIXTEEN

Rabbi Hart

"I've never been in a synagogue before." Kate followed Cece into the reception area of Beth Shalom Synagogue. Stained glass windows reflected soft colors in contemporary designs on three sides of the hexagonal entry. Similar hues echoed in the carpet leading down three steps into a long hallway to the left. The thick pile of the rug silenced their footsteps, and Kate felt a sense of peace wash over her. "It's beautiful here."

"I'm glad you decided to come with me. We're early 'cause I wanted you to see the place before we start the study. Come on back to the library where we have Torah class." Cece led the way down the hall, past a set of double doors, and into a large room lined from floor to ceiling with bookshelves. A podium on the side of the room held an open scroll, and the middle of the room was taken up by a huge oblong table with ten carved wooden chairs on each side and one chair at the head of the table.

"This is lovely," Kate said as she stood in front of one of the book shelves.

Cece pointed to a set of volumes with leather-bound covers. "This is the collection that makes up the Talmud, the writings that have to do with Jewish religious law and theology." She moved to the next bookshelf and ran her hands along the spines of a group of identical dark blue books. "Each of these books is a Chumash."

"What's a Chumash?" Kathryn asked.

"They contain the first five books of the Bible. We call those books the Torah. The Chumash contains the scriptures plus commentaries. The synagogue keeps a ton of these so we can use them for study sessions." She pulled two of the books out and handed one to Kathryn. "A lot of the books in this room are commentaries on the Torah. Some of them are revered by the Jewish community."

"We have a lot of commentaries too, but I haven't studied many of them. We always went to the scriptures themselves when we wanted to study God's word."

"That's an excellent idea." A clear baritone voice with an eastern European accent invaded the room.

Kate looked around to see a short man with a long beard standing at the door. "Shalom," he said. "I'm Rabbi Hart."

It would be hard to pin an age on the rabbi. His thinning hair under the yarmulke and the gray in his beard would imply something around fifty. But his face was unlined and his dark brown eyes radiated a boyish curiosity, suggesting something younger. He took several bounding steps across the room to Kathryn and held out his hand.

Kate hesitated. She had understood women shouldn't shake hands with a man in Orthodox Jewish custom.

"It's all right," he said. "We're a conservative synagogue. You can shake my hand."

Kate took his hand and he gave it a vigorous shake. "I'm Kathryn Frasier," she said. "Cece's half-sister."

"Yes, I know. Cece and her parents have told me all about you and the history of the family. It's most interesting." His head bobbed up and down as he pulled at his beard.

"That it is," said Cece. "I invited Kathryn to join us for study this morning. I hope it's all right."

"Of course it is!" The rabbi threw his hands up in a gesture of excitement, as if Cece had just handed him the gift of a lifetime. "What could be better than to have a new friend to study God's word with us?"

The room slowly filled with fifteen women. When everyone settled in their places, Rabbi Hart introduced Kathryn and began the session with a Hebrew prayer followed by its English translation. "Blessed are you, Lord our God, who has sanctified us with your commandments and commanded us to engross ourselves in your Torah." Then he proceeded to lead a study of the story of Joseph.

He explained how Joseph's brothers were considering murdering him, but Judah had stepped in to save his life. "Think of it," he said. "Judah saved Joseph's life, and Joseph ended up saving the world from a terrible famine." He looked around the table and made eye contact with each person. "You can see from this story how just one person can change the course of history." He continued by leading a discussion on the various ways they could each save lives in their communities. The class discussed homeless shelters, food programs, and care for widows and orphans.

"The Talmud teaches us that saving one life is like saving the whole world. That's relevant to today's lesson, but it's also critical to us in today's world. We should all consider this wisdom as we serve others on this earth." The rabbi then thanked the class and left.

"Wow. What a powerful lesson," Kathryn said as she and Cece put their books away and left the room.

"Rabbi Hart is a talented teacher and a very sincere man. He spends a lot of his time in the community helping the poor."

"He certainly gave me something to think about." Kate shook her head in awe. "Saving one life is like saving the whole world."

CHAPTER SEVENTEEN

Stan Palmerton

"**S**o Mac is at Hodges Campaign Headquarters to question them about the phone call?" Commissioner Blake parked the car in front of the nondescript building at 180 North Signal Street.

"Yeah." Carlioni nodded. "Me and Mackie flipped a coin to see who would take that assignment. He lost."

Blake chuckled and took a slip of paper out of his shirt pocket. "This guy's name is Stan Palmerton. Do you know him?"

"No. I don't have much to do with private eye types. Seems like they just get in the way." Carlioni made a gesture with his hand like he was brushing something off his trench coat. "But I talked to a few of the guys at headquarters. One of them worked with him over in Bakertown when he was on the force there. He says Palmerton is a real smart guy and a good cop, but he thought he could make more money as a private eye, so he moved to Bellevue a few years ago to give it a try."

"Can't recall I've ever heard of him," Blake said. "He didn't sound surprised when I told him we wanted to talk to him, though." He paused in front of the building and glanced at the paper again. "Upstairs. Suite 201. Let's see what he knows."

The single door at the top of the stairs was labeled Stanley Palmerton, Private Investigator. Blake rang a bell and they heard a buzz as the door was unlocked.

The place had a tiny outer room with a small desk where a secretary should be. A man appeared at the doorway to an office behind the reception area. "Come on in. I'm Stan Palmerton."

Blake took a quick assessment. About six feet tall, shaved head, tan, and obviously in good shape. Outdoors type. Young. Mid-thirties? He wore a tailored dress shirt with sleeves rolled up to his elbows and casual slacks. Sharp navy blue tie. Classy for a PI.

Blake showed him his badge. "I'm Commissioner Blake and this is Detective Carlioni. I phoned earlier."

"Good to meet you fellas," Palmerton said as he shook hands. "I have to register a complaint with you, though."

Blake's eyebrows shot up. "Complaint?"

"Yeah. You're doing such a great job of keeping crime down in Bellevue, I don't get much business anymore. I had to let my secretary go."

"Sorry about that," Blake said with a laugh. "We'll try to let up on the criminals for a while so you can get more business."

Palmerton chuckled and gestured toward his office. "This way." As they entered, he pointed to the chairs in front of his desk. "Have a seat. Do you guys like coffee?"

Carlioni harrumphed. "Not the kind we get at headquarters."

"I'm kind of a coffee nut. Let me get you a cup of this new blend." He disappeared into a kitchenette attached to his office. "Cream and sugar?"

"Heck no," Carlioni replied. "Remember, we're cops."

Palmerton came back with two large mugs. "I remember the coffee at police headquarters. I was on the force in Bakertown until I moved to Bellevue." He handed the mugs to Blake and Carlioni. "You're gonna love this. Fresh brewed. Hope you don't mind, though. It's a pretty strong Columbian blend."

Carlioni took a sip. "Now this is what I call coffee." He turned toward Blake. "Why can't we get something like this at headquarters, boss?"

"Because the taxpayers pay for our coffee, and I suspect this costs a whole lot more than the bargain brand we're drinking. But this sure is good stuff. Thanks, Mr. Palmerton."

"My pleasure. And call me Stan." Palmerton took a seat behind his desk. "Now tell me what's on your minds, gentlemen."

Blake put his cup down on the desk and pulled a small notebook and pen from his pocket. "I'll get right to the point, Stan. We have information indicating you made a phone call to the Bellevue Hotel on Thursday evening and asked for Al Hadecker's room. Is that correct?"

"Yes. That's true."

"I suppose you're aware of a news story that Al Hadecker was murdered in Bellevue Friday night?"

"I heard that."

"Why don't you tell us your purpose in calling him at the hotel."

Palmerton bit on his lower lip. "Commissioner, this is a private matter. Al Hadecker was a client of mine and our conversation was confidential."

"Understood. But we're investigating a murder." Blake paused. "You know I can get a court order if I have to."

"No need for that. Al Hadecker hired me about six months ago to investigate his wife's trips to Bellevue and some of the surrounding communities. He had reason to believe she was ... let's say, participating in unwifely activities."

"You mean he suspected she was carrying on an affair and wanted you to get proof?"

"Right."

"Probably a pre-nup," Carlioni said. "I'm guessing he could get out of it if he could prove his wife was cheating on him."

"I don't know the details about their marriage. From my point of view, it's a job. My clients pay me. I take pictures."

"So what happened?"

"Hadecker and I were supposed to meet when he came to Bellevue so I could show him what I had, but the meeting didn't take place."

"Why not?"

"I had nothing to report. I followed Mrs. Hadecker on several different occasions when she came to Bellevue in the past, but there was never any hanky-panky going on. She has an autistic brother in the Bellevue Mental Institute, and she comes to town to check on him. Every now and then she would meet some friends for lunch or do some shopping. Those kinds of things. I called Hadecker at the hotel and told him I'd mail in my report. No need for a meeting."

"You spoke to him, then? When you called the hotel." Blake made a note.

"Yes. That's when I briefed him and gave him the final figure for my services. I was surprised when I heard about the murder. I guess that means I won't get the last payment." He sighed and gave a resigned smile. "The perils of being a private investigator. Do you have any suspects?"

"We have a person of interest, but we still have to check on other people who had contact with Hadecker when he was in Bellevue. You know, we need to touch all the bases."

"Yeah. I understand."

"Do you remember where you were at the time of the murder?"

"What time would that be?"

"Friday evening somewhere between eight o'clock and midnight."

Palmerton paused and looked at the ceiling, steepling his fingers together. "Let's see. I was here finishing up paperwork Friday night. That's my usual routine. I probably left around ten o'clock or so. Stopped at the restaurant on the corner for a bite to eat before heading home."

"Anybody see you?"

"The cleaning folks can verify I was here, and I know the staff at the restaurant. They'll probably remember I was there Friday night." He drummed his fingers together. "Oh, and I paid the check with my credit card, so they'll have the receipt."

"Can you give us any idea why someone might want to murder Al Hadecker?"

Palmerton shook his head. "Like I said, I didn't know the guy. Most of my dealings were through his attorney. I talked to Hadecker on the phone a few times, but I have no idea why somebody would take him out."

"Did he ever say anything to you about being in danger? Or his life being threatened? You know, along those lines."

"No, nothing like that."

"How about his wife? Did he ever express concern about her? Like she might have a reason to see him dead? You know, insurance or inheritance?"

"He never said anything like that to me. I get a lot of business from people like him. You know, husbands who are suspicious of their wives or vice versa. It's a simple business arrangement. They pay me to follow someone and take pictures. They don't tell me why they're doing it, and I don't ask." Palmerton leaned forward and put his forearms on his desk. "But Al Hadecker was my client, so I feel some responsibility to know what happened. I'll let you know if I remember anything that might bear on the case." He pulled a business card out of a holder on his desk and handed it to the commissioner. "And I'd appreciate it if you'd keep me in the loop. Call me if there's anything I can do."

"Thanks. If you come up with anything, you know how to get in touch with us. And by the way ..."

"Yes?"

"Did you mail your report to Hadecker?"

"Yeah. I sent it registered mail." He opened the top drawer of his desk and rummaged around. "Here it is. Sent Friday around one o'clock." He stood and handed the receipt to the commissioner.

Blake looked it over and nodded. "Okay." He handed it back. "That's all for now." He shook hands with Palmerton. "We'll be in touch."

As the commissioner and his detective walked down the stairs and out of the building, Blake asked, "What do you think, Carli?"

"I'll get Mac to check his alibis, but he seems reliable. He could be useful to us. He had a relationship with Hadecker, and he has some experience in law enforcement. He knows the ropes."

"That's what I was thinking. Maybe we can get him to do some snooping for us." Blake unlocked his car and they both slid in. "Besides, he was shadowing Mrs. Hadecker. If she was involved in any way, he might be useful in figuring it out."

"I'll tell ya one thing, boss. I sure am glad I'm not a PI. Must be a lousy job following rich women around to prove they've been unfaithful to their husbands. Not something I'd want to do."

"Yeah. I agree." Blake turned the ignition and pulled out into traffic. "But if Hadecker was suspicious of his wife, it means the marriage might have been on the rocks. She's coming in to identify the body as soon as she returns from Europe. It'll be interesting to see how she handles it."

CHAPTER EIGHTEEN

Saving One Life Is Like Saving the World

T he GPS system ordered Kate to turn left onto Oakleaf Lane. "We're almost there."

"Remind me. Who did you talk to?" Cece asked.

Kathryn turned left at the next corner and continued down the block. "Brad's mother-in-law. She's the one who told me the police took Brad in for questioning. Apparently, his in-laws are staying at his house with his little girl during all this chaos." She pulled over to the curb. "Here it is—4230 Oakleaf Lane." They peered at the house. It was a small ranch home with a garage attached. The front landscaping looked neat and well cared for.

Kate and Cece walked toward the front door on a stone walkway with a few weeds emerging around the edges. The house looked like it had a fresh coat of white paint with blue trim. Kate took a deep breath and rang the doorbell.

She heard a heavy tread. *Maybe Brad has been released,* she thought. But the door was opened by a heavyset man wearing a green plaid shirt and blue jeans. His face radiated a kind of irritation like a person who had happened onto a bothersome insect. Or a bothersome visitor.

Kate cleared her throat. "Hello. I'm Kathryn Frasier. I called earlier and talked to Mrs. Weatherspoon." She held up the casserole. "My sister and I wanted to bring something by to express our sympathy for your loss."

A woman appeared from behind and stepped in front of the man. "I'm Thelma Weatherspoon. I remember you, Kathryn. I worked with your mother on a couple of PTA projects at the high school, and she told me a lot about you." Thelma pushed the storm door open and motioned them into the house. "This is my husband, Earl."

Earl Weatherspoon nodded and stepped back to make way for their entrance.

Kate introduced Cece and then held out the covered dish. "It's spaghetti. I hope you like it."

"We love spaghetti. Thank you so much for thinking of us." Thelma put the casserole in the refrigerator and returned to the living room. "Earl, isn't it nice of these young women to stop by?"

Earl barely nodded. "I have some chores to do back at home." He grabbed a baseball hat from a hook by the door and stomped out.

Thelma Weatherspoon grimaced. "You'll have to forgive Earl. Ellie's death was such a shock to him. You see, she was our only child. Earl just about came apart when she died."

Cece nodded. "It must be so hard for both of you. I didn't know Ellie, but Kathryn tells me she was a beautiful girl."

"We thought she was perfect." Thelma sighed, then seemed to regroup. "But where are my manners? Please have a seat. Let me move these things." She picked up a stack of blue work shirts from the sofa. "I was mending some of Brad's work shirts. He's always losing buttons off his shirts. Keeps me busy sewing them back on."

Kate and Cece settled on the living room sofa just as a small child tiptoed in from the hall. The little girl immediately ran to Thelma and grabbed her hand. "Telly?" she said.

"It's all right, Sara. These ladies are friends who brought us a nice casserole." She turned to Kate and Cece. "This is my granddaughter, Sara. It's been hard on her these last months." She turned toward the child and kissed the little girl's head. "But she's a good girl, aren't you, pumpkin?"

Sara shyly approached Kate. "Were you a friend of my mommy's?"

Kate reached out and took the young girl's hand. "I knew your mother when I was in high school."

Sara climbed onto the couch and turned toward Cece.

"Did you know my mommy?"

Cece reached out and took the child onto her lap. "No, I didn't know her, but I understand she was very pretty. I bet you look a lot like her." Cece brushed Sara's blonde hair back away from her face.

Sara's face broke into a wide smile. "Telly says I look exactly like her." She pointed to a framed picture on the end table. "That's my mommy." She turned back to Cece and looked up into her face. "What's your name?"

"I'm Cece and this is my sister, Kathryn. We're glad to know you, Sara." Cece's voice was warm and uplifting.

"Now, Sara," Thelma said, "get down and let the ladies alone."

"Oh, no. I'm fine." Cece gave the child a hug. "Sara and I are already friends."

"Would you like to come to my room and see my favorite doll baby?" Sara's voice became happy and animated. "She has blonde hair too!"

"I'd love to!" Cece turned to Thelma. "Is it all right?" Sara had already hopped down and was pulling Cece's hand.

"Of course." Thelma's face melted into a smile as Cece and Sara disappeared into the back room. She turned to Kathryn. "Your sister is amazing. Sara has never responded to anyone like that before."

"Cece is one of a kind. She seems to have the ability to form a bond with everyone she meets. I've never known anybody like her."

"Sara certainly can use some joy in her life. She was here when the police came and took Brad in for questioning."

"They don't think he had anything to do with the murder, do they?"

Thelma sighed and sat on the edge of the easy chair. "I don't know what they think, but sometimes I think Brad must have been born under a curse."

"Why do you say that? I remember he was popular in high school."

"Maybe in high school, but everything has gone wrong for him since then. Poor thing. I'm sure you know Ellie was addicted to drugs."

"I heard that."

"It ruined their marriage. All their friends turned away from them. Brad worked hard to get her off drugs. He even took out another mortgage on this house to send her to a rehab center. They just went further and further into debt." Thelma sighed.

"I'm so sorry."

"Ellie was my daughter and I loved her, but the drugs turned her into a different person. I want to cry when I think of what she did to Brad. And of course Sara will always bear the burden of her mother's behavior."

"She's very fortunate to have you as her grandmother."

"Thank you, Kathryn. Earl and I are determined to make her life as good as we can."

"I guess your husband must be pretty upset about the police arresting Brad."

Thelma blushed. "Unfortunately, Earl blames Brad for everything. He was against the marriage from the start. He thought Ellie should marry somebody with money who could give her a good life. Brad was a nice boy, but he was going to work stringing lines for the phone company, and Earl thought that was beneath Ellie. He always thought Ellie got into drugs because she was so unhappy with her marriage to Brad."

* * *

"Do you think he did it?" Cece settled into the passenger seat of Kate's car.

Kate frowned and shook her head. "Brad? No. Absolutely not. The boy I knew would never take a life. It doesn't fit his personality."

"You never know what somebody will do when they're defending a loved one. He must have been furious at the guy who sold his wife drugs. Maybe he decided to take revenge."

"Thelma said he loved Ellie so much, he was willing to do anything to get her off her addiction. But murdering someone wouldn't bring her back, and Brad would know that."

"What a tragedy. I wish we could have helped her, but there's nothing we can do for her now."

Kate started the ignition. "No, but maybe there's something we can do for Brad."

"What do you mean?"

"Maybe we can help find out who did this thing."

Cece's face wrinkled up. "You don't mean you want us to try to find the killer, do you?"

Kate turned to face her sister. "Cece, I owe a debt to Brad Lassiter."

"What debt?"

"I don't really want to talk about it now, but I feel like I have a responsibility to help him."

"But we decided we didn't ever want to do any detective work again, remember?"

"Yes. But if Brad is innocent, the cards are really stacked against him. Look, we probably can't solve it, but maybe we can find a few things to help the police."

Cece raised her eyebrows. "This wouldn't have anything to do with our Torah study, would it? You know, what Rabbi Hart taught us. 'Saving one life is like saving the world.'"

"Yeah." Kate nodded. "What do you think, sister? Shall we save the world?"

Cece shrugged. "Somehow I knew you were going to say that." She sighed. "Lead on, Nancy Drew."

CHAPTER NINETEEN

Lunch with Mike

K ate spotted Mike Strickland as soon as she pushed the door open to The Pointe Grille. He was sitting at a booth on the right side of the restaurant. He immediately stood and came to her, extending his hand. Still the handsome, smooth campaign manager. Always at ease.

She pressed his hand. It was warm and soft and she remembered how he had gently touched her face after the scary events at the political rally. Was that only a couple of months ago?

"Kathryn, thanks for coming." He brushed her cheek with his lips and gave her the charming young-man-in-charge grin that had attracted her before.

"Hello, Mike."

"We're right over here." He took her elbow, led her to the booth, and they sat across from each other. "I ordered unsweet iced tea for you. I remember you said you like that."

"Yes." She settled in and took off her jacket.

The waitress came and they ordered. Kate waited.

Mike cleared his throat and fingered the cocktail napkin under his Coke. "I wanted to see you. See how you're doing. If you've gotten over that awful day at ArcTron Labs when Gavin pulled a gun on you."

"I'm fine. I've had a lot of support from my friends." She paused to let it sink in. "And I've come to terms with Gavin's illness and my parents' deaths."

"I'm sorry."

"Sorry for what?"

"Sorry for what I did. Or rather, sorry for what I didn't do. I wasn't there for you when you needed support. I want you to know how bad I feel."

She stared at him, not sure what to say.

"I was a jerk back then. But that's not who I really am, Kathryn. That's what I wanted to tell you." He looked down at his hands. "I'm making a big change."

"What sort of change?"

The waitress returned and set burgers and fries down in front of them.

Kate fiddled with the fries. She could feel Mike staring at her.

"I'm leaving the campaign."

Kate's head snapped up. Mike Strickland, the quintessential chief of staff, leaving the side of his beloved candidate? Impossible. "I thought you said you loved the give and take of politics. Why on earth would you leave it?"

"I didn't realize how much I'd changed until I looked back at the past few months. I never would have done those things ten years ago. I don't particularly like the person I've become."

Kate chewed on a french fry. "So what are you going to do now?"

"I'm buying some land in Bellevue. I'm going to return to farming."

"I thought you told me you grew up on a farm and you hated farming."

"Actually, what I said was I hated seeing a hog slaughtered. There's a lot about farming I like. I love planting and watching crops grow. I like the idea of producing something that's essential for life. And I want to live where people are honest and they're not trying to score political points. I've missed that." He grinned. "I'm just not gonna raise any hogs."

"Ha. Good idea."

His grin faded, and he reached over to put his hand on hers. "I want to settle down and make a real life for myself."

Kate gently removed her hand from under his and adjusted her napkin. "That sounds like a terrific idea, Mike. Where's the land you're buying?" Kate sipped her iced tea.

"I put in a bid for half of the Barringer farm."

Kate swallowed hard and almost spit out the tea. "The Barringer farm? That's the land Al Hadecker was trying to acquire to subdivide into housing units."

"Yes, I know. Al Hadecker was apparently murdered, and the police have been out to talk to us about his murder."

"Why did they want to talk to you?"

"Hadecker called me last Friday afternoon. He wanted to talk to me about my offer. He wanted to meet."

"You met with Hadecker?"

"No. I told him I wasn't interested and hung up. Did you know him?"

"Not exactly. Cece and I were the ones who found his body." Kate dropped a french fry back into the pile on her plate. "Can you tell me about your phone call with Hadecker?"

"Sure. I was surprised when he called me. I knew he had been in touch with Jeremy about contributing to the campaign, but he and I had never talked. Then I got this strange phone call."

"Strange? How do you mean?"

Mike downed a big bite of hamburger. "He tried to get me to pay him off."

"Why would he want you to pay him? Isn't it usually the other way around? Somebody wants to bribe political figures?"

"Right. But this wasn't political. It was about the farm. He wanted to buy it and subdivide it into little plots, but I had an offer on the table for half the farm. He told me if I'd give him fifty thousand dollars, he'd drop his offer altogether, and that would probably allow me to buy the acreage I want at a lower price."

"Why would he be willing to drop his offer for the farm? I thought he was going to make millions by subdividing that land."

"I don't know. Maybe he got into financial trouble and wanted to back out of the deal and make some money on the way out. I doubt he did it to be a nice guy. You should have heard him. He sounded like a first-class con man."

"What did you do?"

"I hung up on him, of course. I've had people try to buy political influence, but I never had somebody personally do something like that."

"Did you report it to the police?"

"No. It wasn't a political violation, so I wasn't required to report it, but the police had phone records and they showed up at headquarters yesterday and questioned me."

"What did you tell them?"

"Same thing I told you. They wanted to know if I had an alibi for Friday evening when the murder took place. Fortunately for me, I was with Bob all afternoon and evening. We were all over in Markerton for a rally."

"All?"

"Bob, Liz, Jeremy, and me. We were there from five o'clock until around ten."

"Were you all together the whole time?"

"No. We usually make an appearance at the start of the thing and then split up. I spend some time mingling with the crowd or hanging around in the back room waiting for it to get over."

"So you're all in the clear then?"

Mike shrugged. "I guess so."

CHAPTER TWENTY

Kate and Cece Get Onboard

"Commissioner Blake's office is at the end of the hall." Kate led her sister down the long corridor.

"I never liked this place," Cece said. "It's so sterile. The only pictures on the walls are photos of police cars. There's nothing to soften the hard lines of law enforcement."

"Nicely put, but there was a potted plant by the front door. That's something."

Cece looked back. "That plant doesn't look healthy to me. Negative vibes from the bad guys are probably killing it."

"More likely it isn't getting watered properly." Kate chuckled as they approached the office at the end of the hall. "Here we are." They stopped outside the closed door.

"I hear voices," Cece said. "I wonder if he invited somebody else to this meeting."

"Well, there's one way to find out." Kate knocked.

Blake opened the door and stepped aside. "Kathryn, Cece, welcome." He motioned them into the room.

"We can come back later if you're in the middle of a meeting."

"No, not at all. This is Detective Carlioni. He's one of my men. We were talking over some recent cases."

Carlioni nodded "I've heard a lot about you two." He pulled at the frayed edges of his jacket. "I've been checkin' my 401k just in case he hires you to replace me."

"Ha! Now that's something that would never happen." Blake clapped his detective on the shoulder. "You know I can't replace you, Carli." He motioned to a second man standing on the opposite side of the room. "This is Detective MacMillan. He's my other star."

"Hi there." MacMillan nodded and blushed. "It's nice to meet you."

"Have a seat," Blake said. Kate and Cece sat in the chairs in front of his desk. Carlioni remained standing and leaned against an upright file cabinet. MacMillan stood opposite him.

Blake took a seat behind his desk. "How's everything going? I take it you two weren't terribly traumatized by finding the body in the park last weekend."

Cece shook her head. "It wasn't exactly the way we thought the day would go, but it wasn't really upsetting since we didn't actually fall over a dead body."

"Thanks for your concern, commissioner," Kate added. "The only real problem was Cece's sprained ankle, but she's pretty much recovered."

"Good, I'm glad to hear it. Now why don't you tell me what you wanted to meet with me about."

Kate pressed her lips together. "We heard that you brought someone in for questioning. Brad Lassiter."

"That's right. Do you know him?"

Kate nodded. "I knew him from church camp when I was growing up, and we went to the same high school. He was a year or two older than me. I was surprised when I heard about it because I'm certain Brad Lassiter wouldn't have anything to do with a murder."

Blake put his forearms on his desk and leaned forward. His bright blue eyes took on a sudden intensity. "Why do you say that, Kathryn?"

"He was a very honest and decent guy. He was always trying to help other people. He'd go out of his way to help the younger kids at camp."

"I see. Did you have a relationship with him in any way? Did you date him?"

"No. I didn't know him well. But I did tutor him in a math course."

"You tutored him? Didn't that give you a chance to get to know him? I mean on a more personal level?"

"Not really. It was very businesslike. We met in the school library twice a week, but he was usually in a hurry because of his other activities. We would go over the lessons and then he would leave."

Carlioni walked over and propped himself on the front of the desk. "Did he ever try to get you to help him cheat? You know, do his homework for him or something like that?"

"No. Definitely not. He was very honest."

Carlioni leaned forward. "Honest people commit murders, Miss Frasier. That's not an alibi."

"I know. But I can't imagine Brad committing murder."

"Did you know his wife?" Blake looked down at the legal pad in front of him with notes. "Her name was Earlene, right?"

"People called her Ellie. I knew who she was, but I didn't really know her. She and Brad were going together in high school. She was a cheerleader. They were like this perfect couple. I think they were married pretty soon after they graduated."

"Did you know anything about their marriage? Were they happy?"

"I really don't know. I was busy with school and then I went away to college and didn't see either of them again. I was shocked when I found out Ellie had died. I guess I've been so wrapped up in my parents' deaths that I didn't hear about it."

"Did you read the cause of death?"

"We heard it was related to drugs."

Blake frowned and looked down at his notes again. "Earlene Lassiter died of an overdose of heroin. She was a drug addict."

Kate frowned. "I'm sorry to hear that. But what does that have to do with Brad?"

"We think Al Hadecker was dealing drugs."

"Dealing drugs?" Cece's mouth fell open. "I thought he was a real estate guy."

"Apparently he may have had another business going on the side." Blake shook his head. "You won't believe the people who get involved in these illegal activities."

Cece's blue eyes were wide. "This whole thing gets weirder and weirder."

"It gets even stranger," Blake said. "See, Hadecker had texted Earlene Lassiter about a drug deal, apparently not knowing she was dead. Brad Lassiter answered the text and set up a meeting in order to kill him."

"Brad told you that?" Kate asked.

"Yes, he did. Flat out. That's what's called motive, ladies," Carlioni said. "His wife died from an overdose of drugs and he murdered the dealer. Open-and-shut case."

"Oh." Kate's frown deepened. "Brad told you he murdered Mr.Hadecker? I can hardly believe it."

Blake folded his hands together. "He didn't admit to murdering Hadecker, only that he intended to kill him. He denies he actually did the deed."

"Well, there you go. Brad obviously couldn't go through with it."

Carlioni straightened up. "Just because he didn't admit to the murder doesn't mean he didn't do it."

Blake held his hand up to quiet Detective Carlioni. "Kathryn, I can see you want to believe in Lassiter's innocence, but we're not so sure. Still, I want to assure you we'll be fair and unbiased."

"Thank you, commissioner. I don't know what I can do, but I want to help Brad. You know I'm a software developer. I work from home and my hours are flexible, so I can work on this in my spare time."

"Kathryn, I'd prefer it if you let us handle this case. But if you feel strongly, you might want to talk to this man." He handed her

Stan Palmerton's business card. "He's a private investigator who had some dealings with Al Hadecker. He might be able to help."

"Thanks. I'll talk to him." She examined the card. "In the meantime, can I visit Brad in jail?"

"Yes. That'd be fine."

* * *

"What do you think, Cece?" Kate looked at her sister when they got into her car.

"I think they don't want us nosing around. You heard the Carlioni guy. They're convinced Brad is guilty, and they're not going out of their way to consider anything else."

"I agree. I think we're on our own." Kate looked at the business card she was still holding in her hand. "Maybe this man can help. Oh, and there's a meeting of the Keep Bellevue Beautiful group tonight."

CHAPTER TWENTY-ONE

Keep Bellevue Beautiful

"This is where you went to high school?" Cece asked as she and Kate made their way into the building.

"Yep. Nice, isn't it?" Kate pointed the way down the hall to the left. "The library's over there."

"I figured that out all by myself," Cece said. "I think it's the hordes of people heading in that direction."

Bellevue High School's library was big and beautiful. Five thousand square feet of shelves flush with books and CDs occupied one half of the room. The other half housed rows and rows of tables lined with monitors and keyboards. Extra chairs had been set up all around the room to accommodate the crowd.

"I'm guessing more than a hundred people. What do you think?" Kate asked.

"Mm-hmm. I agree." Cece turned her head to scan the room. "That's a lot of suspects."

Jonathan Katz stood at the lectern and called the meeting to order. Despite the this-is-serious-business frown he stuck on his face, his wispy straw-colored hair and bony frame made him look more like a scarecrow in Adidas 3-Stripes warm-ups than a protester. "We can't let our guard down," he said. "Alexander Hadecker may not be with us anymore, but the Barringer farm is still up for sale and there's bound to be another real estate guy out there ready to buy it and turn it into ticky-tacky shacks."

"Interesting that he brought up Hadecker's name right off the bat," Kate whispered. Cece nodded in response.

A thirtyish man in the second row raised his hand. "Have you heard of anybody else, Jonathan?"

"No, but I had lunch with Councilman Grayson today, and he says he'll keep me informed if anything comes up. He's definitely on our side."

"What should we do next to ensure we protect ourselves?"

"Good question. Please stay vigilant and let me know immediately if you hear anything. We need to cut off any new threat before it can take root. And we need to know where our political leaders are. If they don't support us, we'll take action."

After an hour of discussions about marches, protests, and letter-writing campaigns, the meeting wrapped up, and Jonathan Katz began gathering papers from the lectern.

"Excuse me." Kate and Cece approached him and introduced themselves. "We were wondering if we could ask you a couple of questions."

Katz continued sifting through the papers. "You're not reporters, are you?"

"No, we're not." Kate smiled. "But we were looking into Mr. Hadecker's murder, and we thought you might be able to help us."

Katz dropped the pile of papers on the lectern, and his eyebrows shot up above his wire-rimmed glasses. "You're from the police?"

"No, no," Cece said and laughed. "We're the two people who found the body, and we're interested in looking into the murder."

"Oh, I see." The eyebrows descended back to more agreeable territory. "I read about you in the paper. It said you were out running when you noticed the body. Must have been a terrible trauma to you both."

"Well, it wasn't any fun, that's for sure," Cece said.

Kate pulled on her ponytail. "Mr. Katz, do you think anyone in this organization would go so far as to harm Mr. Hadecker to stop him from buying the Barringer farm?"

The eyebrows headed north again. "Violence? Absolutely not! We're a group of successful and honest people. No one in this organization would even think of such a thing."

Out of the corner of her eye, Kate saw a man enter the library and walk toward them. He approached the little group with a frown. "Jonathan, we have to talk," he said.

"No problem. Have a seat in the conference room. I'll be right there." Katz checked his watch and turned back to face Kate. "Ladies, you'll have to excuse me now. I have to meet with Jeremy Dodd."

* * *

"So, what do you think?" Kate and Cece walked down the silent corridor to the parking area.

"On the one hand," Cece said and grinned, "me thinks he doth protest too much."

"You mean when he said none of that group would be involved in violence?"

"Yeah. Did you see how red his face got?"

Kate turned a corner and put her hand on the door handle. "Maybe he got mad that we suggested it." She pushed the door open. "I wonder what Jeremy Dodd wants with Jonathan Katz."

"Money."

"You really think so?" They walked to the car and she slipped into the driver's seat.

Cece opened the passenger door and hopped in. "I'm guessing he can get some big contributions from this crowd. Didn't you notice the cars when we drove in? I thought we were in a BMW dealership. I bet every one of these people has an ivy league degree and a high-tech, six-figure salary."

"So they'll contribute to Hodges if he promises to fend off the cheap real estate developers?"

"You got it."

"Do you think any of them could have killed Hadecker?"

Cece clicked her seat belt in place. "Jonathan Katz looks like he'd be more comfortable behind a computer screen than a firearm. He'd probably run for cover if a balloon popped. We may not like their attitude, but I bet the most violent thing that bunch would do is sponsor a voter registration drive."

CHAPTER TWENTY-TWO

Mac's Update

Commissioner Blake took the last bite of his egg salad sandwich and gulped down a swig of coffee. He peered into the paper lunch bag for any clue of a cookie. Finding none, he put his hand in and rummaged around. "Gee whiz, Marsha," he said under his breath. "One cookie wouldn't hurt." There was a tap on the door. "Come on in."

Detective MacMillan pushed the door open. "You wanted to see me, boss?"

Blake nodded. "Have a seat and give me the scoop on the Hadecker investigation." He crumpled his lunch bag and tossed it in the trash.

MacMillan folded himself into the chair in front of Blake's desk. "I questioned the staff at Hodges Campaign Headquarters. Nobody admitted making the call to Hadecker's hotel room, and there's no way to identify who called him. That's a dead end."

"Yeah. That's what I thought. How about the search at Lassiter's house?"

"Mr. and Mrs. Weatherspoon were there when we arrived with the warrant. They didn't give us any grief. We did a thorough sweep of the house."

"Find any guns?"

"Several. A rifle and two handguns. We checked and Lassiter has a license for all of them."

"Did you confiscate them?"

"Yep. One of them was a Smith & Wesson. It had been fired recently."

Blake sat forward in his chair. "Can we tie it to the murder?"

"We can't say for sure 'cause we don't have the bullet that killed the guy. The medical examiner says the shot went straight through and exited out the man's back. However, he says the size of the entry and exit wounds are consistent with what would have been produced by Lassiter's gun."

"Anything else?"

MacMillan leaned forward and chewed on his bottom lip. "One other thing. Kind of odd."

"What's that?"

"When we checked his car, we found a receipt from a car wash in the cup holder. It was dated the day after the murder."

"Why is that odd?"

"It rained all day on Saturday." He scratched his head. "Who gets their car washed on a rainy day?"

"I see what you mean. That is odd." Blake sat back in his chair. "Any more from Lassiter?"

"He's in a holding cell. We're scheduled to do an interrogation tomorrow. Maybe we'll get some information out of him then."

"Good. What about Hadecker's car? Any news?"

"Nothing. The APB is still out on it and we reported it to surrounding states, but nobody's seen it."

Blake drummed his fingers on his desk. "That's one thing that doesn't add up. If Lassiter killed him, why would he take his car?"

"Maybe to make it look like a robbery?"

"Hmm. Maybe. I'll stop in tomorrow to witness the questioning. In the meantime, I have a few other people you need to add to the list to question."

MacMillan pulled a notebook out of his pocket. "No problem. Who are they?"

"Start with Earl Weatherspoon. Since Lassiter's his son-in-law, he might know something."

"Got it."

"Also talk to Jonathan Katz. He's the head of that Keep Bellevue Beautiful crowd. No reason to think one of them may have taken things into their own hands, but the motive is there."

"Got it. Anybody else?"

"Yeah. Have a talk with Jeremy Dodd. Kathryn Frasier called to tell me he showed up at one of those KBB meetings. It's probably nothing, but there's always a chance we can find out more information."

"Will do, boss." MacMillan stood and stretched.

As MacMillan walked out, Officer Fioni poked her head into the office. "She's here."

"Does she have anybody with her?" Commissioner Blake wiped his brow with a handkerchief.

Officer Fioni shook her head. "No. She says she can handle this."

"Tell her I'll be right there." He waited until Fioni left. "Stay calm," he muttered to himself. A woman might think she could handle seeing her husband's dead body, but Blake knew the effect such a shock could have. He took a roll of Life Savers out of one pocket and looked at it. Then he returned it to his pocket, took a stomach pill out of his other pocket, and popped it in his mouth.

CHAPTER TWENTY-THREE

Larissa Hadecker

Mrs. Hadecker was standing in the reception area. After the loud blue and yellow plaid jacket Hadecker was wearing, Blake had expected something similar from his wife. But this woman was sleek and sophisticated with dark, straight hair pulled back into a twist. She looked to be in her thirties. A lot younger than Hadecker. Brown pencil skirt, white blouse under a dark brown leather jacket. *Hadecker had good taste.* As he got closer, Mrs. Hadecker looked up at him with a steady gaze, but her eyes were red and puffy. She held a handkerchief.

"Mrs. Hadecker." Commissioner Blake introduced himself. "I'm sorry to meet you under these circumstances. Would you like a glass of water?"

She stood straight, with her hands folded together at her waist. "No, thank you, Commissioner." Her voice shook a little but had a quiet, determined quality. "I know this is going to be difficult, so I'd like to get it over with as quickly as possible."

"I understand. I'm sure you have a lot of questions, and we can talk after the identification."

"Actually, I came straight from the airport, and I have a limo waiting for me outside. I'm very tired from the travel, so I plan to return home immediately. I'll make all the arrangements from there."

"Yes, of course. You'll want to get back to your home." Blake pointed down the hall. "The morgue is right next door. Do you have someone you'd like to be with you? This might be hard for you to face without some support."

"Perhaps Officer Fioni could be there." Larissa Hadecker nodded at the junior woman detective.

"Fioni, is that all right with you?" He'd give her an out if she was uncomfortable with it.

"Yes, sir." She looked serious and professional, even eager, but Blake wondered if she was up to the task. She was twenty-something years old.

"All right, then. This way." The commissioner led the women to the adjoining building and motioned for them to take a seat in the outer room. "Wait here, please. Let me make sure everything is ready for you." Blake entered a key code and pushed open the door to the morgue.

The frigid temperature in the room hit him in the face and made him clamp his teeth together. He held his breath against the antiseptic smell. He'd have this lousy scent on him for the rest of the day. "Afternoon, Forrester. I've got Mrs. Hadecker here to identify the body."

"Hey, come on in, Commish." Forrester Conway looked up over horn-rimmed glasses and displayed an enormous, toothy smile. He had been the medical examiner in Bellevue for over twenty years, and he and Blake maintained a friendly relationship.

Blake was impressed with Conway, a man who spent all his time in a cold, smelly cave of death and yet maintained a happy, even gleeful, exterior. *He must be glad to see a real, live human being.* "Is everything ready?"

Conway took off the rubber gloves and washed his hands. "Yep. I've got him all set up for her." Conway dried his hands on a paper towel and led Blake to a separate wing that held the viewing table. "The body's in good shape," he said as he pulled back the cover. "We can lower the sheet enough for her to verify the ID. Head and shoulders will do the trick. Then she won't have to see the autopsy incisions. Or the bullet wound." He spread the covering back over the body.

Blake nodded and walked back to the door. He motioned for the two women to come into the room and gently took Mrs. Hadecker's arm to lead her across to the table.

"This is Mr. Conway, the medical examiner. He'll be able to answer any questions you may have."

Mrs. Hadecker nodded to the ME. "Thank you, Mr. Conway, for all you've done to take care of my husband's body." She took a deep breath, held her chin up, and stepped forward as Blake slid the covering down to reveal the top part of the victim's body.

"Oh!" Mrs. Hadecker cried out and staggered back.

Officer Fioni was there in time to keep the woman from falling. She quickly stepped in to take hold of Mrs. Hadecker's arm and led her to a chair by the wall.

Larissa Hadecker collapsed into the chair and put her head in her hands. She gasped for air as the medical examiner rushed to get her a bottle of water.

"I know this is a terrible shock, Mrs. Hadecker." The commissioner bent over the distraught woman. "Fioni, please help Mrs. Hadecker to the outer room."

"No!" Larissa shook her head violently. "You don't understand." She took the bottle of water Conway handed her and gulped it. Her hand was shaking.

"You don't understand," she said again, louder this time as if they hadn't heard it. She waved her hand toward the body. "That isn't my husband!"

CHAPTER TWENTY-FOUR

Lunch with Jeremy

K athryn stood in the doorway of Mrs. Fletcher's Fabulous Fried Chicken and scanned the room in search of Jeremy Dodd. He said they should meet here since it was close to the campaign headquarters. *Smooth guy,* she thought. *How did Representative Hodges ever choose him as a campaign manager?* After ten minutes of waiting, she stepped into the fast food line, ordered a chicken sandwich, and took it to an empty booth. She munched her food while keeping an eye on the door.

She was taking the last bite of sandwich when Jeremy appeared at the entrance and took his Ray-Bans off with a little twist of his hand. Kate waved, and he sauntered over and slid into the booth. She noted beads of perspiration on his forehead. *Sweating on a cold day? That's odd.*

"Hello, Kathryn." He gave a half smile and looked around the room. He turned his head to examine the empty booth behind him.

"Aren't you going to get something to eat?"

"No. I can't stay long. Lots of work to do." He pulled his lips back into a mechanical smile.

"You said you wanted to talk to me about something?" Kate noticed he didn't make eye contact.

"Yes. Um, Mike told me you're working with the police on this Hadecker thing." He pulled a handkerchief from his jacket pocket and wiped his face.

"Not exactly. My sister and I are looking into some things. We were the ones who found the body."

"Oh." He made a face. "Horrible. Have you found out anything? Any idea who killed him?"

"No. We really don't know anything. The police are keeping things pretty hush-hush." *No need to tell him about Brad.*

"If you find anything, I'd like you to contact me. I've worked with Al Hadecker a few times, and I'm really upset about this whole thing." He took a slip of paper and a pen out of his pocket. "Here's my cell number." He jotted down his phone number on the paper and clicked the ballpoint pen several times before laying it on the table. "Give me a call if you hear anything." He shoved the paper over to her.

"Sure thing."

He jumped up. "I have to get back to the office. Lots of meetings today. Don't forget to let me know what you find out." Before she could answer, he turned and hurried out.

"Jeremy, you forgot your pen," she called after him, but he had already exited the door. Kate held the red, white, and blue pen up to examine the writing on the side. "Hodges for Governor."

CHAPTER TWENTY-FIVE

Trauma in the Morgue

ommissioner Blake felt a surge of compassion as he knelt
in front of Larissa Hadecker. Part of his job was to help
relatives of murder victims come to grips with their
nightmare. "Mrs. Hadecker, I know this is a terrible shock. Many
times people aren't able to accept the fact their loved one is dead.
They even feel there's been a mistake. Please calm yourself, and
we'll have another look."

"I don't need another look," the woman said. Her lips
trembled. Her right arm shot out and she pointed toward the
table. "That ... that person is not my husband, and I can prove it
to you." She jumped up so suddenly she almost knocked the
commissioner over as she rushed back to the viewing table.

Blake looked over at Officer Fioni. The young woman's eyes
were wide with bewilderment. She stood and followed
Mrs. Hadecker. Blake regained his balance and joined them.

Larissa Hadecker pushed past the medical examiner. She
took the sheet in her hand and paused as if she was afraid of what
she was about to see. She dragged it back timidly, revealing the
upper half of the dead man's body. She stood frozen, staring at
the man on the table, before she spoke.

"My husband has a scar on his left shoulder. It was a deep cut
he got when he was in the army. It was at least six inches long."
She pointed to the left shoulder of the dead man. "Do you see a
scar there?"

Blake could feel the blood draining out of his face. "Are you sure about the scar?"

She turned to face Commissioner Blake and glared at him. "Of course I'm sure. We've been married for ten years. Don't you think I'd know something like that?" She flung the sheet back over the dead man's face. "You brought me all the way here from Europe because you found a dead man who resembles my husband?"

Blake stepped back. *What the heck is going on here? Is this a bad dream? We had the guy's ID.* Conway's gaze shifted back and forth between the dead body and him. Fioni was looking up at him with puppy eyes, waiting for a command that would make everything right.

Blake tried to get control of his voice, but it came out thin and shaky. "I assure you, Mrs. Hadecker, we had information identifying this man as your husband, Alexander Hadecker. If there's been a mistake, we'll get to the bottom of it."

"*If* there's a mistake?" Her face corkscrewed into a mask of pain and she wiped at the tears that were beginning to slide down her face. "What I want to know is, where is my husband?"

CHAPTER TWENTY-SIX

Who's the Dead Man?

L ate afternoon shadows found their way into Commissioner Blake's office. And into his mind. Detective Fioni had looked terrified when he told her to escort Mrs. Hadecker out to her limousine. Even his good friend Forrester Conway had raised his bushy eyebrows and scurried away as if trying to remove himself from the mess. *My mess.*

Worst of all, the mayor had gotten wind of the morgue episode. Blake put his head in his hands. The dead man wasn't Alexander Hadecker? Impossible. Something didn't add up. Larissa Hadecker must be wrong. She was overwrought, not thinking straight. The fingerprints would prove it. His phone buzzed and Carlioni's voice came across.

"We got the results."

"Be right there." Blake set his jaw and briskly left his office.

"You're not gonna like it, boss." Carlioni held up a report as soon as the commissioner walked in.

"Give it to me straight, boys. Nothing could be worse than what happened today."

"We ran the fingerprints. It's not Alexander Hadecker."

"What?" Blake sank into a chair. *Nightmare time.*

"They match a guy named Louis Tinnerman. Small time actor, small time drug dealer. Real slime."

Blake stared with an open mouth. "How could we have been so wrong?"

"He was a dead ringer for the Hadecker dude. Nobody would have figured it out. Besides, he had Hadecker's ID." Carlioni dropped in the chair behind his desk. "It looks to me like this guy Tinnerman tried to pass himself off as Hadecker."

"Brilliant detective work, Carli." MacMillan propped himself on the side of the desk and shook his head. His thick, sandy-colored hair was a mass of confusion where he had been running his hands through it. "But why would he want to pass himself off as Hadecker? Maybe he just stole Hadecker's stuff and was joy-riding in his car when he got in trouble."

Carlioni twirled his mechanical pencil around his fingers. "Maybe Tinnerman killed Hadecker and was gonna impersonate him in order to get some money."

Blake took a stomach pill out of his pocket and chomped on it. "We need to go back to square one, fellas. What do we know? Al Hadecker was scheduled to come to Bellevue last week. According to his housekeeper, he had an appointment to see the owners of the Barringer farm. Right?"

"That's the way I understand it. He was supposed to meet with the Barringers on Saturday, but he never showed."

"Some guy comes here wearing Hadecker's clothes, or at least duds that look like Hadecker's. And he's practically Hadecker's twin. He signs Phil's repair order as Hadecker and pays with Hadecker's credit card."

"That's right." Carlioni dropped his pencil on the desk.

"Nobody knows where Hadecker is, right? The housekeeper has been calling his cell phone but getting no response."

"Right again."

"Hadecker was from Curtisville, right? The police there know we identified the dead man as Hadecker. Have you contacted them with this latest information?"

"Not yet." MacMillan moved back to his desk.

"Mac, get in touch with the force in Curtisville and fill them in on what we know. If Carli's right about Tinnerman killing

Hadecker, there may have been a murder in their jurisdiction. Also, see if they have any information on Louis Tinnerman."

"Righto. I'm on it." MacMillan tapped a note on his laptop.

"All we've got to go on right now are these phone records." Blake ran his hand through his almost-white hair. "I'm gonna have to call the mayor. I don't think it's gonna go well."

CHAPTER TWENTY-SEVEN

Interrogation 1

C ommissioner Blake peered through the one-way mirror. The identification mess was yesterday's problem, but they still had a murder victim and a suspect. It was time to move on. He took a sip from the paper coffee cup. "Ugh. What do they make this stuff out of, Carli? It tastes like mud warmed over."

Carlioni snorted. "That's about the nicest thing you can say about it," he said and tossed his own cup into the trash. "I sure could use a cup of Palmerton's coffee right now."

"Me too." Blake nodded and dropped the rest of his coffee in the waste bin. A sound from behind the mirror brought them both to attention. "Here we go," Blake said.

Detective MacMillan escorted Brad Lassiter into the interrogation room and gestured for him to sit in a chair on the other side of a small table so he faced the one-way mirror. "Can I get you a cup of coffee or a glass of water?"

"No." Lassiter shook his head. "I'm fine."

Blake examined the man's face. Some suspects like to puff themselves up and put on a defiant show of bravado. But most shrink to a smaller version of themselves when they're seated in that straight chair in the unadorned interrogation room. Lassiter was somewhere in between. He had lost the contempt, but his face wasn't giving away anything that was going on inside.

MacMillan walked to a video device on the side of the room. "I'll be recording our conversation, Mr. Lassiter." He clicked on the device. "Detective MacMillan interviewing Brad Lassiter." He returned to the table and took a seat at an angle so Blake could have an unobstructed view. "I'm going to repeat what you heard from us earlier, Mr. Lassiter. You have the right to remain silent. Anything you say may be held against you. You have a right to legal counsel, but you have waived that right. Correct?"

"Correct." Brad Lassiter's voice was so low it was barely audible.

"Would you speak up, Mr. Lassiter. We want to ensure we get every word."

Brad lifted his head and boomed out his answer. "Correct."

"Thank you." MacMillan took a small notebook out of his shirt pocket and peered at it. "Mr. Lassiter, we need to clarify something. We originally told you the victim's name was Alexander Hadecker. Do you remember that?"

"Yes. I remember."

Blake glanced at Carlioni. "Let's see how he reacts to the name." He focused on Lassiter's face.

MacMillan looked up from his notebook and leaned in toward Lassiter. "The victim was not Alexander Hadecker. The murdered man was Louis Tinnerman."

Lassiter shrugged. "Doesn't matter to me."

"Did you know Louis Tinnerman, Mr. Lassiter?"

"No."

"Huh." Blake rubbed his chin. "No reaction. I guess he didn't know either of those guys. As far as he was concerned, all he wanted to do was kill the man who was supplying drugs to his wife. Makes sense."

"Either that or he's one heck of an actor," Carlioni replied. They turned their attention back to the mirror.

"Now, Mr. Lassiter, I'm going to walk you through the events of last Friday night." MacMillan glanced at his notes again. "You stated that you noticed a text that had been sent to your wife's phone. Is that correct?"

"Yes. I noticed it when I got home from work."

"Were you in the habit of monitoring the texts that came to your wife's phone?"

"Yes. I checked her phone every day after she died."

"Why?"

Lassiter's face sagged. "My wife was a drug addict. She died of an overdose. I suspected a pusher might try to contact her."

"But since your wife had already died, why would you want to know about a drug dealer trying to contact her?"

"I wanted to make sure he didn't ruin anybody else's life." Brad rubbed his hand across his eyes.

"How were you going to do that?" MacMillan's voice was steady and soft.

"I was going to kill him."

Carlioni looked at Commissioner Blake. "I never saw anything like this, boss. He's telling us his motive right off the bat. The guy's either stupid or crazy. You want me to go in?"

"Not yet. Why don't you let Mac have some more time with him. We might get a confession now."

* * *

MacMillan felt a lump in his throat and he coughed to clear it. He wasn't supposed to feel compassion for a suspect. His job was to get at the truth. But MacMillan's own sister had died of a drug overdose, and he knew the rage that came with losing someone you loved to a slimy monster who kept feeding them poison. He took a deep breath and gulped water from a bottle. "Mr. Lassiter, are you sure you don't want an attorney present? It would be a good idea."

"No. I'm going to tell you the truth about what happened. The truth will set me free."

MacMillan frowned. This wasn't smart, but it was Lassiter's decision. "So you saw the text on your wife's phone on Friday. Did you recognize the number?"

"No."

"Did you know who sent the message?"

"No."

"What did the message say?"

"You have the message. You know what it said." Lassiter's tone was changing. He was getting impatient.

"Yes, we know. But I need you to tell me." MacMillan's voice remained steady and quiet.

Lassiter shrugged. "It said 'Drop tonight 8:00. Where?'"

"And what did you think it meant?"

"I thought it meant the dealer wanted to sell her drugs. He thought she was still alive."

"So you answered the text?"

"Yes."

"And what did you say in your response?"

"I said 'RR Terminal back lot.'"

"And why did you say that?"

"I wanted to meet him behind the old railroad terminal. It's deserted there."

"Did you want to buy drugs from him?"

"No. I told you. I wanted to kill him."

"Did you kill him, Mr. Lassiter?"

CHAPTER TWENTY-EIGHT

Interrogation 2

B lake and Carlioni both leaned forward toward the mirror. MacMillan asked again, "Did you kill him, Mr. Lassiter?"

Lassiter's face was contorted with pain. "No. I didn't kill him."

Blake put his hand on Carlioni's shoulder. "Time for you to make your entrance, Carli. This guy's on the edge. You might be able to push him over."

Lassiter turned his head when the door opened, then dropped it back down.

"This is Detective Carlioni," MacMillan said. "He's going to help me with the questioning."

Lassiter nodded but didn't speak.

"Sorry I'm late to the party." Carlioni's voice was upbeat as he placed his bottle of water on the table. "Can I get you something, Mr. Lassiter?"

"No. I'm good."

Carlioni stood by the side of the table and put his foot up on a chair. "Why don't we go back over what's been said so far."

While Carlioni sipped his water, MacMillan summarized. "Mr. Lassiter says he drove to the deserted lot behind the old railroad terminal on Friday night with intent to murder Mr. Tinnerman."

Lassiter's head jerked up. "I didn't say it was Mr. Tinnerman. I didn't know who it was."

"All right," MacMillan continued. "Mr. Lassiter said he intended to kill the man who had sent his wife a text message. He assumed that man wanted to sell drugs to Mrs. Lassiter."

"Let's start right there." Carlioni's voice became clipped and impatient. "You were angry and you had made up your mind to commit murder."

Lassiter nodded and a line of sweat appeared on his forehead.

Carlioni's voice notched up. "Isn't that right, Mr. Lassiter? You'll have to speak up."

"Yes. That's right." Lassiter's voice rose to match. "I already told him." He gestured toward MacMillan.

Carlioni leaned in. The corners of his mouth turned down in derision. "Well now, you're gonna have to tell me."

Lassiter looked to MacMillan for support, but Mac was hunched over his notebook, writing something.

Carlioni stood and walked around to the other side of the table behind MacMillan. "What time did you arrive at the deserted lot, Mr. Lassiter?"

Lassiter shifted in his chair and wiped away the perspiration on his face. "Around eight o'clock. I'm not sure exactly what time it was."

"And was the other man there?"

"No. I was alone in the lot."

"Okay. You were alone in the parking lot behind the old railroad station at about eight o'clock Friday night. Then what happened?"

"I waited five or ten minutes. Then a man drove into the lot."

"What kind of car was the man driving?"

"I don't know. It was dark. I didn't pay attention."

"Then what happened?"

Lassiter sat back in his chair and stared out into space. His hair was wet with perspiration. "He got out of his car and came over to mine. He opened the passenger door to my car."

"And?"

"He wanted to know where Ellie was."

Carlioni put his hands on the table and leaned in with a sneer on his face. He was less than a foot from Lassiter. "Didn't that make you mad? That he knew your wife's name?"

Lassiter looked at Carlioni and his face reddened. "Yeah. That made me real mad."

Carlioni stood upright and threw his hands up in the air. "You were *real* mad? If that had been my wife and some lowlife jerk had come along selling stuff to her, I wouldn't have been real mad. I would have been in a rage. You must have been more than mad."

"I was furious. I've never hated anybody that much."

"So you shot him." Carlioni's voice was matter-of-fact. A that-makes-sense, sure-I-understand tone designed to make the suspect agree with the justification of it all. Designed to get the big C, the confession.

"No!" Lassiter shouted. "I wish I had, but I couldn't do it. I yelled at him. I told him I was going to kill him and all the other pushers I could find. I told him he didn't deserve to live."

"You didn't shoot him? After what he did to your wife?" Carlioni planted his hands on his hips, a dubious expression on his face. "You want us to believe that?"

Lassiter's head drooped. "I wanted to kill him. I wanted to blow his head off. I felt sick he even touched my car. I couldn't stand the thought of Ellie meeting this man and buying drugs from him. I thought I was going to lose my mind."

Carlioni pursed his lips in disgust. "So what happened next?"

"He laughed at me. He looked at his watch and said he had another appointment. Then he called me a couple of names and left."

"He drove away?"

"Yeah."

"And you let him go?"

"Yeah."

"Then what did you do?"

Lassiter put the heels of his hands over his eyes.

"Mr. Lassiter, I need you to answer the question. What did you do after he left?"

Lassiter's voice cracked. "I cried."

CHAPTER TWENTY-NINE

Stan Joins the Team

"Here it is," Kathryn said as she pulled the car over to the curb. "180 North Signal Street."

"Stanley Palmerton sounds like a pretty ritzy name for a private eye," Cece said as they walked to the front door. "I wonder if he's one of those guys who solves murders for fun. Like Lord Peter Wimsey in the Dorothy Sayers mysteries. Maybe it's Lord Stanley Palmerton. Wouldn't that be a hoot?"

"I think he'd be in a fancier office building."

They rang the bell at the second-floor office and were buzzed in.

A tall, fit man appeared from the inner office. He looked them over with hazel eyes and smiled a handsome, dimpled grin. "Hi. I'm Stan Palmerton."

Kate cleared her throat. "I called earlier. I'm Kathryn Frasier and this is my sister, Cece Goldman."

"Nice to meet both of you. Commissioner Blake told me about your interest in the murder. He was very complimentary." He motioned them toward his office. "Come on in. You're in time for a fresh cup of coffee."

"Look at that." Cece pointed to a poster of the Agatha Christie movie *And Then There Were None* on the side wall. "I had a part in the stage play five or six years ago."

"Really?" Stan said. "What role did you have?"

"I was Ethel Rogers, one of the servants." Cece changed to a cockney accent and quoted a line from the movie. "Wot they don't know won't 'urt 'em."

"Ha! Very good." He applauded. "Naturally, I love mysteries, and that's one of my favorites." He nodded toward the poster. "The audience doesn't understand what's going on, but there's a mastermind behind the murders. Clever plot." He gestured to chairs in front of his desk. "Have a seat. I just made a pot of Hawaiian blend. Smoothest I've ever had. Would you like to try a cup?"

"Sounds great," Kate said as she and Cece settled into the chairs.

Stan returned and placed steaming mugs in front of them. "I have no silver and gold, but what I do have I give to you."

Kate smiled up at him. "That's a Bible verse."

"Yeah. My mother was a Sunday school teacher. She made me memorize a bunch of verses. They always seem to bubble up at the right time." He walked behind his desk and sat in his large executive chair. "Cream and sugar are there."

Cece sipped her coffee. "Wow. This is the best coffee I've ever tasted. Maybe you should quit the PI business and open a coffee shop, Stan."

"Believe me, I've thought about it. It'd probably be a lot more fun than detective work. And more profitable." His expression turned serious as he focused on Kate. "Commissioner Blake tells me you're interested in the murder investigation. He says you think Brad Lassiter is innocent, and you want to help him."

"That's right." Kate put her cup down. "He said you might be available. If so, we'd like to employ you to help us."

"What do you think I can do for you?"

"We're not professionals." Kate gestured at Cece. "We're trying to find the truth behind what happened, but we're not sure how to go about it. We thought you could give us some direction."

"So you're basically asking for guidance? Someone to check in now and then to see if you're doing what you need to do?"

"Yes. That's right." Kate nodded.

Stan spent several seconds gazing intently at Kate. Then he leaned forward, picked his cell phone up from the desk, and scrolled through a couple of screens. "I tell you what. I can't give you the details, but I have a special interest in this case." He looked up. "I was planning to do some investigating on my own. If you like, we can join forces. No charge. If it looks like it'll take longer than a few days, we can discuss a fee."

"Are you sure?" Kate asked.

"Yes. First, I want to get to the bottom of this crime. It's personal. And second, I could use some good press. It never hurts to have the public know you helped solve a murder case. It'll do my business a lot of good."

"That would be great, Stan. Having a professional on our side would give us a lot of confidence since we really don't know what we're doing."

"Good. It's a deal." He smiled at Kathryn. "Have you had a chance to visit Lassiter, Kathryn?"

"No. I haven't gone yet."

"That's just as well. I heard they're starting the interrogation today. Knowing what I do about police interrogations, he'll probably be ready for a friendly face soon."

Kathryn stared at her new team member. "What do you think about this case, Stan? Do you think Brad is guilty?"

"I don't know." He shrugged. "But from what they told me so far, it sounds like they've got a solid case against him."

Cece's eyebrows shot up. "Don't tell Kathryn that. She believes Brad is incapable of murder."

"First rule of detective work: stay uninvolved." The corners of his mouth turned up in a slight smile. "It's nice to support your friends, Kathryn, but you need to look at the case as if he's a stranger to you. Otherwise you lose your objectivity."

"I understand," Kate said. "But I'm going to have to be convinced Brad's a murderer. I know there's a lot of evidence pointing to him, but it's circumstantial. There's no proof he pulled the trigger that killed Al Hadecker."

"Whoa. Haven't you heard?" Stan looked back and forth between the two women. "The dead man wasn't Al Hadecker."

"What?" Kate and Cece both spoke at the same time.

"It was some guy named Louis Tinnerman."

Cece's mouth dropped open. "They misidentified the dead man? How did that happen?"

"Don't ask me. I don't have any official responsibility here. I heard that from one of my contacts in the police department."

Kate shook her head. "It doesn't matter. Whoever the person was, there's no real proof Brad killed him."

Cece leaned forward in her chair. "Listen, Stan. You have to understand Kathryn. Her motto is 'Never give up.' You wouldn't believe how stubborn she is." She reached over and laid her hand on Kate's arm. "Sorry, sister. I didn't mean stubborn, I meant determined." She turned back to Stan. "They could be marching Brad Lassiter to the gas chamber and Kathryn would still be turning over every leaf trying to prove his innocence."

Stan folded his hands together. "To tell the truth, you may be right. I have a feeling the police are taking the easy way out on this one. And if that's the case, we should work together to find out everything we can to help the guy. Give me a little while to collect my thoughts and check with some of my contacts on the police force. I'll give you a call." He took a business card from the holder on his desk. "If you need to get in touch with me, I'll write my personal cell phone number on the back of this." He scrounged around his desk. "Where's a pen when you need one?"

"Here." Kate reached in her bag. "Jeremy Dodd accidentally left this one." She handed it over.

Stan examined the pen. "Who's Jeremy Dodd?"

"He's Representative Hodges's campaign manager and has tons of that kind of stuff around."

Stan jotted his cell number on the back of the card and handed the pen and the card back to Kate. "Here you go. Call or text me anytime."

Stan Calls

K ate opened the door to the freezer. "We're running low on frozen dinners," she said to Cece who was sitting at the kitchen table reading a news story on her laptop.

"What's in the freezer?"

Kate turned around and grinned. "Ice."

Cece laughed and leaned back in her chair. "I guess it's about time for another trip to the store. In the meantime, I could fix us an omelet for dinner. We have eggs and I think there's a tomato and some fresh spinach."

"Perfect. I vote yes." Kate opened the refrigerator and pulled out a carton of eggs. "I am so glad you moved in with me. Not only is it great to have my own sister in the house, you actually know how to cook!"

Cece got a bowl out of the cabinet. "I'm not a great cook, sister, but I'm glad you think so."

Kate's phone sounded Mozart's *Eine Kleine Nachtmusik*. "I wonder who this is."

"Kathryn, hi. This is Stan Palmerton."

"Oh, hi, Stan." She looked at Cece and raised her eyebrows.

"Hey. I wanted to call and tell you how much I enjoyed talking to you and Cece today. You two got me interested in this case, and I'm looking forward to working with you."

"That's wonderful, Stan. We really appreciate you helping us out. We don't know anything about detective work, so having you to work with is fantastic."

"Good. I'm glad you feel that way. I think we may want to start by talking to Brad's in-laws. I hear they're staying at his house while he's being held by the police. Could you make an appointment for us to talk to them? I'm free Monday morning if it works for you and Cece."

"Sure. I'll give Thelma a call right now and let you know. I get the impression they're looking for help, and I'm sure they'd be willing to talk to us."

"Great." There was silence on the line for a few seconds, then Stan cleared his throat. "Um. One other thing, Kathryn."

"Yes?"

"I was wondering if you'd have dinner with me tomorrow night. I know an Italian restaurant where the atmosphere is authentic and the food is great. It'd give us a chance to talk about the case and get to know each other better."

"Oh." Kate felt herself blush. "Thanks for the invitation, Stan." She scrunched up her face and looked down at her feet. "Actually, though, I'm in a relationship with someone, and, um, we've decided not to see other people."

"Oh, sorry," he said. "I didn't know." He cleared his throat again. "Let's go ahead and meet with the Weatherspoons, though. Let me know if you can set it up."

After Kate clicked her phone off, she turned to her sister. Cece stared at her wide-eyed. "He asked you out, didn't he?"

"Yes. You heard it. I told him about Phil and me."

"I knew he was interested in you. I could tell by the way he was looking at you in his office. Do you suppose he's helping us so he can get to know you better?"

"I doubt it. He says he wants the three of us to meet with Thelma and Earl Monday morning. If it works for you, I'll call them and set it up."

"Works for me, sister." Cece grinned and shook her head. "This whole thing gets more and more interesting," she said as she cracked an egg and dropped the contents into a bowl. "I wonder what Phil will say when you tell him."

CHAPTER THIRTY-ONE

Kate Visits Brad

"This is the first time I've ever been in a jail." Kathryn smiled weakly at the massive prison guard who didn't respond but simply motioned her toward the metal door. *I guess he only hears that one about a million times a day,* she thought as she followed him through the door and down a long, austere hallway. He opened a door on the left side of the hallway and held it for her.

"Sit there." He pointed to a row of chairs. "You're in number twelve."

"Thank you." Kathryn nodded to him. Her running shoes made little chirping sounds on the marble floor as she proceeded down the line of chairs until she found number twelve. She perched on the edge of the chair and hugged her sweater to her. *I wonder if he'll be in handcuffs.* She took two deep breaths. *I wish Cece was here. I could use her support.* But prison rules allowed only one guest at a time, so Cece remained in the outer office.

A guard led a man over to the chair on the other side of the Plexiglass partition. The person who slouched over with downcast eyes couldn't be Brad. *What did you expect? A touchdown celebration?* She chided herself on her own naivete. *This is a jail, not a football field.* His hair was uncombed, and his mouth had descended into an upside-down U. After he took the seat opposite her, he lifted the phone receiver as if it were an effort and met her eyes.

Kate picked up the phone on her side of the partition. "Hi, Brad. Maybe you remember me. I'm Kathryn Frasier."

The mouth slowly changed to an almost smile. "Of course I remember you, Kathryn. Thelma told me you'd be coming over."

Kate shifted in her chair and cleared her throat. "I was sorry to hear about Ellie. Are you okay?"

He made what sounded like a cough, but she took it for a laugh. "I guess I'm about as good as anybody can be who's being questioned about a murder. It's not exactly the Hilton around here."

"Yeah. I can see that."

His eyes were vacant. "Why are you here, Kathryn? You don't want to get mixed up in this mess. You should go." He turned to call the guard.

"Brad, wait. Listen to me. I want to help you. I owe it to you."

He smiled sadly and turned back. "Kathryn, I know you're a real nice person, but you don't owe me anything. Let it go."

"I can't let it go, Brad. I have to do this." She paused and waited for him to focus back on her. "But first I have to know. Did you kill him, Brad?"

He jerked his head up so fast, she sat back in her seat. His eyes burned into hers. "Do you think I could be a killer?"

"No."

He made the little coughing sound again and looked down at his hand. "Good. That makes one person in the world who thinks I'm innocent. Maybe you can convince the jury."

"Did you kill him, Brad?" She had to hear him say it.

"No." He looked up at her. "I wanted to, and it sure looks like I did. You wouldn't believe the evidence they've got that points to me."

"I know."

He shook his head. "Sometimes, Kathryn, I think God himself must hate me."

"Why would you say that?"

His eyes lost focus and he stared past her. "Ellie and I started out so great. We were on this wonderful path in life. And then it all went wrong. And it kept getting worse and worse. Now it looks like I'll be convicted of a murder I didn't commit." He refocused on her. "You know, Kathryn, I wish I had killed that man. At least I'd be guilty of the crime they're going to convict me of."

"You don't mean that, Brad."

"I messed up big time, Kathryn. I couldn't make my wife happy, and she finally took all her frustrations out in drugs. Now I can't even take care of my little girl." He clenched his teeth. "I failed at everything. Sara's going to have to live knowing her father is in prison for murder. What kind of life will she have?"

"Listen, Brad. If you didn't kill Louis Tinnerman, we'll find a way to prove it. But do me a favor."

"What?"

Kathryn put the palm of her hand on the divider. "Don't give up. Give me a chance."

He stared at her for a long minute. Then he put his hand up to meet hers.

"Time's up." The big guard motioned to Brad. He stood and walked to the exit door. He looked back at her for several seconds before he left the room.

No problem. I just gave some hope to a hopeless man. Now all I have to do is find a killer.

CHAPTER THIRTY-TWO

Cece Rides a Horse

I don't think this was such a good idea." Cece sat holding onto the saddle horn with both hands.

"You'll be fine." Ben held the lead line he had tied to Lady's bridle and mounted his own horse. "Relax. Lady is the gentlest creature in the world."

Kathryn and Phil rode up behind them. Kathryn smiled at Cece. "I can't believe Ben talked you into getting on a horse. I'm so proud of you."

Cece wrinkled up her nose and stiffly turned her head toward Kate. "Don't be proud. Just stay close by in case Lady decides to dump me."

Ben laughed and clicked to his steed. "Nobody's gonna dump you, pretty one." He led the others out to the trail behind the barn.

Thirty minutes and a mile later, the trail opened up into a wide glen next to Hyde Park Lake.

"How're you doing, blue eyes?" Ben stopped his horse and leaned over toward Cece.

"I'm still on board, so that's a good sign. By the way, what happened to Kathryn and Phil? I thought they were going to come with us to the lake."

"I think they took a detour a ways back. Maybe they were looking for a place to be alone."

"Seems like they're always wanting to be alone."

"Maybe they wanted us to have a chance to be alone together, too."

Cece tilted her head in mock surprise. "Why on earth would we want to be alone with each other?"

Ben resettled his Stetson back on his head. "So we can get to know each other better. A horseback ride on a pretty day has a way of bringing people together." He grinned. "Even us." He dismounted and walked to her side. "Come on, I'll help you down and we'll let the horses get a drink. Hyde Park Lake is one of the deepest lakes in the country and it has the sweetest water. It's fed through natural springs and runs off into the river over there." He pointed down to the left.

Cece swung her leg over Lady's rump like Ben had taught her. He caught her by the waist and lowered her to the ground. Cece smiled up at him, surprised she didn't feel icky being around the horses.

Ben handed her Lady's lead line and they walked to the edge of the lake. "Lady loves this water. We'll have to be careful she doesn't drink the whole lake—" He didn't have time to finish his sentence when Lady began to pull back away from the water.

"Oh, Ben, help me!" Cece held onto the lead line, but the horse was pulling her back.

Ben stepped around and quickly grabbed the line from her. "What's wrong, girl?"

"What's wrong? She was getting ready to drag me back to the barn!"

Ben shook his head. "I'm not talking to you. I'm talking to the horse."

"Oh. Sorry. I thought you said she liked it here."

"She does. That's what I don't understand." He tied his horse to a pine tree and led Lady toward the lake. When they got within a few feet, she pulled back again, but Ben held her firm. "Funny. Lady's never acted like that." He stared at the surface of the water. "And I never saw that before."

"What?"

"It looks like there's oil floating on the lake. Maybe that's what got her spooked."

"Look, Ben." Cece pointed toward the water. "There's something there."

"Where?" Ben tied Lady to another tree and stood behind Cece with his hands on her shoulders while she pointed.

"There. It looks like something's submerged in the water."

"Yeah. I see it just under the surface." Ben picked up a rock and tossed it toward the object. When it sank, they heard a thud. "There's something there all right. Cece, do you have your phone?"

"Yes."

"Call the police. I think Commissioner Blake may want to take a look at this."

CHAPTER THIRTY-THREE

The Car

"That didn't take long. What do you think he found?" Kate turned to Phil.

"We'll know soon enough."

They had tied the horses to trees out of the way, and they watched the diver as he came to the surface and stepped out of the lake. He pulled his face mask off and flippered over to Commissioner Blake. The diver turned back toward the water and motioned with his hand, pointing down and over. Blake nodded to the policemen who were standing next to him. Two of them taped the area with yellow police tape and the third man went back to his squad car to make a call.

"Uh-oh," Cece said. "This can't be good." She moved closer to Ben.

Ben put an arm around her shoulders. "No use guessing," he said. "Let's wait to see what the commissioner has to say."

Blake walked over and motioned for them to move to the side. "We'll need to cordon this off. It's already been spoiled with the horses and cars, but we need to preserve whatever we can."

As they walked out of the glen, Kate asked, "What did he find?"

"It's a car," Blake said. "The back axle got caught on a tree stump. If it hadn't been for that, we'd never have found it. It'd be at the bottom of a very deep lake."

"Do you know what kind of car it is?" Phil asked.

"It's a Jaguar."

* * *

Kate got as close as she could to the scene and peered into the lake as the diver re-emerged and walked to the shoreline. He pulled off his mask and flippers and nodded to Commissioner Blake.

Blake motioned to the tow truck driver. "Pull her out, Bob. But take it easy. We don't want you pulling the bumper off."

The chain between the truck and the water slowly straightened. As it became taut, Kate saw the driver hang out of the truck door to watch the progress. He gunned the engine, but nothing moved. All at once, the truck jumped forward a foot and began a slow progress away from the lake. A flock of starlings leaped from the trees, sounding an alarm, and flew north to a better retreat.

The truck groaned under the weight of its burden. As the back bumper appeared on the surface of the water, Kate, Phil, Cece, and Ben moved in for a closer look. The driver stopped and Kate heard him shout.

"Keep goin'?"

"Yes," Blake shouted back. "Pull it out to the edge of the lake."

The truck revved again and moved forward until the entire black Jaguar sedan emerged.

"What a waste of an outstanding piece of mechanical engineering," Ben said and shook his head.

The driver's side door dropped open as the car was being hauled out, and water gushed out. More water poured out from under the carriage. Kate craned her neck and stepped forward.

"Commissioner Blake?"

Blake turned toward her.

"I noticed something that might be important."

"Yes. What is it?"

Kate pointed to the driver's seat. "It looks like the driver's seat is pushed all the way back. It's a lot farther back than the passenger side. Like a tall person must have positioned it there."

Blake looked toward the car, then back to Kate. "Yes. I see what you mean."

"But you told us Louis Tinnerman was a short guy. He wouldn't have the seat that far back. Doesn't that mean the murderer must have been a tall person?"

"You're saying the murderer killed Tinnerman, then got in his car, pushed the seat back, and drove it into the lake?" Blake rubbed his chin. "Makes sense."

"But Brad Lassiter isn't a tall man. He's about average height. He wouldn't have done that."

"Now wait a second, Kathryn. You're jumping to conclusions. Tinnerman may have had the seat back all along. Or it may have gotten bumped when the murderer drove it into the lake. We can't let Lassiter go based on the position of the seat."

"I understand. I just thought it might be important."

"We'll keep it in mind." He turned away from her. "Simon, be sure to get the odometer reading on this car and compare it with the information Phil had. That'll tell us how far the car was driven between the time it was in Phil's shop and the time it was driven into the lake."

"Right, boss." Police Officer Simon started toward the car.

Blake intercepted him. "Oh, and Simon, take photos of the interior so we know exactly where everything was when the car was driven into the lake."

"Yes, sir." Officer Simon took out his camera and began snapping pictures. "Look at this, boss. The keys are still in the ignition."

"That's a help." Blake pulled them out, walked to the back of the car, and opened the trunk. "Well, what's all this?" he said.

Kate peered over his shoulder. "Is that a watch?"

Blake took a handkerchief out of his pocket and used it to carefully lift the mud-covered timepiece by its wrist strap. He held it at eye level. "The dead man's watch," he said.

CHAPTER THIRTY-FOUR

The Weatherspoons

K ate parked outside the Lassiter home and looked in the rear-view mirror. "Stan's pulling in right behind us. I'm glad he'll be here when we talk to the Weatherspoons. I don't feel comfortable around Earl."

"Me either." Cece wrinkled her brow.

The three of them approached the front door together. Thelma Weatherspoon answered the bell.

"Hello, Kathryn, Cece. Come on in." Her voice sounded anxious. Was she worried about Earl's behavior?

"Thelma, this is Stan Palmerton. He's a private investigator, and we're working together to see if we can find anything that will exonerate Brad."

"Thank you, Kathryn. You and Cece have been such a great help to us already. Mr. Palmerton, please come in and have a seat. I'll call my husband."

"You don't have to call me. I'm right here." Earl Weatherspoon walked into the room, and any hope he would be cooperative left. His face was as dark as a thundercloud as he approached Stan. "I heard what Kathryn said. I don't know what you can do for Brad."

Palmerton nodded and smiled. "Sometimes we're not sure what we're gonna find until we find it." He held out his hand. "I'm Stan Palmerton."

Earl took his hand and shook it, but he looked away.

"Please have a seat," Thelma said. "Earl, help me move these things."

"More blue shirts to be repaired?" Cece asked.

Earl picked up the laundry basket from the couch and dropped it on the floor. "Thelma spends more time mending Brad's shirts than doing anything else."

"Oh, I don't mind. Brad has a hard job and the buttons are always coming off."

"Are those the ones you use?" Stan picked up a button from a little bowl containing dozens of blue ones and dropped it back in the pile.

Thelma smiled sweetly. "Yes. I keep a whole supply on hand."

"Well, I say it's a waste of time. Especially now." Earl remained standing. "Go ahead and ask your questions. I have work to do."

Stan took a seat in a straight chair. "Mrs. Weatherspoon, were you here the night Brad left to meet Louis Tinnerman?"

"No. Sara was sleeping over at a little friend's house, so Earl and I were at our own home."

"Did you hear from Brad that afternoon or evening?" Stan took out a small notebook.

Thelma knitted her brows and glanced at Earl. "No. I don't believe we talked to him at all that day. Earl, do you remember?"

"I didn't talk to him that day."

Stan jotted a note. "The two of you were alone at home? All afternoon and evening?"

"Yes," Thelma nodded.

"Where is Sara now?" Cece asked.

Thelma gestured toward the house next door. "We asked the neighbors to watch her for a few minutes today while you were here. We didn't want her to hear our conversation about Brad."

"Mr. Weatherspoon." Stan turned toward Earl. "Can you tell us about Brad's behavior leading up to the day of the shooting?"

Earl's words split the room in two. Him against everyone else. "I already told the police. Brad and I didn't get along. I stayed away from him as much as I could. I didn't see him or hear from him the day of the shooting."

"Do you think Brad could have killed Louis Tinnerman?"

"Can't say. If you think you're gonna get an opinion out of me, you're dead wrong. I'm leaving the entire matter up to the police."

Stan turned back to Thelma. "Mrs. Weatherspoon, I take it you're here a lot and know this house pretty well."

"Oh, yes. I take care of Sara and keep the house in order."

"Did you notice anything unusual the day after the shooting? That would have been on a Saturday. Any unfamiliar object you hadn't seen before?"

Thelma paused and chewed on her lower lip. "No. I don't think so. Why do you ask?"

"No reason." Stan stood and looked at Kate. "Kathryn, do you or Cece have any other questions for the Weatherspooons?"

Kate nodded. "One more thing before we leave. Mrs. Weatherspoon, can I see Brad's car?"

"Of course. It's in the garage."

As the group entered the garage, Stan issued a low whistle. "That's quite an array of building supplies," he said and nodded toward the shelves against the back wall.

"Brad's real handy around the house," Earl said. "He added the porch on the back. Even did the electrical work." He pursed his lips together and muttered, "At least that was one thing he could do right."

While Stan examined the building materials, Kate walked around the car and tried the passenger door. It opened easily. She bent down and tried to imagine Louis Tinnerman leaning in.

"Are you looking for anything in particular?" Thelma asked.

"I just wanted to get a feeling for the car." She walked around to the driver's side, opened the door and slid into the driver's seat. "Has anyone driven Brad's car since he was arrested?"

Thelma nodded. "I took it to the grocery store one day when Earl wasn't here." She looked at her husband. "Earl, didn't you take it to get gas a couple of days ago?"

"Yeah. You told me it was on empty when you came back from the store. I took it around to fill it up." He shrugged. "Why? Is it important?"

"Probably not. But the driver's seat is pushed all the way back. Is that the way Brad drove it? Or did one of you change it?"

"Goodness me." Thelma shook her head. "I have no idea how Brad drives, but I wouldn't have changed anything."

Earl shrugged. "I'm not sure. I'm a big guy, and I might have moved the seat back without thinking about it. Why are you asking?"

"No reason. Just curious, that's all." Kathryn got out of the car. Earl closed the car door. "Of course, the police were here."

"Did they drive the car?" Stan had rejoined the group.

"No. They looked around it like she did. But I suppose one of them could have changed the position of the seat."

Stan nodded to Kathryn and turned to face the Weatherspoons. "Thanks for your time. If you think of anything that might help Brad, you can contact one of us." He handed a business card to Thelma.

* * *

"So, what do you think?" Kate asked as they walked to their cars. "Any hope of getting help from them?"

Stan responded quietly, "Earl's not going to help anybody, and Thelma doesn't seem to be the type who would notice anything."

"She's so focused on Sara, she probably wouldn't see a train if it was coming right at her," Cece said.

They stopped between their two cars. "So this was a waste of time?" Kate asked.

"Not necessarily." Stan pulled his keys out of his pocket. "You never know what might be useful."

Cece's brows had wrinkled up. "Stan, why did you ask Thelma if she noticed anything unusual in the house the day after the murder?"

"Murderers sometimes take something off their victim after they've killed him. Like a key chain or lapel pin. I learned about that when I served on the murder squad in Bakertown. There are criminals who get some kind of sick excitement out of holding on to a reminder of their crime. It's like a souvenir."

"A souvenir?" Cece's eyebrows shot up. "You're kidding."

"No, I'm not kidding. It's a strange thing, but true. If Thelma saw anything unusual in the house, it might have helped us get to the bottom of this." He checked his watch and walked toward his car. "Better run. I've got another meeting. Have a good afternoon. Call me if you hear anything."

CHAPTER THIRTY-FIVE

The Letter

"You're really going to take a riding lesson?" Kate turned her car onto Shady Lawn.

Cece nodded. "Yep. I'm going over to Ben's place tomorrow. It'll be a chance to prove to myself I'm not a complete klutz." She shrugged. "Besides, after finding that car in the lake and meeting with mean ol' Earl, I'm beginning to think a horseback riding lesson won't be so bad after all."

"Maybe it'll get your mind off the murder."

"Yeah. Watching them pull that car out of the water was spooky." Cece shuddered.

Kate pulled up in front of her house. "Would you grab the mail?"

Cece reached out of the window and opened the mailbox. "Looks like you got a water bill, an electricity bill, insurance bill ..."

"Another exciting day at the mailbox."

"Hey, what's this? Something different." Cece held up an envelope. "No return address. The only thing on it is your name and address in big, bold type." Cece raised her eyebrows in mock excitement. "Maybe you won the lottery."

"I think you have to enter to win. Too bad about that." Kathryn took the envelope and shook it. "Nothing ticking, that's a good sign." She put her finger under the flap of the envelope and opened it. Her smile disappeared.

* * *

"'Curiosity killed the Kat.'" Phil read the sentence out loud. "You got this out of your mailbox?"

"Yes. Cece and I stopped to pick up the mail on the way back from the grocery store and this was one of the letters." Kate and Cece stood in front of Phil's desk at Warren's Auto Repair Shop.

"No return address. And they spelled 'cat' with a *K*. I don't like this, Kathryn." Phil frowned and turned the paper over in his hand.

"You don't suppose it could have something to do with that guy—Jonathan Katz—do you? Could this be a warning about him?" Cece asked.

"I don't know," Phil said. "But I don't care about Jonathan Katz. I only care about Kathryn."

Ben poked his head in the office door. "Well, look who's here." Seeing Cece, he grinned and sauntered over to her side. "Why didn't you tell me you were coming over? I'd've baked a cherry pie."

"Very funny," Cece said. "But something happened today we thought Phil should see." She pointed at the paper Phil was still examining. "We're not sure, but it looks like somebody isn't happy about Kathryn getting involved in this murder investigation."

"What?" He took the paper from Phil. "'Curiosity killed the Kat.' That's all it says?" He turned the paper over. "Was there anything else in the envelope?"

"No. That's all." Kate took the paper back and held it up to the light. "And I don't see any marks on the paper or anything unusual."

"I don't like this. I think we should call the police," Phil said.

"I don't know." Kate sat in one of the chairs in front of Phil's desk. "It could be a practical joke."

"Well, for a practical joke, it sure isn't funny." Ben's face tensed into a frown that matched Phil's.

"Or it could be some kind of marketing thing." Kate flipped the paper over.

"Kathryn, what kind of marketer mails something like that?" Phil's scowl deepened. "I think you're trying to talk yourself into thinking this isn't a problem when it is."

"No, really." Kate pulled at her ponytail. "A month ago I was out running and when I got back to my car there was a paper underneath the windshield wiper. It had big, bold letters that said, 'You could be next!' It scared me when I saw it."

"You never told me that," Phil said. "That sounds dangerous."

"That's exactly what I thought until I turned the paper over. It was an advertisement for a 5K run. The other side of the paper said 'You could be the next winner of a trip to the Caribbean. Enter the Campbell Park 5K now.' Or something like that." She shrugged. "It scared me at first, but it was just a silly flyer. I wonder if this is the same thing."

"But there's nothing on the other side of this," Cece said. "Let's take a vote. Report it to the police or not. What do you think, Ben?"

"Definitely report it to the police. Better safe than sorry. I think we all know what Phil's vote is."

Phil nodded. "Absolutely, report it. It might not be anything, but it sure is a strange coincidence you got that letter while you're nosing around in a murder investigation."

Cece raised her hand. "I'm with the guys on this one, Kathryn. Let's report it and let the police decide whether or not it's important."

Kate chewed on her lower lip. "Okay. For the record, I don't think it's important, but you've outnumbered me on this one. I'll give Commissioner Blake a call and let him decide whether to follow up."

"We'll call him right now." Phil picked up his phone. "No more excuses."

CHAPTER THIRTY-SIX

The Riding Lesson

"**H**ey there." Cece spotted Mattie walking back to the house from the greenhouse with a tub full of winter squash.

"Hi." Mattie smiled and made a sideways motion with her arm.

"Need some help?"

"You can open the door for me."

"Sure thing, ma'am." Cece sprinted up the stairs and pulled the front door open. "Ben around?"

Mattie gave a knowing smile. "Yep. He's in the barn. Said you'd be coming by for a riding lesson. I thought he was kidding."

"I promised Ben I'd give it a try. I felt so dumb when he had to lead my horse around like I wasn't really riding it, so I'm gonna go through with it before I lose my nerve." Cece laughed and rolled her eyes. "You know, this really isn't my thing."

"Oh, pshaw. I bet you'll be riding like a pro in no time at all. They say Ben is a top-notch trainer." She grinned impishly. "And I think you're going to be the teacher's pet." She turned and made her way into the house. "Good luck. Don't fall."

Yeah. Great. Saying "don't fall" to me is like saying "have a good flight" to a brick.

"Hey." She heard Ben's voice. "What are you doin' up there on the porch? The horses are down here in the barn."

She waved and skipped down the stairs to meet him. *Courage. Courage. Be strong and courageous.*

"Ready for your first lesson?" He pulled a red bandana from around his neck and wiped his hands on it.

"I guess."

"That doesn't sound very enthusiastic." He stopped in front of her. "Where's your hat?"

"What hat? I never wear a hat."

"You need a hat if you're going to be riding outside. You can pick one up later. We'll be spending most of this lesson in the barn."

Cece wrinkled her nose. "I'm gonna be riding around inside the barn? Is that safe?"

Ben put his hands on his hips. "No, you're not gonna be riding inside the barn. You're gonna be learning about horses and how to tack them up."

Cece's eyes got big and she sucked in a lungful of air. "Tack them up? Won't that hurt them?"

Ben shook his head and took her hand. "This is gonna take more time than I thought. Come on, sunshine. We've got a lot of work to do."

* * *

Cece led Lady from her stall into the main aisle of the barn. Ben showed her how to hold the halter and lead line so the horse wouldn't step on her feet.

"You'll need boots, too. They'll protect your feet and legs."

Cece held herself away from Lady as Ben tethered the mare between two posts. "Sounds like I'm gonna need a whole new wardrobe if I want to ride a horse."

"You only need to pick up a few things," he said and handed her a brush. "Take this and watch me." He used his own brush to smooth the horse's neck and sides. "Give her a gentle brushing."

Cece cooed and talked quietly to Lady as she brushed her. The mare whinnied softly.

"See there, she likes you. Look here." Ben walked to the front and gently stroked Lady's nose. "She'll fall in love with you if you rub her face and scratch behind her ears."

Cece reached up and gently smoothed the mane behind the horse's ears. Lady tilted her head like a dog. "Oh, look. She's liking this." Cece patted the mare's neck and looked up into the luminous eyes. "I can see why they call you Lady. You're very proper. You and I are going to be great friends."

"I've already cleaned her feet, so you don't have to do that. Here. Take this." Ben handed Cece a blanket. "Put it on her back."

Cece threw the blanket over the horse the way she had seen cowboys do in the movies.

"Perfect. I knew you were a natural."

"Yeah. Thanks to Clint Eastwood."

"Now comes the saddle." Ben pulled a western saddle down from the rack. "You can use this one." He held it out. "See if you can hold it. Put your arms under it like I have mine."

She reached under the saddle and got a good grip. "Okay. You can let go." Ben removed his hands. "It's heavy," she said.

"You'll get used to it. Think you can swing it up onto Lady?"

"No way."

"Give it a try."

Cece tried to lift the saddle to Lady's back, but she only managed to bump into her side. "Help."

Lady turned her head around and looked at Cece.

"I think she's laughing at me."

Ben took the saddle and gently laid it on Lady's back. "Don't worry. You'll get the hang of it."

"Yeah, right after I get the hang of brain surgery."

He chuckled and showed her how to cinch the saddle. Then he put Lady's bridle on. "Now we're all set. It's time to ride, cowpoke."

CHAPTER THIRTY-SEVEN

Stan Warns Phil

*1*80 North Signal Street. Suite 201. Phil checked his GPS and found the unassuming building with a brick facade and a metal door designed to keep out intruders. He pushed it open and climbed the stairs. *So this is where the guy works who asked Kathryn out.*

The only office on the second floor was labeled Stanley Palmerton, Private Investigator. He rang the bell and heard the buzzer unlock the door. Stan walked out of a side office to welcome him.

"Hi. You must be Phil Warren. I'm Stan Palmerton. Thanks for coming over." He walked briskly across the lobby area and extended his hand.

Phil nodded but didn't smile. He took the outstretched hand. It was firm. Maybe even hard. Phil returned one to match. "Good to meet you, Stan. You made it sound like there was something important you wanted to talk about."

"Right. Come on in my office." Stan led the way. His desk sat in front of a window at the other end of the room facing out toward the lobby. Papers and file folders littered the desk and the top of a set of file cabinets.

Stan closed the door behind Phil and pointed to a chair. "Have a seat. Can I offer you a cup of coffee? I just made a pot of gourmet blend. It's really good."

"Thanks, but I've already had my quota for the day." Phil took a seat. *No need to get chummy. I've got work to do.* "Now, tell me what you wanted to talk to me about."

Stan took a seat behind the desk and folded his hands. "Phil, I take it you and Kathryn Frasier are pretty close, maybe even serious about each other."

"That's right. Everybody knows I'm crazy about her."

"I'm guessing she told you I asked her out."

"Yeah, she told me that."

Stan held up his hands, palms out. "One of the reasons I wanted to see you was to let you know I'm not trying to cause any trouble. I saw she wasn't wearing a ring, and I figured she was available. I didn't realize you and she were a couple."

"Thanks, Stan. I appreciate you telling me that."

"Watch your step, though." Stan winked. "You two break up, and I'm definitely gonna make a move."

Phil faked a smile. "Sorry about that, but nothing's gonna come between us. We're in it for the long haul."

"Well, you're a lucky man. Kathryn's a great girl. I've gotten to know her a little these last few days, and I'm impressed with her intelligence. And her persistence." Stan took a swallow of his coffee and his expression went dark. "But that persistence can get her in trouble, Phil. Can I be frank with you?"

"Yes. Of course."

"I want you to know I'm concerned about Kathryn's attitude. She's taken it on herself to find Louis Tinnerman's murderer, and I think she's putting herself in danger." He paused and his frown deepened. "Commissioner Blake told me about the note."

"Do you think it was a warning?"

"I haven't seen the note, but from what Blake told me, it's definitely a warning."

Phil felt his shoulders tense. "I don't like this any more than you do, but Kathryn's a real determined woman."

"I gathered that. That's why I called you. Maybe you can talk some sense into her. I don't think she understands how dangerous this is."

Stan's voice knifed into Phil. "Why don't you tell me how dangerous you think it is."

"Phil, I've been in this business long enough to know when a criminal learns somebody's on his trail, he'll stop at nothing to get away. Kathryn's life could be on the line, and she doesn't seem to want to listen to reason."

"She's convinced Brad Lassiter is innocent, and she's determined to prove it. If you could find a way to get him off the hook, I think she'd give up."

Stan put his elbows on his desk and propped his chin on his hands. "Personally, I think she may be right. But somebody might want Lassiter to take the fall for the murder, and Kathryn is getting in the way."

"Do you have any idea who would do that?"

Stan pointed to a file folder on his desk. "I've been nosing around to see what I could find out."

"Tell me."

"I don't have anything specific yet, but it could be any number of people. One possibility is a drug kingpin. We know Louis Tinnerman was dealing heroin. Any time illegal drugs are involved, there'll be a lot of bad actors who don't want to be discovered. Could be one of them wasted Tinnerman, and now he's got the perfect cover since Lassiter bungled into the situation."

Phil's body went cold, and he gripped the arms of his chair. "You're scaring me."

"That's what I want to do." Stan's jaw tightened. "And that's not all. There are other possibilities."

"Such as?"

"The Lassiters didn't have the kind of money to support Ellie's drug habit. I figured she must have been getting money from somewhere else. I suspect Ellie Lassiter was seeing another man who was giving her money to buy drugs. This makes the case more complicated than a simple murder. A third party might not want Kathryn exposing all kinds of ugly facts about Ellie and her habit. Whoever's after her might not have Brad's interest in mind at all."

"Have you told the police about this? Why aren't they following up?"

"The police think they have this case all wrapped up. They're not gonna be interested in any theories I have until I get more solid evidence. I'll be working in the background, and I can keep you informed as things proceed." He locked his eyes on Phil's. "In the meantime, you need to convince your girlfriend to let the police and me handle the investigation."

"I'll do what I can, but you've already seen how determined she is. She's like a pit bull getting hold of a rag doll. She'll never let go. You know, they say marathon runners are the most persistent people around, and I can believe it, knowing Kathryn."

"She's a marathoner?" Stan's jaw relaxed and he sat back in his chair, looking interested.

"She signed up for the Vancouver Marathon next month, and she's running the Bellevue Women's Half-Marathon this weekend to tune up for it."

"No kidding. I used to run some races in town, but I'm more into white water rafting now." He pointed to a picture behind his desk showing a group of men in front of a line of kayaks.

"Looks like fun," Phil said.

"It is." Stan picked up his phone and tapped the screen. "As far as Kathryn's race, I've got an early meeting on Saturday, but maybe I can stop by in time to see her come across the finish line. That's always a thrill. Do you know what time she's shooting for?"

"She says she can finish in less than an hour and a half."

"Wow. That's fast. I'm definitely gonna stop by. She might win a medal."

"You don't think there's any danger in her running that race, do you?"

"Nah. There'll be a huge crowd. It'll be the safest place in Bellevue."

CHAPTER THIRTY-EIGHT

The Cowgirl

Cece looked up at the fully saddled and bridled mare. She was going to have to maneuver this tall creature around without the aid of Ben leading her. *No way.* "Gosh, Ben, I've learned so much already. Maybe we should call it a day and I'll get the first riding lesson next time."

"Nice try. Come on. Take the reins and lead her out to the corral. I'll be right here."

As they walked out of the barn, a white Mustang convertible pulled in and parked, and a young woman jumped out. "Hey, Ben," she called and waved. She was wearing a navy blue cowboy hat and matching boots. She had a white silk shirt with a denim vest. And the tightest pair of blue jeans Cece had ever seen. She did a fashion model strut toward them.

"Ginger, hi." Ben tipped his hat. "Come here and meet Cece."

The young woman was aptly named with her long, strawberry-blonde hair. Cece glanced down at her own sweatshirt, warmups, and running shoes and realized how foolish she must look to this cowgirl goddess.

Ginger looked Cece up and down. "Lesson?"

"Yes. This is Cece Goldman. She's about to take her first riding lesson."

"Ooh, you're lucky. Ben is the best instructor around." She linked her arm in his and planted a coquettish smile on her face. "He taught me to ride."

Ben unhooked himself from the newcomer and adjusted Lady's bridle strap. "Ginger boarded her horse over here when her father's barn was being repaired. How's everything going?"

"I showed Montana Ray last weekend, and he was perfect." She continued to gaze at Ben and stepped in front of him with her back turned to Cece. "You should have been there, Ben. We came away with a couple of ribbons, and Daddy was so proud."

Ben moved around to stand next to Cece. "Great. Thanks for stopping by. We need to get on with our lesson now."

Ginger's eyes flickered. "Sure. I understand. First-time students can be so demanding." She put a hand on his arm. "Oh, I almost forgot, I brought back that bridle I borrowed from you."

Cece watched as Ginger did an exaggerated hip-sway back to her car. *Maybe she's gonna get a rope and hog-tie him right in front of me.*

Ben followed Ginger and met her halfway to retrieve the bridle. "Thanks for returning it. Say hello to your dad for me."

"Sure, Ben. I'll stop by again when you're not so busy." She turned toward Cece and gave a little-girl wave. "Bye now."

* * *

I should probably give up this whole stupid thing right now. Cece waited for Ben while he returned the bridle to the barn. *I can never be a good rider, and I'll never look like Ginger.* "Sorry, Lady," she said and patted the mare. "You're stuck with a loser. Maybe we can get this over with fast, and I can go back to being Uptown Girl."

"Okay, are we ready?" Ben strode back from the barn.

"I don't know, Ben. I'm having second thoughts about this. I could never be a good rider. Not like your other students."

Ben looked down at her with a knowing smile. "'The fool doth think he is wise, but the wise man knows himself to be a fool.'"

"*As You Like It.* But what does that have to do with my riding a horse?"

Ben put his arm on the saddle and leaned down toward her until his face was inches away from hers. "It means you know you're a beginner. You're conscious of your own shortcomings." He stood upright. "Some students come here thinking they're God's answer to Roy Rogers, and they never achieve the level they should because of their own arrogance."

"Ginger?"

Ben rechecked the cinch on Lady's saddle. "Ginger's a frisky young filly who's full of herself, but she's not teachable. She'll never be a proficient rider until she's willing to deal with her own shortcomings. Both in and out of the saddle." He led the horse over to a small wooden box. "Come on, now. Stand on this box and put your left foot in the stirrup. Then swing your right leg over the saddle." He held the stirrup for her.

Cece grabbed onto the saddle horn and bit the fear out of her bottom lip. The leather creaked as she put weight on her foot in the stirrup and swung up into the saddle. Then she took the reins in her hands. "'Our doubts are traitors and make us lose the good we oft might win by fearing to attempt.'"

"Now you're talking my language, cowgirl." Ben squeezed her ankle. "*Measure for Measure*."

CHAPTER THIRTY-NINE

Looking for Clues

"**L**ooks like the police have removed all the yellow tape." Kate parked her car by the side of the lake. "Are you sure this is a good idea?" Cece wrinkled up her nose. "You know, Phil's concerned about you doing all this snooping around."

"Phil's just being protective. And he told me it's okay as long as I include Stan in anything we're doing. Besides, it's the middle of the day. What can happen?" Kate got out of her car and Cece followed.

Kate was looking under a bush and Cece was scanning the edge of the lake when Stan pulled up in his Jeep Wrangler and hopped out. He was dressed in a black turtleneck sweater, black jacket, and blue jeans. "Hey, ladies. Been here long?" He jogged over.

"We got here about ten minutes ago, and we've been looking around to see what we could find."

"Come up with anything?"

"No." Kate shook her head. "The only things we found are dead ends."

"Now you're learning what being a detective is really like. A lot of hard work and not much reward." He smiled. "You said you want to do some brainstorming."

"Right."

He nodded. "So what's the plan?"

Kate gestured around the area. "I thought it might help to get some ideas by being here at the scene of the crime. At least the place where the car was driven into the lake." She grinned at Stan. "You can tell us if we're all wet."

"Sounds good," Stan said. "Let's review the facts." He pointed toward the road. "The body was found over in the park about a mile from here next to a road." He turned back and pointed to the lake. "The car was found in the lake." He shoved his hands in his pockets. "We all know Brad Lassiter admitted he wanted to kill the victim. So let's hear your theories."

"Theory Number One." Kate walked to the middle of the clearing and held up her index finger. "The murder took place on the road by the park. Maybe Tinnerman picked up a hitchhiker who robbed him, shot him, dumped his body into the ravine, and then drove his car over here and into the lake."

"Makes sense to me." Cece shrugged and looked up into her sister's face. "And that would exonerate Brad since Brad couldn't drive both cars at once."

"The robber theory is a good one," Stan said. "And it could have been two robbers. They pretend to have car trouble, flag down Tinnerman to help them, and then kill him. That way one of them could drive Tinnerman's car over here and the other one could follow in his own car."

"True," Kate said. "But it couldn't be robbers."

Stan raised his eyebrows. "Why not?"

"Because of what the police found in the trunk of the car."

"What?"

"They found the credit cards from Hadecker's wallet, and they also found the dead man's watch and phone. Whoever killed Tinnerman took the cash out of the wallet, threw the credit cards, the watch, and the phone in the trunk, and then planted the wallet with the driver's license on the body. Robbers wouldn't do that."

"Maybe not." Stan shrugged. "But don't discount the robber theory so quickly. Could have been inexperienced thugs looking for cash. Maybe they opened the trunk to see if there were any other goodies there and just threw everything they didn't want into the trunk. You'd be surprised at the crazy things people do when they're committing a crime." He tilted his head at Kate. "But that's a good haul of evidence. Did the police get any clues from it?"

"No. Commissioner Blake said everything was ruined by water and mud."

Stan's face took on new animation. "If the police found Tinnerman's watch, maybe they can tell what time the murder took place. Or at least the time the car was driven into the lake."

"No." Kate shook her head. "It wasn't a regular watch with hands. It was a plastic digital one. Completely ruined by the water and mud."

"Too bad," Stan said. "Tell me what else you have in mind."

"Theory Number Two." Kate held up two fingers. "The murder took place here." She pointed to the ground by her feet. "Suppose the killer was in his own car, and he made an appointment to meet Tinnerman here because this place is so deserted, nobody would ever come here. There's a road on the other side of the ravine, so he couldn't meet him there. Somebody might come driving by."

Stan threw his hands up in the air. "You don't want to go with that one. You're describing the exact scenario the police will use to convict Brad! They think he followed Tinnerman from the railroad terminal and ended up here."

Kate stopped and chewed on her lower lip. "But if Brad had done it, he would have put the body in the car and driven it into the lake."

"Maybe. Maybe not." Stan shoved his hands back in his pockets. "But let's hear the rest of this theory."

"The killer murders Tinnerman and drives the car into the lake, thinking it will never be found because the lake is so deep. Of course, we know the car got caught on a tree stump, but the killer wouldn't have known that."

Cece shook her head. "But then there's a dead body lying on the ground. That's a bit inconvenient."

158 • KAY DIBIANCA

"Hmmm." Kathryn rubbed her chin. "So the killer loads the body into his own car, drives around to the ravine, and dumps the body there."

"That's a great theory, Kathryn," Stan said. "But why would somebody do that? The killer obviously didn't think the car would be found. So why not leave the body in the car and drive the car into the lake?"

Kate walked around in a circle with her hands clasped behind her back. "Good question." Then she stopped and snapped her fingers. "Of course! The killer *wanted* the body to be found and knew somebody would happen on it in the park."

"Yeah," Cece snorted. "Like me. Remind me to thank the murderer for being so considerate when we meet him. Or her."

Kate straightened up. "Do you think it could be a woman?"

"Sure, why not?" Stan said.

"I never thought of that." Kate turned around and began circling in the other direction. "There's something that's bothering me about this whole thing, though."

"Let's hear it."

"It's hard to believe the killer met Tinnerman here. This place is so deserted, and Tinnerman wasn't from Bellevue. I don't know how he could have found a clearing in the woods without some signs. Maybe the killer met him somewhere else, killed him, took his body to the ravine, and then brought the car here and drove it into the lake." She tilted her head and looked at Stan and Cece. "That would work."

"Now you're making this complicated," Stan said. "And complicated doesn't usually work in murders. Besides, once the killer drives the car into the lake, he's stuck here in this place, miles away from anything. How does he get back to his own car? Someone might see him walking along the road."

Kate rubbed her chin and looked out to the lake. "Theory Number Three. There's a game warden cabin over there on the other side of the lake." She pointed to a small house directly opposite them. "Suppose the killer met him there and killed him.

Then he put the body in Tinnerman's car, drove over to the ravine, dumped the body, then drove the car into the lake here and went back to the cabin."

Stan knitted his brows together. "That's another good theory, but the last step doesn't work. How's he gonna get back across the lake? He can't swim across. It's freezing in that water. And he can't walk around the lake. It's too big."

They all walked down to the edge of the lake. "Stan's right," Cece said. "It must be a half mile across this lake. You'd freeze to death trying to swim it."

"Hmm." Kate looked down at her feet, then her head snapped up. "I've got it! Theory Number Four. There wasn't one killer. There were two. They murder Tinnerman at the cabin, then the accomplice can drive the second car." She grinned at Stan. "That would work, wouldn't it?"

Stan didn't smile back. "I don't think you want to go there, Kathryn."

"Why not?"

"Think about it. Brad could have had an accomplice. Somebody else who would like to have seen Tinnerman dead."

Kathryn hesitated, then said quietly, "Earl."

All three were silent for a minute, then Kate started toward her car. "I'm going to drive around to that cabin across the lake and have a look."

Stan stepped in front of her. "No, you're not. You've already received one threat, and I promised Phil I'd keep you out of trouble. If somebody sees you nosing around over there, you could be in real danger. I'll drive over to the cabin later today and see what I can find out." He leaned toward her and put his hands on her shoulders. "Besides, Phil told me you're running the half-marathon this weekend, and you need to concentrate on getting ready for that."

Cece nodded. "Stan's right, Kathryn. You had some good ideas, but you know how worried Phil is. Stan needs to be the one to handle this." She linked her arm through Kate's. "Let's make sure you're ready to run this weekend."

"Okay." Kate patted her sister's hand. "Thanks, Stan. I really appreciate you doing this. You'll let me know if you find anything, won't you?"

"Sure thing. I'll grab some lunch, and then I'll do some snooping around that cabin."

CHAPTER FORTY

The Cabin

K ate took a right turn out of the glen next to the lake. In the rear-view mirror, she saw Stan turn in the opposite direction. She and Cece drove for a few minutes and she took another right turn.

"This isn't the way back to your house, is it?" Cece made it sound more like a statement than a question.

"No. I want to drive around the lake and get a look at that cabin before we go home."

"Kathryn, you know you shouldn't do this. Phil's gonna be mad at both of us if something happens."

Kate made another turn down a dirt road. "All I want to do is take a quick look. If anybody's there, we'll turn around and leave." She slowed the car as they approached a gravel driveway that led down to the cabin. The house was hidden by a thick grove of evergreen trees, but Kate could see a small dock that stretched out onto the lake. No cars. No people. She turned onto the long drive leading to the cabin. The tires clattered over the pebbles as they drove down the rutted path.

Cece leaned forward. "It's awfully dark here."

"It's a little wooded, that's all. Nice spot for a cabin." Kate pulled the car to the end of the drive. "Oh, look. We can park in that grove of trees and nobody will see the car." She maneuvered into the hidden area and parked. "Let's see what's here." She opened her door and stepped out.

Cece followed her. "Okay. But at the first sign anything's wrong, let's leave."

"It'll only take a second." The cabin's main door was located on the side of the house. Kathryn stepped up on the small stone porch and knocked. No answer. She knocked again, louder this time, and listened for sounds of movement inside. She tried the door knob, and it turned with a rattle, but didn't open. With Cece on her heels, she moved down from the stoop and walked over to a window that was next to the door. They tried to look in, but curtains were drawn and they couldn't see anything inside.

"Hmm," Kate said and continued around to the back of the cabin that faced the lake, with Cece right behind. They walked onto a small patio that butted against a sliding glass door. But that door was locked too, and drapes were drawn over the door. Kate knocked again. Nothing.

"Oh, look. There's a shed. I wonder if that's where they keep a canoe or something." The shed was locked with a combination lock. Kate shook it, but it didn't budge.

"This is enough for me. I don't enjoy snooping around other people's houses, especially this one." Cece turned. "I'm going back to the car, and you need to—"

The sound of tires on the gravel path brought them both to attention.

"Uh-oh." Cece grabbed Kate's arm. "Now what are we going to do?"

The two women stood like statues as the sound of the car grew closer.

Cece's eyes were so wide Kate could see the whites all around her blue irises, and she wondered if she looked as scared as her sister. She whispered, "Wait. Maybe they'll go away." They crept onto the patio, close to the glass door.

The sound of the engine died, and they heard the car door open and close. Footsteps crunched on the gravel and scraped against the small porch. Someone knocked on the door and rattled the knob.

Kate could hear Cece's breath growing louder, and her own heart was thudding against her chest. The footsteps moved off the porch and stopped again. Whoever it was must be looking in the window the way they had. When she heard the person walking toward the back of the house, Kate grabbed Cece's hand and pulled her around to the far side. They tiptoed along and stopped at the front corner of the cabin. Kate put her finger to her lips. Once more they stood still, trying not to breathe. There were no more sounds of footsteps.

Cece peeked around the corner. When she turned back to motion to Kate, she looked past her and screamed.

CHAPTER FORTY-ONE

Caught Snooping

"What do you two think you're doing?" Stan Palmerton stood with his feet apart and his hands planted firmly on his hips. He wasn't smiling.

"Oh, Stan." Cece put her hand over her heart. "It's you. Thank goodness."

He shook his head as he walked toward them. "I was about a mile down the road when it occurred to me you were going to come over here even after I told you not to." He stopped right in front of them. "Kathryn, I wasn't being nice. You could be putting yourself and Cece in danger. Don't you realize that?"

Kate felt her face grow warm with embarrassment. "I'm sorry, Stan. I guess I got carried away trying to figure things out."

He crossed his arms over his chest and frowned at her. "Cece, would you mind if I talk to Kathryn alone for a second?"

"No problem." Cece scooted away and called back over her shoulder, "I'll wait in the car."

Stan shoved his hands in his pockets. "Listen, Kathryn, I told Phil I'd take care of you, but you're making this hard. If you do anything else without me being there, I'm going to have to talk to him. You don't want that, do you?"

"No, but you have to realize how important this is to me. I know Brad Lassiter couldn't have committed murder, and I've got to find a way to prove it."

"Okay. I get that. But you need to see how dangerous it is." He paused and she heard him take a deep breath. "I'm worried about you."

She lifted her head and looked into his face. His hazel eyes were dark with concern.

He pressed his lips together. "Look, I'm not trying to come between you and Phil. It's just that you're special. You're smart and dedicated, and you're trying to help your friend." He put his hands on her shoulders and leaned in. "But you're being careless. I feel responsible, and I don't want anything to happen to you. Now will you please promise me you won't do anything else unless you check with me first?"

"I know you're trying to help, and I appreciate it." Kate sighed. "I'll do better."

"You and Cece go on home. I'll look around here, and I'll let you know if I find anything." He shook his finger in her face in mock anger. "Be a good girl."

He took her arm and led her toward her car. As they got within a few feet of the driveway, Kate stopped. "What's that?"

"What?"

"There's something on the ground next to the pine tree." She pointed.

Stan stooped to pick up the object and held it up so Kate could see it. It was a ballpoint pen. "Did you drop this?" he asked.

"No. We didn't walk over here." She took it from him, but she didn't need to see the writing on the side of the red, white, and blue pen. She knew what it said. "It's a Hodges for Governor pen."

Stan examined it. "It's like the one you let me use in my office. Who did you say had these?"

"Jeremy Dodd has tons of them."

"Hmm." Stan turned the pen over in his hand. "Anybody could have dropped this, but I'll turn it over to the police. It could be another piece of the puzzle."

CHAPTER FORTY-TWO

Just Start This Thing

"How do you feel?" Phil said. "You were quiet on the way over here."

Kate smiled up at him as they walked toward the runners queuing up at the starting line. "I was going through the race in my mind. But I feel great. I got a good night's sleep, and I'm ready to run."

"Thirteen miles?" Cece shook her head. "I can't believe you do this for fun."

"It is fun." Kate smiled and hugged her sister. "At least it will be when the race starts. The waiting is the hardest part."

"Good luck! I hope you do well." Cece gave her two thumbs up and walked with Ben to the sidelines.

"You're sure you're ready for this?" Phil put his arm around her waist and looked intently into her face. "You're not gonna fall and hurt yourself, right?"

Kate laughed. "Not if I can help it. I trained for it, and I'm ready." She bounced up and down to warm up her legs. "At least I hope I am." She wrinkled up her nose and gave him a big smile.

He leaned down and kissed her. "I'll be waiting at the finish. Now don't try to win this thing."

"Okay, boss." She saluted and turned to make her way into her starting corral. "I'll see you at the finish line." *He's going to be so surprised because I am going to win this race.*

She wouldn't have thought it was possible if it hadn't been for the phone call from Coach Siler last week. "Kathryn," he had said, "I saw the participant list for the women's half-marathon, and I was thrilled to see your name on it."

"Thanks, coach. I've been training for the Vancouver Marathon for the last four months. I'm using this race as my last tune-up, and I think I'm ready."

"Do you have a target time you're shooting for?"

When she told him her anticipated finish time, she had heard him draw a deep breath.

"Are you sure?"

"I've been using a training plan from *Runner's World*. I think I can do it."

"Kathryn, that's a winning time. You know there are a lot of other races going on around the country right now, so most of our best women runners are in Denver or Las Vegas this weekend. I've checked out the folks in this race, and you won't have much competition. You could be first across the finish line!" His voice was high with excitement, much like the days when he coached her on the cross-country team. "You're at the top of your game. If you pace yourself, you'll take home the gold."

"Do you really think so?"

"Absolutely. The only woman who could be close to that time is Shirley Setkoff. She's in this race too."

"Setkoff? She's a world-class marathoner. I wouldn't have a chance against her."

"Shirley used to be world-class, but that was a lot of years ago. She's thirty years older than you. The only way she'll be a threat is if you go out too fast and run out of fuel. If you pace yourself, you'll win."

"Thanks, coach. I'll do my best."

"Listen, this is your first half-marathon, so anything can happen. I don't want to create any false expectations, but you have a great chance. I'll email you mile split times, and I'll be there to cheer you on."

Now, Kate spotted Coach Siler on the sidelines talking to one of the high school runners. He looked up and they made eye contact. He gave her a high sign and she waved back. *Okay, coach, I got your split times, and I'm gonna pace myself through this to the gold medal.* She smiled as she stretched her quads. What would Phil's expression be when he saw her come across the finish line first?

The early morning chill and dry conditions meant this would be a fast race. The trees tingled with a breezy encouragement. *Go for it.*

The crowd was small, only a couple hundred runners. Less than a lot of 5Ks she had run. Coach Siler was right. This would be her race to win—or lose.

Women runners finished their strides and found places in the starting area, trying to stay warm and loose, making small talk, and waiting.

Kate found herself next to a young woman who was stretching her arms over her head. She stood over six feet tall and had bright red hair pulled into two curly pigtails. She looked to be a teenager. Kate nodded to her as she loosened up her shoulders.

"You run many half-marathons?" the other woman asked.

"No. First time for me. How about you?"

"I've done some 5Ks, but nothing this long. I'm a little nervous." She leaned over side to side to stretch her waist.

Kate rubbed her hands together. "I'm always nervous at the start of a race, but I'm sure you'll do fine."

"I see you're wearing a GPS." The other woman cocked her head and looked at Kate's watch.

"Right. It's a great help." Kate glanced down at her GPS watch to confirm it was ready to start and then pointed to the other woman's wrist. "What kind of watch is that?"

"It's a Galileo." The redhead held up her hand to show off the silvery watch with a large, round face. "I got it just a week ago. It's incredible."

"It's beautiful." Kate tilted her head to get a good look. "Does it have a lot of neat features?"

"It has something no other GPS watch has. It uploads data to a satellite as you're running, so you don't have to upload it yourself later. It's great. When I get home, I'll log into my account on the Galileo website to see all the data."

Kate nodded in appreciation as the announcer came over the PA with a loud, "Good morning, runners!"

There was a roar from the crowd in response. Some applauded, some whooped or raised their arms to signal their excitement.

Kate's new friend smiled sweetly. "I'll see you at the finish line. Have a good race."

"You too."

The announcer gave them some basic rules. "No shoving, move to the right if you want to walk, stay in the marked areas." Kate checked her own GPS again and put her right index finger on the start button.

"Are you ready, runners?" The announcer was shouting into the microphone now.

"Yeah!" Two hundred voices responded as one. Everyone was pumped.

Kate knew what was going on in the minds of the runners all around her. The same thing she was thinking. *Just start this thing!*

The announcer began the countdown. "Thirty seconds ... twenty-five seconds ..."

The crowd came alive around Kate as the runners gelled into a tight mass at the starting line.

"Five seconds ..." Then the horn sounded and four hundred feet began their trek through thirteen miles of trails.

CHAPTER FORTY-THREE

The Race

Kate was one of seven women in the lead group as they reached the three-mile marker. She barely slowed her pace to grab a bottle of water from the volunteer table, then continued. It was like a dream, the small group running smoothly while the rest of the field lagged behind.

The lead changed hands a dozen times. They may have been in competition, but they kept up a stream of friendly conversation as they ran.

"Nice day for a run, eh?"

"Great. How do you like those Nikes?"

"They're good. Probably should have broken them in before the race, though."

"Anybody have plans for an ice bath when you get home?"

"Not on your life!"

The back-and-forth took their minds off the boredom of the first miles when it's all about keeping yourself under control even though you're tempted to break out and run free. But soon the strenuous job of distance running took over and they quieted down, each runner digging deeper to find the ideal pace and stick with it.

"Feeling okay?" Kate asked the young redhead she had befriended in the starting corral.

"So far, so good." But the answer was gasped out, and by the time they reached the five-mile marker, the other woman had dropped behind.

A small brunette broke out of the remaining group and sprinted ahead. Kate felt the urge to chase her, but she knew better. Within a mile, the brunette had wilted and fallen back behind the others.

Kate checked the split times she had written on her arm. *Right on schedule.*

At eight miles, Kate moved into the lead. *Five miles to go.* She rolled her shoulders to release the tension and concentrated on her breathing. She recited psalms in her head to avoid thinking about the slowly building pain in her legs. *The Lord is my shepherd.*

As she passed the ten-mile marker, she grabbed a bottle of Gatorade from the volunteer table, gulped it down, and glanced back over her shoulder. The group had thinned out like Coach Siler said it would. The closest runner was at least a quarter mile back, but Kate was tiring. *Three miles to go. Don't think about the pain.*

She rounded a turn into a heavily wooded section of the course and welcomed the cool air, undisturbed by the heat of the sun. She blinked like a moviegoer entering a dark theater.

It was an odd thing to leave the sunshine of the meadow with spectators sprinkled around the course shouting encouragement and enter this deep shade with its eerie silence. Alone in the tree-lined tunnel, the only sounds were the rhythmic *thump, thump* of her Sauconys on the pavement and the measured draft of her breaths. *Lead me on a level path.*

Sunshine beckoned from the next turn a quarter mile ahead, then it would be about two and a half miles through open air to the finish line. She felt the urge to run hard to the light and escape this gloomy silence, but she knew the key was to keep herself under control. *Steady to the last mile, then pick it up and push hard to the finish.*

She checked her posture. Arm swing was comfortable. *Run like a gazelle.* Her shoes continued their soft pounding, and she wondered how many more steps it would take to the finish. *Let's see. Around a thousand steps to a mile. That's about three thousand steps to the win.* She smiled to herself and repeated the mantra she had used so often in the months after her parents' deaths. *Never give up. Never give up.*

A rustle and a loud snap brought her back to the moment. Up ahead to the left, was that a person standing in the shadow of the trees beside the trail?

CHAPTER FORTY-FOUR

Back in Bellevue

C ommissioner Blake's rubber-soled Naturalizers squeaked on the tile floor as he walked toward the office at the other end of the hall. *I gotta get new shoes. I sound like a sick mouse every time I walk on this floor.* Carlioni's call had sent Blake scurrying down the hall to the detectives' office.

Carlioni was sitting behind his desk squinting at a sheaf of papers. MacMillan was hunched over his laptop, pecking away. They both looked up.

"So what's all this about new information? Tell me it's good news," Blake said.

Carlioni waved the papers. "I don't know if you'd call this good news, but it sure is surprising stuff we got from the police in Curtisville." He shook his head. "You're not gonna believe this one, boss."

"Yeah?" Blake leaned against a file cabinet. "I can believe just about anything now."

MacMillan wheeled around to face the two of them. "Wait'll you hear it."

Blake raised his eyebrows. "Okay. Lemme have it."

Carlioni laid the papers on the desk in front of him and glanced up over his reading glasses. "Louis Tinnerman did have a relationship with Al Hadecker after all."

Blake stood upright. "They knew each other?"

"Better than that. They were brothers."

"Holy mackerel, Carli. Are you sure?"

"It's right here." Carlioni tapped the document with his finger. "We've printed another copy of the entire Curtisville police report so you can read it at your leisure. In the meantime,"—he gestured toward a swivel chair in front of his desk—"have a seat and I'll give you all the good stuff."

Blake dropped into the chair. "Shoot."

"Seems Al Hadecker's father was an important real estate guy. Made a lot of money in the big land boom. When he died, he left everything to his son, Al."

"So where does Louis Tinnerman come into this picture?"

MacMillan coughed behind a chuckle, his sandy-colored hair sticking up in all directions where he had been pulling at it. "According to the report, the senior Mr. Hadecker was doing more than selling real estate. He apparently had a girlfriend on the side."

"Okay, I see where this is going." Blake nodded. "He fathered a child with his girlfriend and then paid her to get lost?"

"That's it. Her name was..." Carlioni glanced back at the report. "Heather Tinnerman. She moved to L.A. and gave birth to a son named Louis. He was trouble from the get-go. Grew up with a bad crowd and started dealing drugs. Worked a few small jobs in Hollywood."

"Did he know his father was actually a rich guy?"

"Apparently not. There's no indication he knew anything about the Hadeckers until a couple of years ago. His mother may have done the confession thing before she died because he started making trouble for Al Hadecker shortly after that."

"Let me guess. He goes to Al Hadecker and demands money. If he doesn't get it, he claims he'll ruin the elder Hadecker's sparkling reputation."

"Bingo. Classic blackmail. Not only does he look like Hadecker's twin, he has the DNA to prove who he is and pushes hard for money."

"And Hadecker isn't thrilled to learn he has a brother, right?"

"Right again, boss." MacMillan ran his fingers through his hair. "Hadecker must have given him some money to keep him quiet, but Tinnerman kept coming back. Hadecker probably realized this was never going to end. They think he decided to put a stop to it."

"They?"

"The police in Curtisville." Carlioni took off his reading glasses and rubbed his bloodshot eyes. "They found Hadecker's body yesterday. It was in a remote cabin Hadecker owned up by Curtisville Lake. It had been set up to look like a robbery, but the cops aren't buying it."

Blake took out a roll of Life Savers and popped one in his mouth to dispel the lousy taste that had settled there. "They think it was Tinnerman?"

"Yep. They'll have the fingerprint and DNA results back in a day or two. Their theory is the two men met there periodically so Hadecker could pay Tinnerman off. This time, he refused, and Tinnerman took matters into his own hands. The gun they found at the scene was Hadecker's, but there appeared to be a scuffle and Hadecker has some marks on his body consistent with a fight. The police concluded Tinnerman killed Hadecker and planned to use his car and ID to get as much cash as he could before disappearing."

"The ugly side of brotherhood." Blake sat back in his chair and exhaled. He hadn't realized he was holding his breath. "What about Mrs. Hadecker? Did she identify the body?"

"Yep. You'll be happy to know she identified the body as Al Hadecker. Must have been quite a shock to go through that twice."

"Anything else?"

"There was one weird thing," MacMillan said. "They found a watch tossed in the trash at the cabin. Another one of those cheap plastic digital ones."

"So the Hadecker boys had one thing in common after all." Carlioni's eyelids drooped. "They both liked cheap watches."

CHAPTER FORTY-FIVE

The Wire

A pair of legs was visible underneath the lowest branch of an evergreen hemlock. *What's he doing here?* Kate thought. *Ignore him. Don't let him throw you off your pace.*

She turned back to concentrate on the trail, but she sensed the person in the shadows was watching her. A prickly tingle made its way up her spine. *Don't get spooked. It's probably some guy using nature's facilities.* She tried to recite Psalm 91, but her mind had shifted to another gear. She couldn't remember the words.

At this point in a race, she knew any distraction could disrupt a runner's cadence. She looked at the birch trees ahead in order to focus on something else and get her mind back on the race. *Run to the light.* But as she came even with the unknown being, the mysterious figure lured her eyes, and she turned her head again toward the trees.

Without warning, something ripped into her left foot just above her shoe. There was no time to react. Her feet came out from under her and she flew forward, arms beating the air. The ground came up to meet her and she slammed down on the paved path. Her right knee hit first, then the heel of her hand as she skimmed along the pavement. Her head banged onto the trail, and she fell over in a heap on her side. She turned to see what had tripped her and saw a wire lying across the trail. She squinted to make out the man in the trees, but he was gone.

Kate rolled over and pushed herself up, shaking her head to overcome the fuzziness. The wire was tied to a tree on one side of the trail and disappeared into the woods where she had seen the man. *He tripped me.* She pulled the wire over to the opposite side of the trail and threw it down so nobody else could trip on it. Then she took a stiff-legged step forward, trying to run again, but her right knee hurt. She limped forward for a few steps, but each time she put weight on her right foot, a fire ignited in her knee. She felt warm liquid on the side of her head and reached up to wipe the blood away. She clenched her teeth. *Never give up.*

"Are you okay?" A woman's voice pulled her out of the fog.

Kate looked around to see an older woman coming up beside her.

"Yes. I'm fine." Kathryn was wiping at her face where gravel was encrusted on the side of her head. Her right arm was scraped from the palm of her hand to her elbow and her right knee was bleeding and swelling.

"You're not all right, honey," the woman said. She looked to be in her sixties with gray hair under a white visor. Her body was long and lean, and Kate could see the distance runner's muscles outlined on her arms and legs.

Kate shook her head. "You need to go ahead. I don't want to ruin your race for you."

"I've run a million races. I don't need to win my age group in every one. It's more important to get you taken care of."

Two other women ran by, but neither of them stopped.

Kate looked into the face of the woman who was helping her. "I know you. You're Shirley Setkoff. You've won major marathons."

"You're pretty perceptive for someone who just got smashed into the pavement. What happened?"

"A guy was standing in the woods. When I ran by, I think he tripped me with that wire." She pointed to the wire coiled next to the birch tree.

"I was coming around the turn when I saw you fall. I thought maybe you tripped over an uneven place in the trail."

"Look." Kate showed her the front of her left foot where the wire had scraped her leg. "That's where the wire got me. My knee hurts when I try to run, but I think I can walk it. I don't want to drop out. I'm okay."

"You're not okay, but we're within three miles of the finish. I'll stay with you. If you begin to hurt, we'll stop and I'll call a medic." She walked beside her. "Do you know who would want to hurt you?"

Kate grimaced as she took a couple of slow steps. "I don't know who, but I think I know why."

CHAPTER FORTY-SIX

The Finish Line

P hil checked his watch. "It's close to two hours. She said she'd be done in less than an hour and a half." He frowned at Ben. "I don't like this."

Ben put his hand on his friend's shoulder. "I don't think you have to worry about Kathryn. She's an excellent runner and it's a safe course. She probably got tired and decided to slow down." But his face went cloudy with concern.

Phil turned toward Cece. "What do you think, Cece? Should I go looking for her?"

Cece shook her head. "Not unless you want to embarrass her to death. Kathryn is a real independent person. She wouldn't want to think you don't trust her enough to believe she can run a race without help." But Phil noticed the frown on Cece's face as she turned back to scan the group of runners coming into the finishing chute.

Phil stopped pacing. "It's over two hours now since the race started. I'm going to look for her."

"You won't have to." Ben pointed toward a couple of people walking. "There she is." Kathryn was limping toward the finish line. There was a woman walking beside her.

As they got closer, Phil saw the blood running down Kate's leg. He jumped over the rope that held back spectators and ran toward her.

"Hey, you can't go on the course," a young volunteer yelled at him.

"Kathryn, what happened? Are you all right?" He reached out to hold her arm, but she held up a hand.

"Don't help me. I have to finish the race on my own."

The woman next to her crossed over to talk to Phil as they continued toward the finish line. "Somebody used a wire to trip her. I tried to talk her into getting some medical attention, but she insisted on finishing the race. We can go right to the medic tent as soon as she crosses the line."

Phil picked Kate up after she walked across the finish mat under an enormous banner that read "EVERYONE'S A WINNER!"

* * *

Kate lay on the cot in the medical tent. "I'm all right, really. A couple of bumps and bruises. That's all." She tried to sit up.

The medic gently held her down. "No, you don't. You got a pretty good bang on the head and we'll need to take you to the hospital. It could be a concussion."

"I want to know what happened." Phil leaned over her.

"I was running by myself ahead of the others when I thought I saw a man standing behind a tree. The next thing I knew I tripped over a wire and fell." She held her foot up where the wire had bruised it. "By the time I got up, he was gone."

"The guy who sent the letter. He's here." Phil jumped up.

"Wait a minute, Phil." Ben put a hand on his arm. "You stay here with Kathryn. I'll see what I can find. Cece, call the police."

* * *

Kate sat up on the gurney. "I feel fine and I'm ready to go home. Besides, I'm hungry. I haven't eaten anything since early this morning."

"No way." Phil stood by her side. "You're not going anywhere until the doctor takes a look at those X-rays and releases you. He said he'd be back in a minute."

"I hope he hurries. I'm dreaming of a hamburger."

Cece pushed a chair next to the bed and sat down. "I'll buy you the biggest hamburger in town as soon as they let you go."

"Thanks, sister. I'm already planning what I want on it. Pickles, onions, tomatoes ..." There was a soft knock at the door. "Oh good. Must be the doctor."

The door opened slowly. It was Ben. "How's the patient?" As he walked to the side of the bed, he briefly put his hand on Cece's shoulder.

"I'm fine. Waiting for the doctor to come back and release me."

"Did you find the guy?" Phil asked.

Ben shook his head. "No. I ran around to the side of the course by the woods and asked people if they had seen anybody come out, but they said people had been milling around all over the place since the start of the race. When the police got there, I told them what I knew. They found the wire. I suspect they'll find Kathryn's blood on it, but it's too thin to have fingerprints." He stood at the foot of the bed and put his hand on the rail. "Phil, I think you're right. Somebody's real serious about getting Kathryn out of this murder investigation. I have an idea about how we can keep her safe."

CHAPTER FORTY-SEVEN

Kate Faces Facts

"I'm okay. The doctor said there was no concussion." Kate stood in the guest room at Ben's ranch and pretended to knock on the side of her head with her bandaged hand. "Benefits of a hard head."

Phil frowned. "Yeah. But he also said you have to rest for a few weeks to be sure nothing else comes up."

"I know. I'll be a model patient and take some time off."

"And no more snooping around to help the police."

"Don't worry. I'll be good." She held up two fingers. "Scout's honor." She smiled at Phil and tilted her head, but he didn't respond. "It was great of Ben to offer to let Cece and me stay here until this whole thing blows over. And his house is wonderful. An entire guest wing just for Cece and me."

Phil placed her suitcase on the bed while she hung up the clothes she had brought over on hangers and put her duffel bag on the floor. He paced from one end of the room to the other several times, then turned back to face her.

"Make sure somebody is always here with you. I don't want you to be alone in the house."

"No problem. I'll be fine." She gave him the most confident smile she had. "Please don't worry."

Phil stood, arms akimbo, staring at her. Finally he rubbed the back of his neck with his hand. "Kathryn, we need to talk about this. You getting involved in a murder case. It isn't safe. Now we know how dangerous it is."

"Phil, I need to help my friend. I can't quit just because somebody tried to scare me. It wouldn't be right."

He walked over and put his hands on her shoulders. "Kathryn, he didn't try to scare you. He tried to hurt you. It could have been worse."

"I know." Kate swallowed hard. She could almost feel the wire as it caught her foot, forcing her to lose control and crash onto the ground. She clamped her jaws together, determined not to show weakness.

Phil's hands tightened on her shoulders. "Kathryn, you mean everything to me, but I'm not sure I can handle this. I want a lifetime with you. I don't want to be worried every day that somebody's gonna take a pot shot at you. That's not the life I want us to have."

"Phil, you know I have to lead my own life. I can't be somebody else's idea of me."

Phil gently held her out at arm's length. "I know that. You can be whatever you want to be. But I don't want you to put yourself in danger. That puts our relationship at risk. I don't want to lose what we have."

Lose our relationship?

He turned away from her.

She blurted out, "Phil, I don't have a choice. I owe Brad Lassiter."

He turned back to her, his face a combination of surprise and shock. "What do you mean? Were you and Brad ..." He paused, but she knew where he was going. "Did you have a relationship with him?" His eyes searched her face.

"No. Nothing like that."

His jaw softened. "Tell me. What is this all about? I need to know."

"I will tell you. But give me some time to collect myself first. I need to make you understand how important this is to me."

He picked his jacket up off a chair. "All right. I'm going to get some fresh air. We'll talk about this as soon as you're ready." Then he left.

Kate limped into the bathroom and splashed cold water on her face while she listened to the sounds in Ben's house. She could hear Mattie humming in the kitchen, but no men's voices. Ben and Phil must have gone outside to join Cece on the porch.

She shook her head, put both hands on the counter top and looked hard at her reflection in the mirror. The face that stared back at her was bruised and sad. So different from the Kathryn who had bounced up and down to warm up before she confidently started the half-marathon. Sure of the win. *Pride comes before the fall.* She gently touched the bandage on her head and winced.

But Phil. Why couldn't he understand she needed to find the truth? She was trying to save a man's life. Not just any man. She had a debt and it was time to pay it.

Barkley wandered in and sat at her feet, looking up at her. He had jumped out of the car as soon as they opened the door and scooted around the corral as if it was his own domain, playing tag with the horses and sniffing everything in sight.

"What d'ya think, Barkley? Am I going to end up looking like Frankenstein?" The dog thumped his tail on the floor. "You don't have to always be so agreeable, you know." She bent down and ruffled Barkley's ears. *Can I do this? Am I risking my relationship with the man I love? Am I crazy?*

"They tell me that saving one life is like saving the whole world." She walked back into the bedroom and sat on the edge of the bed. "Life is complicated, Barkley, and I don't know what to do. If a friend of yours were in danger, would you risk your life to save him?" The dog wagged his tail so hard his whole body swayed. "Easier said than done, my friend, but I'm glad one of us is happy about this." She patted his head. "Go on out and play in the corral with the horses." She shooed him out of the room. "I'll be out in a minute."

CHAPTER FORTY-EIGHT

Barkley Faces Death

Kate finished washing up. Her knee felt better after the nurse had wrapped it in ice at the hospital. She still sported an ACE bandage, but she barely limped as she walked out onto the porch where Phil, Cece, and Ben were sitting. By the looks on their faces, she knew they had been talking about her. And she knew what they were saying.

Phil pulled her onto the swing next to him and put his arm around her. He didn't speak, but looked off in the distance thoughtfully while he pushed the swing back and forth with his foot.

Mattie appeared with a pitcher of lemonade and plastic cups. She carried on about how spring was here already and it was time to start thinking about summer. She was obviously trying to put everyone at ease, but it wasn't working. The whole group sat in melancholy silence. Mattie retreated, shaking her head.

Ben leaned against the front porch rail, sucking on a piece of straw. "Looks like the horses are shedding already," he said. "I guess that means an early summer."

Cece picked up the beat. "That's wonderful. I've decided to make a real effort to learn to ride this summer." She nodded her head firmly and looked at Kate. "Kathryn, will you come riding with me after Ben teaches me how to stay on a horse for more than five minutes without falling off?"

Kathryn cleared her throat. "Look, I know you're all trying to be nice and avoid the elephant in the room, but let's get it out in the open. The doctor says I have to take it easy for a few weeks." She tried to swallow the lump in her throat. "But Phil thinks I should give up trying to investigate Louis Tinnerman's murder altogether and let the police handle it. Cece, you're the voice of wisdom in my life. What do you think?"

Cece got up from her chair and knelt in front of Kate. "Kathryn, you're my dear sister, my only sibling. I waited a long time to finally meet you, and I don't want anything bad to happen to you." She put her hand on Kate's. "I would definitely advise you if I knew the answer. But, sister, this is a decision only you can make. Whatever you decide, I'll be there."

Kate's eyes teared up, and she squeezed Cece's hand. She wiped at her face and looked at Ben. "Ben, how about you?"

Ben tossed away the piece of straw. "Kathryn, Phil is my best friend. I know how he feels about you." He gave a weak smile. "Heck, I couldn't live around the guy if something happened to you. I vote you give it up."

"Thank you, Ben. I appreciate your honesty." Kate stood and walked to the edge of the porch. For a long minute she stared out at the corral, the distant mountains, and the countryside she loved.

What would her pastor, Reverend Whitefield, advise? And how about Rabbi Hart? Was she living out her faith? Or was her pride somehow involved?

And what would her parents have said? They had always taught her to know herself and be true to who she was. But how did that work when repaying a debt might threaten the most important relationship she'd ever have? Phil. More than anything, she wanted a lifetime with him. She turned and walked back to the swing. "Phil, I've thought this over and—"

All of a sudden, the corral exploded with an uproar of horses snorting and screeching. The four friends jumped to their feet. Cece put her hand to her heart. "What the heck?"

"Rattlesnake." Ben calmly pointed to the edge of the corral where a snake was coiled. The terrified horses wheeled and lurched frantically into each other on the other side of the corral, trying to get away. Barkley raced to confront the intruder. The hair on his back stood straight up as he thrust himself stiff-legged between the horses and the snake, lowering his head to the level of the serpent and barking furiously.

"Wait here," Ben said. "I'll get a gun." He ran into the house.

"Barkley, no," Kate shouted and ran toward the corral with Phil and Cece right behind her. "Barkley, get away." But the dog paid no attention to her.

The horses were panicking, stomping, and kicking up a cloud of dirt that hung in the air. A big roan mare, her eyes wild with terror, slammed against the wooden rail, trying to break out to get back to the barn.

The snake pulled its head back and lunged. Barkley whipped to the right. He spun around, planted his paws again, and snarled in fury. The snake coiled again, its rattle threatening disaster.

"Barkley, come here! Now!" Kate screamed, but he didn't respond. The snake pulled back again, and its entire body flew forward toward the dog. Barkley sprang to the side and pivoted again, standing in the breach to confront the enemy face-to-face.

The corral turned an eerie black-and-white. Horses covered in dust shrieked like ghostly apparitions while particles of dirt swirled around the two combatants. Barkley stiffened and snapped viciously at the serpent while it shook its ominous rattle.

Kate grabbed a shovel leaning against the fence and climbed through the rails, running toward the snake. "Stop it, stop it!" she yelled as the serpent drew its head farther back, its mouth wide open, fangs bared.

"Kathryn, no!" Phil shouted as he and Cece climbed through the fence, but they couldn't catch her.

* * *

The acrid smell of dust and fear hung in the air as Ben ran out of the house with his shotgun and raced toward the corral. Late afternoon clouds had covered the sun, and a dark haze hung like a curtain around the group in the center of the enclosure.

Ben climbed inside the fence but stopped short when he realized death had made a visit to his homestead. Phil and Cece were kneeling on each side of Kathryn, who was sitting on the ground holding Barkley in her lap. She was stroking the dog's head and back and murmuring to him.

Barkley lifted his head and licked her face, then he hopped off her lap and pranced around the corral. He yapped at the horses and paraded around like a prince among his subjects.

The rattlesnake, chopped into five grisly pieces, lay next to the fence.

Phil stood and pulled Kate up. "Barkley saved the horses, and you saved Barkley. I'd say that's a pretty good day's work." He held her close and stroked her hair. "You're the bravest person I've ever known."

She looked up into his face and smiled. "Let's go inside. I need to tell you about Brad."

Stan Helps Out

Commissioner Blake looked up from his desk when he heard the door to his office squeak open.

"You wanted to see us, boss?" Carlioni stuck his head into the commissioner's office.

"Yes. Come on in, guys."

"What's up?" Carlioni pushed the door open and MacMillan followed him in. "Something new?"

Blake nodded. "Maybe. Stan Palmerton called and said he might have some information for us."

"About the Tinnerman murder?" Carlioni picked up a paperweight from the front of Blake's desk and shook it. Little flakes of snow drifted down on the miniature Rocky Mountains. "What's he got?"

"Don't know. But I wanted you guys to be here."

A knock at the door brought them all to attention. MacMillan opened it.

Stan Palmerton stood in the doorway.

"Stan, thanks for dropping by. Come on in." Blake stood behind his desk. "You remember Detective Carlioni. And this is Detective MacMillan."

Palmerton nodded to Carlioni and shook hands with his partner.

Blake sat back in his desk chair. "I wish I could offer you some coffee, but you wouldn't want the stuff that we drink around here."

"Ha." Stan grinned and nodded. "I don't have much time anyway. I'm on my way out to a job, but I wanted to stop by and talk to you about the Tinnerman case. I came across some things that might be useful."

Blake leaned forward. "Oh?"

"I was out at Hyde Park Lake with Kathryn and Cece last week. Kathryn wanted to look around the area to see if we could come up with any fresh ideas. While we were there, she got it in her head to go over to that little ranger cabin."

"Why'd she want to go there?" MacMillan asked.

"She had some theory about the murder that included that place." Stan shook his head. "She has a lot of theories, you know."

Carlioni rolled his eyes. "Yeah, we know. She should write detective stories."

Stan pulled a small plastic bag out of his pocket. "In this case, she may be on to something. We found this pen over by the cabin." He handed the bag to Blake. "It's one of those Hodges for Governor pens. There're a million of those things out there, but Kathryn immediately thought of Jeremy Dodd. She says he's always carrying a bunch of these around."

Blake turned the bag over in his hands. "I don't suppose we could get any fingerprints off this."

Stan gave a grimace. "Sorry about that. I picked it up and she and I both touched it. The only fingerprints on it are probably hers and mine, but you could give it a try."

"Thanks, Stan. We'll take a look at it." Blake held the plastic bag up and peered at it. "That cabin stays empty until summer. Don't know why somebody would be out there."

Carlioni harrumphed. "Could be kids. Who knows? Besides, we got our man."

"Not so fast," MacMillan said. "We need to consider every piece of evidence." He picked up the bag with the pen in it. "You taught me that, Carli."

"There's something else," Stan said.

The other three men turned their attention back to him. "Oh?" Blake said.

Stan put his hands on his hips. "Phil told me about how Kathryn got injured in the half-marathon. He said somebody tripped her with a wire."

"That's right. It was electrical wire tied to a tree on one side of the trail. Somebody pulled it tight when she got to that place," Blake said. "What about it?"

"Kathryn and Cece and I were over at Lassiter's house to talk to Earl and Thelma a week or so before the race. When we went in the garage, I noticed a lot of building materials, including rolls of electrical wire. Seems Lassiter does a lot of work on his house himself."

"I think I see where you're going with this," Blake said.

Stan put his hands up, palms out. "Look. I'm not accusing anybody, but Earl has access to Lassiter's house and to all those building supplies. Seemed suspicious to me."

Blake frowned. "But why would Earl want to trip up Kathryn? She's trying to get his son-in-law off."

"Seems crazy to me too," Stan said. "But Earl's made it real clear he doesn't like Brad. Maybe he doesn't want him cleared."

"Hmm." Blake crossed his arms over his chest. He noticed MacMillan fidgeting like he always did when he was thinking hard about something. "Anything bothering you, Mac?"

MacMillan flung out his long, skinny arms and planted his hands on his hips. "This whole investigation doesn't make sense to me."

"What do you mean?"

"We're getting clues all over the place, but they all point in different directions. It's like we're trying to put a puzzle together, but the pieces don't fit."

Stan shrugged and looked at his watch. "Well, I'm glad it's your puzzle, guys, and I don't have to solve it. See you around."

CHAPTER FIFTY

Sylvia and Harry

"Where's Mattie?" Cece found Kathryn sitting on the couch in Ben's living room.

"She's in her guest house. She said she'll be back in a few minutes and we can have lunch." Kate dropped the magazine she had been reading and picked up her laptop. "This sitting around isn't much fun."

"I was thinking about that." Cece sat beside her sister. "You promised Phil you wouldn't get involved with the case, at least until the doctor releases you, right?"

"Right."

"I think I've found a way we can keep going." Cece sat up straight and gave Kate a thumbs-up. "I can take your place."

"Cece, that's not a good idea. Ben wouldn't want you snooping around in place of me. You'll be in the same danger."

"Negatrons," Cece said with a big smile. "Don't forget I have a superpower."

"What superpower?"

"Disguise. I can go anywhere in a disguise and no one will know me. Maybe I can find out a few more things."

"Gee, Cece. I don't know."

They heard the back door open. "Mattie's coming back. Think it over, and we'll talk later."

* * *

Kate and Cece were helping Mattie put dishes away. "Now don't overdo," Mattie said to Kate. "You've been through a lot and you need to rest."

"It's been three days since the race, and I've been getting more rest than I can stand." Kate smiled. "It feels great to be doing something for a change."

Cece's phone jangled. "Ah, this is the call I've been expecting," she said and left the room to answer it. In a few seconds she was back, her blue eyes sparkling. She took the dishtowel away from Kate and grabbed her two hands. "Are you up for a surprise?"

Kate laughed at her sister's exuberance. Always something new with Cece. "I'm not so sure I'm ready for another surprise," she said.

"You're gonna love this one. Now stay right here and don't come out in the living room until I tell you. I'll be right back." Cece skipped out of the kitchen, and Kate could hear the front door opening. There were muffled voices, then Cece popped back into the kitchen. "Okay, you can come out now."

Kate came out to the living room, and there stood Sylvia and Harry Goldman, Cece's adoptive parents. Kate held her arms out and ran to Sylvia. "Oh, Mrs. Goldman. What a wonderful surprise!"

Sylvia Goldman's face held its usual serene and pleasant expression, but it was tinged with concern. She put her arms around Kate and hugged her hard.

Kate recalled the first time she had met the Goldmans, when Sylvia had stood in front of her clasping her hands together in an attitude of delight, as if meeting Kathryn was the most wonderful thing that could happen to her.

Sylvia stepped back and surveyed Kate's face. "Well, Cece told me you had a nasty fall, but you still look as beautiful as ever, even with that bruise on your forehead."

Harry Goldman moved forward. Kate knew he was a reserved gentleman, but today he put his arm gently around her shoulders and gave a little squeeze. "We wanted to see you for ourselves," he said. "Sylvia had our bags packed about five minutes after Cece called."

"Oh, you're so kind." Kate hugged Sylvia again. "Seeing you is like seeing the sun shine. It makes me so happy." She stepped back and motioned Mattie over. "This is Mattie O'Shaughnessy. She's Ben's housekeeper and the best cook ever."

"I know. We've heard all about Mattie," Sylvia said.

"And I've heard about you too," Mattie said. "Kathryn and Cece have filled me in on everything. I am honored to meet you. Won't you come in and have a spot of lunch?"

"No thank you, dear," Sylvia said. "We came straight from the airport so we could see Kathryn and assure ourselves that she's all right." She turned back to Kate and held her hand. "She's practically our second adopted daughter, you know." She patted Kate's hand. "But we need to go to the apartment we rented here to unpack and set up housekeeping. We'll be able to stay in Bellevue until we finalize the sale of Harry's jewelry business."

"Cece tells me you plan to move to Bellevue," Mattie said.

"That's right." Sylvia reached out and pulled Cece to her. "We've put our home in Denver up for sale, and we plan on moving to Bellevue permanently." She put her arms around both Kate and Cece. "We can't get enough of these two."

"Phil will be so glad to see you," Kate said. "And you'll have a chance to meet Ben."

"We've heard a lot about Ben." Sylvia glanced at Cece.

Kate and Cece accompanied the Goldmans out to their rental car. "Sylvia, why don't you tell Kathryn about our real reason for coming out," Harry said.

Sylvia took Kate's hands in hers. "Kathryn, dear, Cece told us all about this murder investigation and how you've become involved in it. We're worried maybe you've taken on too much. We've invited Reverend Whitefield and Rabbi Hart to our

202 • KAY DIBIANCA

apartment Friday evening for Shabbat dinner, and we want you and Cece to come also. Bring Phil and Ben too. Maybe we can help bring some closure to this."

"That's so kind of you, Mrs. Goldman. But aren't you tired from your trip? It doesn't give you much time to get ready."

"Nonsense. I have all the time in the world. And nothing will give me more pleasure."

CHAPTER FIFTY-ONE

Sara's Day Out

"This was a great idea you had," Kate said to Cece as they approached the Lassiter home.

"This child needs some joy in her life," Cece replied. "At least we can give her an afternoon of fun to keep her mind off all the problems in her family. And you need some time to heal too."

They rang the doorbell and heard a child's steps running to the door. Sara threw the door open and hopped up and down. "You came!" She clapped her hands together. "I was afraid you would forget."

Cece stepped in and caught the little girl up in her arms. "Forget? How could we forget we're going to have an afternoon of fun with our new best friend?"

Thelma came into the room and smiled broadly at the scene. "It's so nice of you two to take Sara to the park and the library. She's been looking forward to this all day. I could hardly get her to eat her lunch."

Kate and Cece walked Sara to the car and Cece strapped her in the booster chair borrowed from Thelma. "Okay, young lady. We're all set. What's your pleasure for our first stop? Library or park?"

"Ooo, let's go to the park. I can swing and climb on the monkey bars."

"Very good," said Kate. "We're off!"

Cece led the singing of kid songs while they were in the car and pushed Sara in the swing when they got to the park. When a little boy asked Sara to do the seesaw with him, Cece retreated to a park bench where she and Kate watched the children play. After an hour at the park, they drove to the library where they all picked out books for Sara to take home.

"I have an idea," Cece said as they left the library. "I know one last thing to make this the perfect day."

"What?" Sara's eyes were wide with anticipation.

"Do you happen to like ice cream?" Cece's eyes sparkled.

"Yes! I love ice cream!"

Cece clapped her hands together. "Hooray! So do I. There's an ice cream parlor right on this block. Let's go."

They dropped the books in the car and the three of them skipped down the block with Sara in the middle holding hands.

"What kind of ice cream do you like, Sara?" Cece asked while they stood in front of the counter of over thirty different kinds.

Sara put her finger in her mouth. "Um. I don't know. What kind do you like?"

"I'm definitely a chocolate person." Cece pointed to the tub of chocolate.

"Me too! I'm a chocolate person!"

"I'll go along with the crowd," Kate said and ordered three chocolate cones.

After they were seated in a booth licking their sweet desserts, Sara said, "This is the best day of my whole life."

Cece and Kate exchanged glances. Then Cece said, "You're going to have a whole lot of good days in your life, little one."

Sara reached over and put her finger gingerly on Cece's watch. "That's a pretty watch, Cece."

"Thanks. Someone very special gave this watch to me." She glanced at Kate and smiled.

Then Sara pointed to Kate's watch. "That's a pretty watch too."

"Thank you, Sara. Someone very special gave this watch to me."

"My daddy has a watch, but it isn't pretty. It's just an ugly black one. He says he doesn't care what it looks like. He says all a watch has to do is tell the time."

CHAPTER FIFTY-TWO

Shabbat Dinner

"It's almost sundown," Harry Goldman said. "Let's get started. Sylvia, where would you like our guests to sit?"

Sylvia Goldman stood at the head of the table and gestured. "Cece, please sit over on this side of the table between Ben and Rabbi Hart. Kathryn, you can sit opposite Cece between Phil and Reverend Whitefield." After everyone had taken their places, Sylvia lit the Shabbat candles and prayed. Harry recited traditional prayers as he poured wine and served challah to each guest. Then they passed heaping dishes of roast beef, potatoes, and vegetables around to everyone's delight.

As Sylvia was serving dessert and coffee, Harry turned to Ben. "Cece told us about your ranch and horses. We were very impressed—actually pretty surprised—that you got her to take a riding lesson."

Ben nodded. "Cece's going to be an excellent rider. She has good hands. She's a little afraid, but she'll get over that."

Cece laughed and elbowed him. "Don't count on it. I don't have the courage to be a good rider."

"But courage doesn't mean the absence of fear, Cece," Reverend Whitefield said. "As a matter of fact, courage is stepping up to do something you're afraid of."

Cece held up her wine glass. "A toast to the many opportunities I have to be courageous then. Because I'm definitely terrified of horses." They all chuckled and offered toasts to Cece's future horse adventures.

Phil put his glass down and turned to Reverend Whitefield. "But isn't it possible to be too courageous?"

"Uh-oh," Kate said. "I think I see where this is going."

The minister patted her hand. "Courage is a wonderful thing, Kathryn. And you certainly have an abundance of it. But it's important to combine our courage with prudence in our lives."

Kate looked toward Rabbi Hart. "But what about the notion that saving one person is like saving the whole world? When I learned Brad Lassiter had been arrested for murder, I felt like that saying was intended especially for me, and I should do everything I could to help him. Doesn't that take precedence over my own safety?"

The rabbi pulled at his beard. "Kathryn, the Talmud teaches us we must always try to save a life, but ..." There was silence as he paused. "We must protect the life that God has given us as well. Many people care for you, and they don't want you to put your own life in danger."

"Kathryn," Reverend Whitefield said quietly, "I think you should tell them about your experience."

"What experience?" Sylvia asked.

The reverend looked at Kate and she nodded. He turned back to Sylvia. "Something happened to Kathryn when she was a child that has influenced her feelings about this situation. This would be an ideal opportunity for her to share it with all of you. I think it would do her good."

Seven pairs of eyes focused on Kate. She glanced at Phil and then at the others. "There's a reason I feel like I need to help Brad Lassiter. Reverend Whitefield has known it for a long time, and I explained it to Phil a few days ago."

"What reason, dear?" Sylvia asked.

"Fifteen years ago, Brad Lassiter saved my life."

CHAPTER FIFTY-THREE

Kate's Story

K ate took a deep breath. "I was twelve years old, and I was at summer camp at King State Park. Brad must have been around fifteen at the time. He was an assistant to the counselors and also acted as lifeguard at the lake.

"There was a girl there, Amy, who must have been about nine or ten years old. She was one of those kids who was the life of the party. Always energetic and full of life. Everybody loved her, and we were all having a great time. Amy was in my cabin.

"The last night of camp, I woke up and saw Amy sneaking out of the cabin in the middle of the night. I followed and caught up with her at the edge of the lake. I asked her what she was doing, and she said she wanted to take one last canoe ride. I told her it was against the rules, but she laughed and told me that's why she wanted to do it. She said Old Feel Bad Filben—that's what she called Mrs. Filben, the camp director—had been mean to her, and she wanted to get the bad taste out of her mouth.

"I knew I should get one of the counselors, but Amy was pleading with me. She made it sound like her camp experience would be perfect if she could do this one thing. She begged me to go with her for a quick canoe ride. Just a little swing out to the middle of the lake and back. Simple. We'd both been in the canoes dozens of times. There couldn't be any danger in it.

"The canoes were lined up on the shore, paddles ready, life vests stowed. There was no wind, and the lake was calm. I stupidly agreed to Amy's plan, but I insisted we had to wear life vests.

"We got in the canoe and paddled out to the middle of the lake, then Amy put down her paddle and suggested we sit quietly for a minute and think about all the wonderful times we'd had during the week before returning to land. I should have realized that was a ploy since Amy was never quiet about anything. As soon as I dropped my paddle, she jumped up and pulled off her life vest.

"Amy started waving her arms around and shouting 'Look at me! I'm free from Old Feel Bad Filben.' She was laughing and jumping. I got mad and told her to sit down, but she just laughed harder. When I stood up to force her to sit down, the canoe tipped to one side and Amy fell."

Kate paused and took a swallow of water. She put the glass down and stared into the candles in the middle of the table. "I can still see it in my mind's eye." She made a gentle arc with her arm. "Amy fell backward and hit her head on the end of the canoe. I'll never forget the sound of the thud when her head hit. She went over the side and disappeared under the water." She paused and tried to swallow the lump in her throat. Phil reached over and squeezed her hand gently. "I knew right then Amy was going to die and it was my fault."

Sylvia's voice was soft and warm. "Kathryn, you can't blame yourself. Young girls do foolish things, and sometimes they end tragically."

"No, Mrs. Goldman." Kate looked into Sylvia's misty eyes. "Other girls do foolish things, but I never did. I was the responsible one. The good girl that everybody could depend on." She shook her head and took a deep breath. "I yanked off the life vest and jumped into the lake. It was pitch black. I couldn't see anything, so I groped around trying to find Amy until my lungs felt like they would explode. When I started to go up for air, someone grabbed my hair and yanked me up to the surface. It was Brad Lassiter."

There was an audible sigh from the others at the table. "Baruch HaShem," Rabbi Hart said quietly.

"Brad was holding Amy and swimming for the shore. He yelled at me, 'Can you make it?' I swam as hard as I ever had. By the time we got to land, Amy was coming to. We didn't even have to give her CPR."

"Thank God," Ben said.

"Brad took us to the infirmary. Before we got there, Amy was cracking jokes. She wasn't even upset. While the camp doctor looked after Amy, Brad took me aside and tried to comfort me. I was so scared and so grateful, I just sat there and cried. He told me he hadn't been able to sleep, so he had gone outside to walk by the lake. He saw Amy fall and swam out to us. He said he was just in the right place at the right time."

Kate paused to take another drink of water and looked around the table. "So you see, Brad Lassiter saved my life that night just as surely as he saved Amy's. If it hadn't been for him, Amy would have drowned, and I would have spent the rest of my life knowing her death was my fault. I owe him for that, and I have the chance to repay him now. I'm in the right place at the right time, and nothing is going to stop me. Nothing."

CHAPTER FIFTY-FOUR

Going Home

C ece grabbed her jacket and kissed her parents. "Thanks for the wonderful evening, Mom. I'll call you tomorrow." Ben shook hands with both of them. "Mr. and Mrs. Goldman, thank you for the dinner. It was a real pleasure to have met you."

"Ben, we're so happy to have had you here." Sylvia smiled up at him while Harry shook hands. "And thank you for staying around while Cece was getting some of her things together so she could ride back to your place with you. You've been a good friend, and we appreciate it."

"My pleasure, Mrs. Goldman. Cece, are you ready?"

"I am."

They rode in silence for a few minutes, then Ben turned to Cece. "Your parents are incredible, Cece. I'm not sure I've ever met people who were so kind and loving. You must have had a wonderful childhood."

"The best." She looked sideways at him. "You know, they aren't my biological parents. I'm adopted."

"Yes, I know. Phil told me. Doesn't matter, though. They seem to adore you."

"I'm a lucky person, and I know it." She shifted in the passenger seat. "Did Phil tell you about how I'm related to Kathryn?"

"He told me some of it." He stopped at a red light and looked over at her. "You don't have to tell me anything if you don't want to."

"Kathryn and I have the same mother. I was the product of a pre-marital affair she had, and I was adopted by my parents when I was a day old. Although I knew about Kathryn for a long time, she never knew about me until after her parents died in that automobile accident a few months ago."

Ben started the truck forward when the light turned green. "You and Kathryn act like you've known each other all your lives. You seem so natural together."

"Yeah. We're different in so many ways. She's tall with dark hair and eyes. I'm short with blonde hair and blue eyes. She loves math and science. I'm into poetry and theater. The first time we met, I was afraid she might be bitter or angry when she learned about me. But it was just the opposite."

"What happened?"

"We were sitting side by side at a table when her lawyer explained the situation. At first, she didn't believe it. But then she reached over and took my hand. At that instant, I felt my life change. Like my family was now complete."

"How did your adoptive parents feel about it?"

"They'd always wanted us to get to know each other. Kathryn's an only child and so am I. We don't have any other relatives in the world. Now we have each other." Cece leaned back in the seat and put her head back. "It's like finding a pearl of great price. Better than that. It's priceless."

"I'd say you're both fortunate."

She turned her head toward him. "Now tell me about your parents. How did they manage to raise somebody who likes Shakespeare *and* automobile mechanics?"

"That's easy." He loosened his tie with his free hand. "My parents were very intellectual people. Both college professors. My dad taught physics, and my mom taught English literature."

"Ah. Hence the interest in Shakespeare."

"Yep. You couldn't live in our house without knowing a lot about Shakespeare *and* Isaac Newton. I got my love of literature from my mom, but it was my dad's interest in physics that inspired me to try to understand how things work. When I was four years old, I had a little rocking chair my mom had bought at a garage sale. You know, college professors don't make much money, so she got a lot of stuff secondhand. Anyway, my chair was kind of rickety, so my dad and I took it apart and put it back together to reinforce the arms and back. He taught me all about how a chair works. It seems simple, but to a four-year-old, it was a whole new world. It's one of my first memories."

He turned right onto Gwinette Street. "When I was seven, I climbed up on a stool and pulled the kitchen clock down off the wall. I took it apart to see if I could figure out how it worked. My folks weren't too happy about that. That's another vivid memory." He grinned. "They told me I'd have to put it back together again."

"Did you?"

"Almost. My dad had to help, but we finally got it running, and I felt like I had invented time itself. It was a heady experience for a young kid when that clock started ticking again."

"That's something we have in common. I used to repair watches in my dad's jewelry shop."

"Did you now?" Ben looked at her with a sideways glance. "I would have thought you sat in the back of the store reading Jane Austen books and trying on your mom's high-heel shoes and feather boas. I didn't peg you for the watch repair type."

"Ha." Cece sat up straighter. "There's a lot you don't know about me, Ben Mullins." She lifted her chin and grinned back at him. "But you still haven't told me about becoming a mechanic."

"It's an extension of my childhood. When I first learned about cars, I immediately tried to take one apart to see it for myself. Working on cars really isn't a job for me. It's fun." Ben took a left on Barnard Road. "You must have the same kind of curiosity if you were working on watches."

"I have to admit, I enjoy taking something that isn't working and fixing it, but I'm really not very good at it. I'm more concerned with people and why they behave the way they do. I've always had a heart to help others."

"You mean people who are broken and need help?"

"That's part of it. But more than that, I enjoy making true friendships."

"Like Kathryn?"

"Yeah. Kathryn is a special person. She has so many talents, but she's hard on herself. Most people don't know this about her, but if she isn't the best at everything she does, she thinks she's failed. You heard that tonight. That's a tough burden for anyone to carry. And now she's in turmoil over Brad Lassiter."

Ben turned onto a narrow dirt road.

"This isn't the way to your house, is it?" Cece asked.

"No, but I want to show you something." Ben slowed as the road turned into a path. "I think you'll like this."

The headlights illuminated a sign and Cece jerked her head around. "Ben, that sign says No Trespassing."

"Yeah, I know. I put it there. This is part of my land." He stopped the truck in front of a fence with a locked gate. He got out, unlocked the gate, and hopped back in the truck. They bumped along across a field until they reached a line of trees and could go no farther. Ben stopped the truck and reached behind the seat to grab a flashlight. "Come on."

"I don't know, Ben. It's awfully dark out there. You know I'm a big chicken when it comes to anything scary."

He walked to her side of the truck and opened the door. "I'll be right here with you."

CHAPTER FIFTY-FIVE

Seeing Stars

"**I** wonder where Ben and Cece are." Kate snuggled against Phil as they sat on the sofa in Ben's living room. "It's getting late."

Phil pulled her closer and nuzzled the side of her face. "I don't think we need to worry about them. They're big kids. Besides, I'd be happy if they don't show up for a while."

"Mmm. Me too." She nestled into his shoulder. "But isn't it going to make it late for you to drive home?"

He pulled his head back and smiled down at her. "No. Ben suggested I bunk here tonight 'cause he and I are going to run some errands tomorrow morning. So I'm staying in the kid's room."

"The kid's room?"

"Yeah. It's a tiny bedroom behind the master." He took her hand and kissed the palm. "When Ben built this house, he had that room added so it will serve as a nursery if he ever gets married and has children."

Kate pulled her head back. "For some reason I thought Ben was a confirmed bachelor."

Phil continued kissing her hand. "Nah. Ben's like me. He's a confirmed once-in-a-lifetimer."

Kate kissed the side of his face. "Okay, I give up. What's a once-in-a-lifetimer?"

Phil sat up straight and smiled down at her. "It's a guy who won't settle for anything other than the love of his life. Ben hasn't found her yet." He nibbled her ear. "But he may be gettin' close."

* * *

Ben took Cece's hand and helped her out of the truck. They walked hand in hand, following the flashlight's beam. "This is a thin border of trees." They stepped through to a tiny clearing.

Cece gasped. Below them was a dark valley, and overhead the night sky sparkled with an array of stars and galaxies. "Oh, Ben. This is beautiful. I've never seen so many stars."

"Yeah. I found this place a couple of years ago. I was able to buy this acreage, and it butts up against my ranch property."

He turned the flashlight off and they stood in complete darkness. "Look up there." He pointed to a bright star. "That's Sirius, the Dog Star. It's the brightest star in the night sky. It's almost nine light years away from us. That means it's roughly fifty trillion miles away."

"Fifty trillion miles? I can't even comprehend something like that." Cece's voice dropped to a whisper.

"Some of the stars are thousands of light years away. Think of it—the light we're seeing from one of them started its journey thousands of years ago. We're not just seeing light. We're seeing time." He squeezed her hand.

"Awesome!"

He pointed to another part of the sky. "And that's Polaris, the North Star."

"Where?"

He pulled her in front of him and pointed so that her eyes could follow. "Draw a line from the outside bowl of the Big Dipper to the tail of the Little Dipper. That's Polaris. It's the star navigators have always relied on. It's constant, fixed in the night sky, and all the other stars rotate around it."

"I see it now." She pointed. "The North Star. I remember a teacher of mine once said, 'Everybody needs a North Star.' Now I know what she meant."

Ben shrugged out of his jacket and spread it on the ground. "Have a seat, m'lady, and I'll give you an astronomy lesson."

They sat for an hour, gazing at the stars in the northwestern sky while Ben pointed out constellations and talked about the history of astronomy.

When he grew quiet, Cece pulled her knees in and wrapped her arms around them. "Tell me more about your family, Ben. Your parents sound wonderful."

"They were. My parents were older when I was born. My dad was already in his fifties and my mom was mid-forties. I think I was a mistake." He leaned back on one elbow and grinned up at her. "Story of my life."

"Sounds like you had a great childhood."

"Yeah. My folks sent my sister and me to live with my mom's brother Fred every summer, since they had to work. Uncle Fred owned a ranch in Texas. He was an older guy, a bachelor who loved horses and ranching. Uncle Fred and I got along great. He taught me to ride and to care about animals. He was almost a second father."

"Not many kids get that. You had a charmed childhood."

"Yeah. At least until my sister died."

"Oh, Ben. I'm so sorry. Was your sister the girl in the picture over your mantel?"

"Yeah." He picked at a few blades of grass. "Cynthia was a sweet thing. She was five years older than me, and she kind of saw me as her own little child. She contracted leukemia when she was thirteen and died a year later. My parents never recovered from it."

"I can understand."

"Dad died two years later from a heart attack. Mom thought it would be best if I stayed with Uncle Fred since she was working all the time. I think it hurt her to see me. I was a reminder of Cynthia."

"Is your mother still alive?"

"No. She passed on ten years ago."

"And your Uncle Fred? He sounds wonderful."

"He was one of a kind. A big, red-headed Irishman with a heart the size of Texas. Mattie was his housekeeper for years. Uncle Fred died five years ago of a massive heart attack. It's because of him I have all this." He made a wide, sweeping gesture with his arm. "He left me everything he had. I sold his ranch, but I kept all the horses and brought them out here when I bought this land." He grinned at Cece. "Lady was just a little filly back then. She was his favorite."

"Ah. And now she's your favorite."

"Yep."

"And Mattie came to work for you."

"Right again. She and I aren't blood related, but she's as much my family as if we were."

For the next hour, Cece lay back on Ben's jacket, contemplating the night sky and listening to Ben's quiet explanations.

"So." He leaned on the palm of one hand and looked down at her. "What do you think of my heavenly theater?"

"It's lovely. I wish we could stay here forever." Cece sat up and brushed grass shavings from her lap. "But I think we should go. Phil and Kathryn will wonder what happened to us."

Ben stood and offered his hand. She took it and pulled herself up. The night was quiet, as if waiting for them to stir the course of destiny. They stood still, inches apart, holding hands and looking into each other's eyes. The only sound she heard was the hushed measure of his breath.

An owl hooted. Cece jumped.

"I think that was your cue to leap into my arms," Ben said and grinned down at her. "I paid that owl to hoot."

She looked up into his face. In the dark she could barely make out his features, but she could see the curve of his lips and she could imagine the crinkle lines around his eyes. "I've always been good at cues," she said, "but I guess I missed that one."

The owl hooted again. This time she didn't miss the cue and stepped into his embrace. He pulled her in and held her so close her body arched against his. His kiss was gentle and warm, his mouth full on hers as the night folded over them. She caressed the nape of his neck and ran her fingers through his hair above his starched collar.

Ben held her head and kissed her hair. She lifted her chin, and his lips slid down to caress her neck and nibble at her ear. She sighed quietly, and he returned to her mouth with a deeper hunger. Her body softened at his touch, and she wondered how she had lived her entire life without ever having known this feeling.

When he pulled his head back, she could see his eyes roaming over her face. "I feel like we're the center of the universe now," she said, "and all the stars are revolving around us."

He kissed her again. "I'm gonna buy a whole herd of those owls."

CHAPTER FIFTY-SIX

Second Thoughts

K ate put her feet up on the ottoman and leaned back on the couch in Ben's living room, opening the copy of *The Adventures of Tom Sawyer* she had pulled from his bookcase.

"Kathryn, are you there?" Cece's voice made its way from beyond the door to the guest wing.

"Good morning, sleepyhead. Yes, I'm here."

"Is Ben out there?"

"No. Ben and Phil said they had to run some errands. They'll be back this afternoon."

"Mattie?"

"Mattie's at the store. You can come out in your jammies if that's what you're asking."

Cece appeared from behind the door in blue jeans and a T-shirt. "I did manage to get dressed." She shuffled across the room. "Is that coffee I smell?"

"Mattie made a big pot of coffee and left it in the thermos. There's also banana bread."

As Cece headed to the kitchen, Kate called after her, "You and Ben were out late last night. What time did you get in?"

Cece returned with a big mug of steaming coffee which she placed gingerly on a coaster on the coffee table. "I don't know what time we got in." She sank down onto the couch. "It was really late." She held her head in her hands.

"Are you okay?" Kate put her book down and turned her complete attention to her sister.

Cece stood and paced in front of the couch. "I am definitely *not* okay." She walked back to the kitchen and returned with a slice of banana bread.

"Cece, what's wrong? You're worrying me."

Cece put the plate on the coffee table and began to pace again. She walked back to the kitchen and came out with a carton of cream. She put a few drops in her coffee and headed back to the kitchen.

"Cece, can you come back here and tell me what's going on? You're wearing a path in the floor."

Cece returned and stood in front of Kate. "Something terrible happened."

"Cece, what are you talking about? Does this have something to do with Ben?"

"This has everything to do with Ben. Kathryn, I made a colossal mistake last night."

Kate frowned and waited. "What mistake?"

"Ben took me to this place overlooking a dark valley, and we talked and everything was so beautiful. The stars were perfect. The trees smelled like honey. I felt like the entire universe was made for that moment in time."

"That sounds wonderful. What could be wrong?"

"He kissed me."

"That's all?"

"All? Isn't that enough? I was locked in an embrace with a man I could never consider a serious relationship with. Before last night, we were friends. Now I've ruined it. He probably thinks I have some kind of deep feelings for him. I feel like a fool."

"Why can't you consider a serious relationship with Ben?"

"Kathryn, you know Ben and I are nothing alike. He's outside, I'm inside. He's all about horses and mechanical things. I'm into poetry. He's cowboy leather, I'm Barbie lace. What am I going to say to him today?"

"Cece, I think you're overreacting. First of all, the attraction between you two is obvious. He can't take his eyes off you when you're in the room. And you're attracted to him, no matter what you say."

"Attraction is one thing. Relationship is something else. You know how much I want to be free to follow my own dreams. I don't want to be tied to a serious commitment that's destined to fail." She paced around the couch and back in front of Kate. "When we got in last night, he looked at me like I was the treasure at the end of the rainbow. And I probably looked at him the same way. Kathryn, I can't lead him on thinking we could have a romantic relationship."

"But, Cece, you yourself told me a relationship between a man and a woman is the highest form of human expression. You can't deny it."

"I know I said that, but it has to be the right relationship. A misguided one would be a mistake that could ruin your life." She rubbed at her temples. "What am I going to do?"

"Whatever it is, you better decide fast. I think I heard his truck pull up outside."

* * *

Cece gripped the edge of the kitchen counter with both hands. *Courage. Be strong and courageous. You have to do this, and you can't put it off.* She had retreated to the kitchen as soon as she heard Ben's truck. She heard the front door open and Ben's voice resonated through the house. "Where's Cece?"

Kathryn stammered, "Um, I think she's in the kitchen. Hey, Phil, can you come out and help me? I think something's wrong with my car."

Ben charged into the kitchen. His eyes were sparkling, and he had that same little-boy expression as if she were one of the stars he'd been describing the night before.

"Hey, you." He walked around the island and stopped about a couple of feet in front of her, still smiling.

"Hey." Cece couldn't meet his eyes. She rubbed at an imagined stain on the granite countertop.

"I bought something this morning I want to show you. Come outside with me." He held his hand out.

Cece gulped and took a step back. *Do it now.* "Ben ..."

His expression changed at the sound of her voice. She saw his eyes go dark. He dropped his hand.

"What is it?"

"Ben ..." She lowered her head. She couldn't face him. She ached to feel the warmth she had the night before. The sense of being home. She wanted to taste his kiss again. A voice inside her head told her to move toward him. But she knew it wasn't to be. "Ben ... About last night." She looked up, knowing she had to face him.

Now he took a step back.

"Ben, I ... I ..."

"It's okay. I understand." He turned and walked back to the other side of the counter. "When you finish your coffee, come on out. I'd like to show you the new horse."

CHAPTER FIFTY-SEVEN

Earl

"Thank you for doing this, Reverend Whitefield," Kathryn said as she rang the doorbell at 4230 Oakleaf Avenue. Reverend and Mrs. Whitefield had been Kathryn's spiritual guides throughout her life and helped her overcome her parents' deaths. Now she hoped he could help another wounded soul.

"No problem, Kathryn. It's my job." The kindly minister smiled and waited, Bible in hand.

Earl Weatherspoon opened the door and invited them in.

Kate swallowed hard. She had no idea how Earl would handle her interfering with his life, but he had said it was all right to bring a pastor by. "Mr. Weatherspoon, this is my minister, Reverend Whitefield. He was a great help to me after my parents died, and I thought you might want to talk to him."

Earl shook hands with the minister and pointed to seats in the living room. "Thelma took Sara out shopping so we could have some time to talk, but you need to know, preacher, I'm not a religious man."

"Thank you for seeing me, Mr. Weatherspoon." The minister's soft brown eyes and quiet voice relaxed them all. "You need to know a lot of my friends aren't religious people."

"Call me Earl." He settled into an easy chair. "I'll be honest with you, Reverend, I probably wouldn't have agreed to meet with you except Kathryn and Cece have been so nice to Sara." His voice caught and he coughed. "I really appreciate how they've made her life better these past few days, so when Kathryn asked if I'd talk to you, I felt like I owed her that much."

"You don't owe me anything, Mr. Weatherspoon, but I'm glad you're going to talk to Reverend Whitefield. I'll be happy to wait outside if you like."

"No. That won't be necessary. You can hear everything I have to say."

"First of all, Earl," the reverend began, "if you don't mind, I'd like to open up our discussion with a prayer."

"No problem. I can use all the prayers you got."

Reverend Whitefield prayed God would bring peace and comfort to Earl and his family and give wisdom to their meeting today. When Kate looked up, she was surprised to see Earl's eyes looking watery.

"Why don't we start with you telling me about your family, Earl."

For the next half hour Earl Weatherspoon related the history of his family. He had been a truck driver and had married his high school sweetheart, Thelma. They had a good marriage. "Thelma's a wonderful woman. She's a hard worker and loves her family more than anything." He paused and chuckled. "And she's patient. Had to be with an old jack—I mean an old mule like me."

Reverend Whitefield nodded. "We give our womenfolk a lot to put up with, don't we?"

"We sure do." Earl's face turned dark. "And Thelma had plenty of heartache along the way. She suffered two miscarriages before Ellie was born. We had pretty much given up on having a baby when Thelma got pregnant a third time and suddenly this beautiful little pink bundle came into our lives." He pulled out a handkerchief, wiped his face, and continued.

"Ellie was a handful, to be sure. She was a strong-willed child, but Thelma kept her on the straight and narrow. When she got to high school, she was so pretty and popular we thought she had the world in the palm of her hand. Our only concern was she might get mixed up with the wrong crowd, but that didn't happen."

"Do you think Brad had something to do with that?" Reverend Whitefield asked. "Kathryn tells me Brad is a serious and honest person. Maybe he kept her from falling in with the wrong crowd."

Earl rubbed his chin. "I never thought of it that way, but maybe he did."

"Then they got married soon after high school?"

"Yeah. Too soon. Thelma and I knew it wasn't a good idea, but they really wanted to get married." He bit on his lower lip. "I hate to admit it, but I think it was Ellie who pushed it. The more I tried to talk her out of it, the more determined she was to go through with it. See, Ellie was a lot like me. She could be real stubborn when she made up her mind about something, and she was stuck on getting married."

"Did you have a good relationship with Brad?"

Earl's chin jutted out. "No. I couldn't stand the fact Ellie had married him. She could have had a lawyer or a doctor, but she settled for this guy who was going to spend his life working manual labor. I didn't like it and I made sure Brad knew it.

"Ellie started showing signs of being unhappy early on, but when Sara was born, we thought everything would straighten itself out. You know, motherhood and all that. But it just got worse. Ellie didn't really take to motherhood. She sank further and further into depression, and we didn't know what to do." Earl blinked hard and clutched the handkerchief in his hands.

Reverend Whitefield didn't respond. He waited. A minute passed. Then another. The weight of the tragedy filled the room.

Earl took a sorrowful, deep breath. "And then she started with the drugs. I blamed Brad. He couldn't buy her the nice things she wanted. I told him he made her unhappy and that's why she started using drugs."

There was another long silence. Earl put his forearms on his legs and leaned forward. "Preacher, I know I made some mistakes talking to Brad the way I did. But I'm a proud man and I wanted him to make more of himself than he was willing to."

"Have you considered reconciling with Brad? You know he's going to need your support."

Earl shuffled his feet and muttered something under his breath.

Reverend Whitefield leaned forward. "Do you think Brad killed Louis Tinnerman?"

Earl hesitated and swallowed hard. "I think it would be good if he did."

"Earl, you can't mean that."

"Yes, I do. Sometimes you have to take revenge when somebody you love is hurt." Earl's eyes were getting red again. "That man deserved to die."

CHAPTER FIFTY-EIGHT

Regrets

*K*athryn may have been the one who was injured, but I'm the one who needs healing. Cece grabbed her jacket from the chair. She and Kathryn had moved out of Ben's ranch and into her parents' apartment on the pretext of being closer to family. But they all knew it was because of the strain between Cece and Ben. "I'm going out for a walk, Mom. I'll be back in a little while."

She closed the door of the apartment behind her and wandered out to the sidewalk. Ben had been so polite through it all. He treated her like a real gentleman would, but the teasing and verbal sparring were gone. Cece knew she had lost a friend, and not just any friend, but one she wanted for life. And no matter how hard she tried to deny it, the thought of him made her breathless and brought her to tears more than once. Sylvia had looked at her strangely the last couple of days, and Cece knew her mother was concerned.

She turned right at the next corner and stopped to watch a group of hummingbirds hovering at a feeder. *It's so easy for you guys. Just whiz around looking for food and company.* She sighed and continued walking.

Kathryn and Phil had gone to a movie after dinner. *Here I am, a grown woman, spending Saturday evening with my parents.* She turned right again and dodged a tricycle left on the sidewalk. *Come on, now. Snap out of it. Head up. Eyes straight ahead.* But the reality didn't match her own counsel. She stopped under a streetlight and pulled an envelope out of her pocket. The return address was The Atlanta Shakespeare Society, but she didn't have to read the letter. She had memorized the entire thing as soon as she had opened it two days ago. She sat on the curb and looked up at the night sky, searching for Polaris. A tear slid down her face, and she wiped it away. *Crying won't help.* But it was all she wanted to do.

When she got back to the apartment, Harry came out from his study. "Have a nice walk?"

Cece smiled and took a seat on the couch. "Yes, I guess so. But I couldn't find the North Star."

Harry nodded. "There are too many streetlights here to see the stars well." He paused and looked carefully at her. "Funny, isn't it?"

"What's funny?"

"That light created by man can sometimes obscure light created by God."

Cece surveyed her father as he moved a newspaper off his recliner and sat down. "I get the feeling you're trying to tell me something."

Harry faced her. "Your mother and I noticed you've been acting withdrawn lately, Cece. Anything troubling you?"

"No. Not really."

Sylvia walked in, bringing her knitting needles, and sat next to her daughter. "Can I join you two? I need to finish this baby cap, and I could use some good conversation to go along with it."

"Sure, Mom."

"I was asking Cece about her mood." Harry folded his hands together on his lap. "She seems unusually quiet to me. What do you think, Sylvia?"

"Definitely quiet." Sylvia turned and smiled at her. "It's not like you, Cece, to stay uncommunicative for such a long time. You may as well tell us now. It's as good a time as any." She patted Cece's hand.

There was a long pause. Finally, Harry said, "It's about Ben, isn't it?"

Cece's mouth dropped open. "How did you know? Has Kathryn been talking to you?"

Sylvia and Harry exchanged a glance before Sylvia said, "No. Kathryn hasn't said anything, but it doesn't take a genius to see how much you like Ben. There's something about a young person in love that can't be denied."

"In love? No, Mom. It's the opposite of that. I think Ben would like a romantic relationship, but I don't want that. I was content with our friendship."

Sylvia put the knitting in her lap. "Friendship and love are closely related, Cece. And you'll need an abundance of both in a marriage."

"But, Mom, I can't get involved with a man who owns a ranch. I wouldn't be happy. I want someone who's urbane and intellectual. Someone who understands my love of theater. Somebody like Dad."

Harry chuckled. "Well, I'm flattered, Cece, but we can't define our perfect partner and have them pop out of a mold. It doesn't happen like that. Sometimes we're surprised by the person God has in mind for us. We call that person our *beshert.* That's Yiddish for 'destiny.'"

"But, Dad, I remember how you used to close the jewelry shop and come home every night so we could have dinner together and you could read with me. You were always clean and neat, and our lives were predictable and steady." She wrinkled her brow. "Don't girls always fall for guys who remind them of their fathers?"

"Oh, Cece." Now it was Sylvia's turn to laugh. "You remember my father. He owned a nursery, and he came home every night covered in so much dirt and grime, it took him an hour to wash up and be presentable. Harry isn't anything like him. I loved my father, but Harry is my beshert."

"You two are perfect for each other." Cece looked back and forth between her parents. She sighed. "But it's too late for me. I hurt Ben deeply. I didn't mean to, but he's been so remote. I feel like the world's biggest jerk, and I don't know what to do."

Sylvia picked up her knitting needles. "Cece, you know what you have to do when you've hurt someone's feelings. You've always known."

Cece pressed her lips together and sighed again. "I have to apologize." She watched her mother's skillful hands.

The knitting needles clicked a soft, constant rhythm. "That's right."

"But suppose he doesn't accept my apology. Suppose he laughs at me or rejects me?"

Harry smiled at her. "Cece, Ben is a good man. I'm sure he'll accept your apology, and you'll be back on a good footing with him in no time. And if it's not God's will for the two of you to be together, that will all work itself out. But in the meantime, telling him you're sorry will go a long way to healing a broken relationship."

Cece took a deep breath and exhaled forcefully. "You're right. I'll do it. I'm going to see him at the street fair tomorrow, and I'll apologize to him then."

CHAPTER FIFTY-NINE

Street Fair

"This is awesome!" Cece twirled around in the middle of Center Street amid the vendor stalls all along the sidewalks. "Do you come to the street fair every year?"

"I've come a few times before, but it's more fun this year." Kathryn picked up a shawl from one of the sale tables. "Look, Cece, this would be ideal for Mattie. The blue would match her eyes."

"It's perfect. Let's get it."

They paid the vendor and Kathryn took the bag. "We're supposed to meet the guys at Cafe Rouge. I hope they can find a parking place with all this crowd."

Cece took her sister's arm and they walked together. "I'm so happy."

"Yeah. I noticed." Kathryn grinned down at her sister. "I'm guessing this has something to do with Ben?"

"I'm so glad we're having lunch with them today. It'll give me a chance to talk to him and get back to being friends again."

"That's wonderful. Everything's working out for the people I love." Her smile disappeared and she stopped. "Except for Brad."

"I know. I'm sorry it turned out this way."

Kate bit on her bottom lip. "I felt sure I would find something to clear Brad, but it hasn't happened. I don't know what else I can do to help him. I feel like I failed him."

"It's not a failure if you tried, Kathryn. Besides, there are other ways to help, you know. Visiting him and letting him know you care about him and his family. And taking Sara out to the park and library. All those things help."

"I guess." They started walking again.

"Oh, look." Cece pointed to her left. "Bellevue Park is full of booksellers. Let's go see if they have any good bargains."

They entered the park and drifted around the tables of books. Cece examined the wares on one of the tables. "Look at this. First edition Wilkie Collins's *The Woman in White* for a dollar! I read this a bunch of years ago." She flipped through the pages and paid the vendor. "Excellent condition too. I can't wait to show it to Ben."

"You shouldn't have to wait long for that." Kate checked her watch. "Let's wander through the sales tables here and then head over to Cafe Rouge."

* * *

"There's Phil." Kate waved as she and Cece approached the table on the patio of Cafe Rouge. "Have you been here long?"

"No. Just got here." Phil stood, pulled Kate to him, and smiled down at her. "You're looking pretty. Walking around at a street fair must be doing you some good."

"Definitely. It feels great just to be outside again."

"Where's Ben?" Cece asked. "Wasn't he coming with you?"

Phil cleared his throat and gave a little cough. "Ben's not going to make it today. He said he had some work to do at the ranch."

"Oh." Cece's face turned pink and she looked down at the book in her lap.

A man's voice broke in to the little group. "Hey. My favorite threesome."

They turned to see Stan Palmerton walking up. "Stan!" Kate said. "What a surprise to bump into you here."

Stan chuckled. "Actually, it's not a surprise. I've been shadowing you and Cece for the last hour."

"Ah," Cece said. "The detective."

"Force of habit. Besides, I want to make sure you two don't get yourselves in any trouble."

Phil nodded. "Thanks, Stan."

Kate scowled at Phil. "You're not paying Stan to follow us, are you?"

Phil grinned and pinched her in the side. "No. But now that you mention it, maybe I should."

She feigned a chilly expression before it changed into a smile. Then she turned to Stan. "Join us for lunch."

"You sure I'm not horning in?"

"Absolutely not. Besides, I want to talk to you about the murder case."

Julie, the waitress, did a happy dance up to the table. "Cece! You're here. I'm so excited. I can't wait to tell you the news."

"What news?"

"Remember when you were here last time and a man took a picture of the two of us and texted it to me? I showed it to the director of the next play at Bellevue Playhouse on the Square, and he gave me a part!"

"Wow, that's fantastic! Congratulations." Cece beamed at the young woman. "What's the part?"

"It's a small one. I only have one line, but it's a start."

"Good for you," Cece said. "You have to start somewhere. And speaking of starts, how about bringing us some menus. I'm starved."

CHAPTER SIXTY

Let's Play Clue

"**L**et's play Clue." Commissioner Blake cleared off the side table in his office and turned to his two favorite detectives.

"Clue?" Carlioni asked. His eyelids slid into a skeptical apathy.

"Yes. You know, the game."

"Sounds good to me." MacMillan nodded and grinned. "Ever played Clue, Carli?"

Carlioni harrumphed. "Not at work."

Blake took a sheet of paper from the printer and held it up. "Clue number one. The letter sent to Kathryn Frasier that we all think was a warning." He put it down on the table.

"That's not the real letter, is it, boss?" Carlioni picked the paper up and examined it.

"No. Of course not. The real evidence is in the lab. We're pretending." He took the paper out of Carlioni's hands and put it back on the table. "What's next?"

"The pen," MacMillan said. He pulled a ballpoint pen out of his pocket and placed it on the table next to the paper. "The pen they found at the cabin."

"Good." Blake nodded approval. "You're getting the hang of my game. "Next?"

"The wire," Carlioni said and looked around the room. He picked up a charger cable lying on Blake's desk and dropped it on the table. "The wire that somebody used to trip Kathryn Frasier in the half-marathon."

"Okay." Blake took a Life Saver out of his pocket and popped it in his mouth. "Who do we suspect in each one of these things and why?"

"I get it now." Carlioni snorted. "It was Earl with the wire at the race. He wants Brad convicted because he hates him, and he has access to plenty of electrical wire, so he tries to injure Kathryn so she'll get out of the picture."

"Good analysis." Blake took an index card and wrote Earl's name on it. He dropped it on top of the charger cord.

MacMillan picked up the pen. "Dodd with the pen at the cabin. He met Tinnerman at the cabin to get some illicit campaign contributions. Things got heated, he killed him, and dropped his pen by mistake."

"Another good analysis." Blake wrote Jeremy Dodd's name on another index card and placed it on top of the pen. "Now how about the letter?"

"That's a tough one, boss," Carlioni said. "Could have been anybody. But my money's on those crazy folks in the Keep Bellevue Beautiful group. Somebody printed it on a laser printer with a fancy font. That's the kind of thing they would do. Maybe that Jonathan Katz guy threatened Hadecker or Tinnerman and doesn't want anybody to find out about it."

Blake put an index card labeled Katz on the letter. "So what does this tell us? Any of these people killers?"

Carlioni rubbed the side of his face. "Jonathan Katz is one of those look-at-me-I-went-to-Harvard types. All puffed up on his own importance. He'll be a genuine hero if it looks like he spoiled Hadecker's plan to buy the Barringer place. For a narcissist like Katz, that's a good motive. He might have sent the letter to scare her off the case, but I can't see him pulling a trigger."

"Me neither." MacMillan ran his hand through his mop. "I also don't see Jeremy Dodd murdering anybody. He's a creep, but I get the feeling he's also a coward. Besides, there are thousands of those pens around. Anybody could've dropped it."

"And the wire?" Blake asked.

Carlioni shook his head. "Earl could probably do the deed, but he couldn't keep his trap shut about it. He'd probably brag about it."

The three men stood for a few minutes looking at the table. "So, what do we make out of all this?" Blake asked.

MacMillan's light blue eyes scanned the index cards on the table. "It looks to me like somebody or maybe several people wanted Kathryn Frasier to stop because they're afraid of what she might find out. Even if Brad Lassiter is guilty, they don't want her turning up any other stuff."

Carlioni took a mechanical pencil out of his pocket. "I agree with Mac. I feel bad about people trying to hurt Kathryn, but that's not our concern. Our job is to find Tinnerman's murderer and bring him to justice." He pointed his pencil at the table. "Besides, all these guys have alibis for the night of the murder."

"Tell me about the alibis." Commissioner Blake walked behind his desk and settled into his chair.

Carlioni retrieved his notebook from his shirt pocket. "Earl says he and his wife, Thelma, were at home all night on the night of the murder. They went to bed early, as usual."

"What time would that be?"

Carlioni flipped a page. "He says they were asleep by nine o'clock. It's their usual routine."

"Hmm." Blake pulled at his shirt collar. "That's a soft alibi. Earl could have left the house after his wife was asleep."

"Yeah. I asked him point-blank if he went outside at all after going to bed. He said he didn't and she backed him up. She said she'd have heard it if he left."

"Wives have been known to lie for their husbands."

"True," MacMillan said. "But if Earl was in on it, did he know Brad was planning to kill the guy?"

"That's where it gets muddy." Blake stood and paced. "Those two both had motive. But if they were working together, why would Brad Lassiter admit wanting to kill the guy?" He leaned against the file cabinet. "How about Jeremy Dodd? Mac, did you question him?"

"I talked to him a couple of days ago," MacMillan said. "He was with Representative Hodges at the rally in Markerton all afternoon and late into the evening the night of the murder."

"So he's clear, then?"

"Not exactly. Those political rallies go on for hours. He could have left, driven back to Bellevue, met Tinnerman, and returned without being missed. There's no way to know for sure."

"Great. Another soft alibi." Blake chewed on his bottom lip. "What motive would he have?"

"Dodd was known to have approached Hadecker for financial support for the campaign. Could have been something underhanded going on that got out of control."

"Does he own a gun?" Blake rubbed the back of his neck.

"No. But I wouldn't put it past him to get a stolen gun if he wanted to kill somebody. We searched his apartment and didn't find anything."

"How about Jonathan Katz? Carli, did you catch up with him?"

"Yeah. Me and Mac both talked to him. He claims he was with his girlfriend all evening on Friday. She backs it up. Says they were in her apartment until late."

"Anybody see them?"

"Nobody we could find. We're back to the same thing. Soft alibis."

"Does Katz own a gun?"

"Nope. But like Mac said, you can always get a stolen one if you want to."

Blake rubbed his chin. "So, give me your bottom-line assessments."

Carlioni nodded to his partner. "You go first, Mac."

MacMillan frowned. "I don't see any of these people as suspects. They might have tried to scare Kathryn Frasier, but I don't see any of them committing murder."

Blake returned to his chair, folded his hands over his waist, and leaned back. "It all comes back to Brad Lassiter. And he's the only suspect we have who doesn't have an alibi."

"That's about it." Carlioni twirled his mechanical pencil. "Boss, I think we're overthinking this case. We've talked to every person who could have possibly been involved. But let's face it, Lassiter's our man."

"Then tell me how it went down."

Carlioni paced in front of the desk. "Lassiter meets Tinnerman behind the railroad station, but he can't kill him there 'cause it's in town. People might hear the shot. So he tells Tinnerman he's afraid the cops are onto the place so he should follow him out to Hyde Park to do the deal. He leads him to the clearing beside the lake. When Tinnerman opens the trunk to get at the goods, Lassiter shoots him. Then he takes the cash out of the wallet, throws all the rest of the dead man's stuff in the trunk, closes the trunk, and drives the car into the water."

"Why get rid of the car?"

"Maybe it had his fingerprints on it. He wanted to be sure there was no trace. And he didn't want to hold on to the credit cards. They're incriminating evidence."

"I'm with you so far. What then?"

"After he drives the car in the lake, he loads the body into the trunk of his own car, drives it around to the ravine, and dumps it there." Carlioni put his pencil back in his pocket and brushed his hands against each other. "Clear as a bell."

"But why move the body? Why not put it in the Jaguar so it won't be found?"

"Easy one. Remember he said how much he hated people who were dealing drugs? He wanted to make a statement to drug pushers everywhere that one of their own was murdered. And he leaves the guy's driver's license on the body so everybody will know who it is."

MacMillan nodded his head slowly. "Carli's onto something. Remember we found that car wash receipt in Lassiter's car? It was from one of those fancy places that cleans every inch of your car, inside and out. If he loaded Tinnerman's body in the trunk of his own car, he would want to get rid of any trace of DNA or blood evidence."

Carlioni leaned against the desk. "Every piece fits, boss. Just like a perfect jigsaw puzzle."

Blake folded his hands together and stared at his two detectives. "Okay, guys, you've convinced me. Let's go for round three. See if you can stretch Lassiter a little further. Maybe he'll break."

CHAPTER SIXTY-ONE

Cafe Rouge

Kate took a bite of salmon salad and looked expectantly at Palmerton. "So, Stan, do you have any information about the investigation?"

"I've been following up on leads, but I haven't found anything substantial." He put down his fork and gazed at Kate. "I was happy when you told me you were going to take it easy for a while. You had me worried there."

"Evidently I had a lot of people worried." She glanced at Phil, then she turned back and sighed. "But I heard the police are going to charge Brad with the murder."

"It doesn't look good for him, does it, Stan?" Phil asked.

"No, it doesn't. Everything points to him. He had a strong motive to kill the man. He admits meeting Tinnerman on the night he was killed. His gun was fired that same night. The only thing they don't have is a confession."

"But there's no real proof," Kate said. "All they have is circumstantial evidence."

"That's true." Stan knitted his brows together. "You know I'm on your side, Kathryn, but I've seen juries convict on the basis of less evidence than this."

Phil put his hand over Kate's. "But if they try him here in Bellevue, he might not be convicted. People here know him and know the circumstances. Juries sometimes react to that, don't they?"

"Yes, I think it's a definite possibility. He could get off."

"But his life would still be ruined," Cece said. "And Sara's life would be ruined too."

The group fell silent for a minute until Stan spoke again. "I hate to bring this up, but we have to face the possibility Brad is guilty."

Kate shook her head vigorously. "I don't believe that. Phil, what do you think?"

"I'm sorry, Kathryn, but I agree with Stan. Brad could be guilty. Good people are capable of doing bad things, especially when someone they love has been hurt. I can even identify with him. I'd probably want to take revenge if it was my wife." He squeezed her hand.

Kate turned to her sister. "Cece?"

Cece looked at the men and lifted her chin. "I'm with Kathryn." She put her silverware down emphatically on her plate. "If she thinks Brad is innocent, then so do I."

"I hope you're right, Cece." Stan looked at his watch and got up. "I hate to leave, but I have plans for this afternoon. I'll take care of my bill."

Phil waved him off. "This one's on me, Stan."

"Well, thanks, Phil. I hope you all have a nice afternoon. If there's anything else I can do to help out, give a call." He nodded and left.

They sat in silence for a minute until Julie, the waitress, bounced up to the table and began clearing the dishes. As she reached over the table, her shirt sleeve slipped back, revealing a long, vine-shaped tattoo on her right arm.

Cece stared. "Wow. That's some tattoo, Julie."

The waitress pulled up her sleeve so they could all admire the vine that slithered up her arm from wrist to elbow. "My boyfriend and I got matching tats a few months ago. It was supposed to be a sign we would always be entwined with each other." She wrinkled her nose and rolled her eyes.

"Let me guess. It didn't work out," Cece said.

"Right. I'd like to get a real vine and strangle him." Julie grabbed her neck with her free hand. "Do any of you have tats? Do you know how to get rid of one?"

They all shook their heads. "Sorry," Cece said. "I think you've come to the wrong table for tattoo advice."

Phil took care of the bill and left to pick up some supplies at the tackle shop, promising to meet Kathryn and Cece in an hour at Bellevue Square. Kate and Cece strolled back through the vendor booths.

"Did you ever think of getting tattooed?" Kate asked as she looked through a display of watercolors on one of the tables.

"Me? Never. I know myself too well to do something like that."

"What do you mean?"

Cece picked up a scarf from the table in front of her and held it out in front of her. "My tastes change from year to year. You know, I'll buy a dress one year and think it's the prettiest thing I've ever seen." She draped the scarf around her shoulders and posed. "I'll wear it over and over. And then one day I'll look at it and wonder how I ever liked it at all." She took the scarf off and dropped it back on the table as if it were an odious rag she was throwing in the trash.

"Um. I see where you're going with this." They moved on to a table of knickknacks.

"I can buy another dress, but a tattoo is permanent. If you decide you don't like it anymore, you're still stuck with it."

Kate picked up a star-shaped refrigerator magnet and looked at it intently, turning it over and over in her hand.

"You can never have enough refrigerator magnets, though." Cece combed through the selection on the table, picked one, and handed over two dollars to the vendor.

Kate stood still, staring at the star magnet she was holding. "Oh my gosh, Cece, I just remembered something."

"You? Miss Never-Forget-Anything? What did you remember now?"

"A tattoo."

"What tattoo?"

"The guy who tripped me in the park. All I could see was a pair of legs behind a tree."

"Yeah. So?"

"I have this mental image of a star. Like a star tattoo on his ankle."

"Great. Now all we have to do is go around and ask all the men in town to show us their ankles."

"That would go over big. Maybe that bonk on my head has me imagining things. A dirty ankle sounds more reasonable." She put the star magnet back on the table. "What's that one you picked up?"

Cece held up the rectangular magnet. "It's a quote from John Wayne. 'Courage is being scared to death but saddling up anyway.'" She put on a weak smile. "Sounds like something Ben would say."

"I'm sorry he wasn't at lunch."

"I know. I've got to face him, but he's obviously avoiding me. I'm afraid if I go out to the ranch, I'll make matters worse."

Kate pointed to the magnet Cece was still holding in her hand. "Saddle up, sister. We're all behind you."

CHAPTER SIXTY-TWO

Saddle Up

Cece stopped her car at the road leading to Ben's ranch. Was this the right time to ask for forgiveness? The big old burr oaks leaned over the road, their leaves waving her on.

But what if he wouldn't forgive? Her spirit sagged under the weight of that thought. She picked up the refrigerator magnet and wrapped her fingers around it. *Courage. Be strong and courageous. Saddle up.* She gulped down the fear in her heart and stepped on the gas pedal.

On the way back to the ranch that starry night, they had ridden in silence, unwilling to disturb the favor heaven had bestowed on them. Before they entered Ben's house, he had held her in his arms as if she were a precious gem. He hadn't uttered the words, but she knew they were in his heart and mind.

She had memorized his face that night. The way the lines around his dark gray-blue eyes testified to his humor. The way one side of his mouth turned up a little more than the other when he grinned at her. The cowlick on the right side of his hairline she had teased him about.

The universe had aligned itself for them that night and all was perfect. At least until she woke up the next morning and her stupid brain had refused to acknowledge what her heart knew to be true. She had walked away from the treasure, like an idiot unwilling to accept a valuable gift because she didn't like the paper it was wrapped in.

She turned onto the access road and drove the final half mile. Sunshine invited her with the assurance that all was well as the lane gave way to the ranch area. But all was not well. Sitting right in front of the house was a white Mustang. *Ginger.* Cece's breath caught in her throat. *This isn't the right time.*

She stopped her car, put it into reverse, and began to back up. *He told you Ginger is nothing to him. She's probably here to see about a horse.* She stopped again and shifted back into Drive. She pulled forward timidly and parked her gray Prius next to the sleek convertible.

She sat for a few minutes, thinking of the little speech she wanted to give. She looked at herself in her car's mirror and practiced. "Ben, I want to apologize." *No. Not strong enough.* "Ben, please accept my apology." *Too formal.* "Ben, can I talk to you for a minute? Alone." *That's it. I'll play it by ear. I was always good at ad-lib.* As she swung out of the car, a sound from the barn caught her attention.

She slipped the refrigerator magnet into her pocket, lifted her chin, took a deep breath, and walked in that direction.

When she got within a few feet of the barn door, she heard movement inside, then she heard Ginger giggle, "Oh, Ben." Seconds later, Ben's voice. "C'mon, baby."

Baby? He's calling her 'baby'? Cece stopped cold. Her heart turned to ice in her chest.

Ginger giggled again, louder this time. Then Ben chuckled, "Oh, baby."

A sob escaped from Cece before she could stop it. She slapped her hand over her mouth and turned and walked quickly toward her car, tears stinging her eyes.

CHAPTER SIXTY-THREE

Interrogation 3

The interrogation room smelled like cleaning fluid mixed with sweat. Detective Carlioni leaned against one of the walls, reading his text messages, when Detective MacMillan entered. "You okay, Mackie?" Carlioni asked.

"Yeah, but this one is taking a lot out of me. I know exactly how Lassiter feels, Carli. I wanted to do the same thing to the monster who sold drugs to my sister."

"Yeah, but there's one big difference. You didn't murder anybody."

MacMillan dropped into one of the chairs. "I'll be honest with you. I know it looks bad for him, but I've been thinking about it, and something inside me says he didn't do it."

"Doesn't matter what you think or what I think. Our job is to get at the truth. I still think there's something he's not telling us."

"I don't want to be too hard on this guy. I'm afraid if you push him too far, he's gonna snap."

"Or confess. Don't get emotional on me, Mac. We have a job to do."

MacMillan looked up and gave him an uncertain smile. "Right. I'm on board."

The door squeaked open, and a police officer escorted Lassiter into the room and pointed to the chair on the far side of the table from the one-way mirror.

"Mr. Lassiter, are you all right?" MacMillan's brows knitted together.

"Yes. I'm fine, but I don't understand why we have to go through this again. I've already told you everything."

Carlioni stuck his chin out. "And you're gonna have to keep telling it till we think we have the whole story."

MacMillan stood. "I'll start the video." He punched a button on the unit. "Detectives MacMillan and Carlioni questioning Brad Lassiter."

The two detectives sat at opposite ends of the small table with Lassiter in between. Carlioni shoved a cup of coffee in front of Lassiter.

"Now tell us again, Mr. Lassiter," MacMillan said. "What did you do after Louis Tinnerman left the parking lot behind the old railroad station?"

"I told you. I was crying and then I left."

Carlioni sipped his coffee. "And where did you go?"

"I drove around for a while. Then I went to the shooting range. I had to do something to get rid of the rage. I felt like I was going to explode."

"Which shooting range did you go to?"

"The one on Cleveland Boulevard. It's the one I always go to."

"What time did you get there?"

"Probably around eight-thirty or so. I wasn't paying attention to the time."

Carlioni took his notebook out of his pocket and scratched a few words on it. "How long did you stay at the shooting range?"

"I don't know. Maybe half an hour. They'd have a record of when I got there and when I left. You can check with them."

"What did you do after you left the shooting range?"

"I went home."

Carlioni stood and leaned over the table. His eyes squinted under the weight of his skepticism. "Mr. Lassiter, I checked the shooting ranges. You're right, you showed up at the one on

Cleveland Boulevard, but it was after nine o'clock when you got there. Can you explain why it took you so long?"

"I don't know. I told you I drove around for a while."

"Doesn't the shooting gallery recommend you clean your gun after you use it there?"

"Yes. I guess so."

Carlioni raised his voice. "But your gun hadn't been cleaned. Why not?"

"I don't remember. I wasn't thinking clearly. I was mad and upset. I hardly knew what I was doing. Why are you asking me all these questions?"

Carlioni scowled. "There are witnesses who say they saw two cars leaving the lot behind the railroad station sometime after eight o'clock Friday night. They saw the first car turn right toward Hyde Park and the second car followed it." He got louder. "You were leading Louis Tinnerman to a meeting place at Hyde Park, weren't you? You got him there and killed him and got rid of his car. Then you loaded his body into the trunk of your car and dumped it in the ravine."

Brad Lassiter placed his hands over his eyes. "No. None of that is true."

Carlioni ratcheted his voice up another notch. "You murdered Louis Tinnerman, and then you went to the Cleveland Boulevard Firing Range so you'd have an alibi for shooting your gun."

Lassiter's face turned deep red.

Carlioni's nose was just a few inches from Lassiter's. "And the next day you took your car to a car wash to wash away all the evidence of the crime."

Lassiter shook his head. "No. I got my car washed to get rid of any speck of that filthy creep. I didn't want to think of Sara getting into a car he had touched."

Carlioni shook his head in disgust. "You killed him. Admit it. Things'll go a lot easier for you if you tell us the truth."

Lassiter put his face in his hands. "I didn't kill him. I swear it."

CHAPTER SIXTY-FOUR

The Apology

"Cece. Cece, wait up!"
Cece glanced back over her shoulder to see Ben jogging toward her. *How did he get away from Ginger's clutches so fast?* She picked up her pace. *I can't face him. I can't stay here.*

But he was at her side before she could reach the car. "Cece, stop. What's up?" He touched her arm and she slowed. "Where are you going?" he said. "Why are you running away?"

She took a deep breath and turned to face him. "Oh, Ben, I'm so sorry. I should have called first before I came." Her voice quivered. "I heard you and Ginger in the barn. I didn't mean to barge in." Her voice gave way and she shook her head. "I feel like such a fool."

"What are you talking about? You're not barging in." He had a tight hold on her arm.

Cece started to pull away when something over by the barn caught her eye. She turned to see Ginger leading a horse out of the barn. There was an older man walking beside her.

Ginger called over. "Hey, Ben. What do you want us to do with Baby?"

"Take her into the big corral. Your dad can harness her to the buggy, but I want to talk to Cece first."

Cece blinked hard and looked from the horse back to Ben. She lifted her eyebrows. "Baby? The horse's name is Baby?"

Ben nodded. "Well, it's really Sultan's Baby, but that's a mouthful, so we just call her Baby." He looked back at the horse. "She's a beauty, isn't she? American Saddlebred. I have a couple of students who want to learn to drive a buggy, and Ginger's dad is an expert. He's helping me train Baby."

Cece looked up into his face and started to laugh. She doubled over and hugged herself, convulsing with laughter.

"What's so funny?"

She wiped away the tears of mirth. "Oh, Ben. I came to talk to you. But when I got close to the barn, I heard Ginger giggling and I heard you saying 'baby,' and I guess I thought you and Ginger were engaged in some ... extra-equine activities."

Ben cocked the hat back on his head and looked down at Cece with a wide grin. "You thought Ginger and I ..."

"Yeah. It sounded pretty intimate."

"Ginger was laughing because Baby kept trying to lick my hands while I was leading her out of her stall. I think the horse smelled the apple pie Mattie fed me after lunch." Ben shook his head. "I never had a female go after me like that before. Maybe I should eat apple pie more often."

"Oh, Ben. I'm so stupid. Can you forgive me?"

"Forgive you for what? For misunderstanding?"

She looked up into his eyes. "For being stupid and for hurting you and thinking we ..." Her throat felt full and she couldn't get the words out.

"For thinking we weren't exactly meant for each other?"

She gulped down the sorrow. "Yes."

Ben let his hands drop to his sides. "There's nothing to forgive, Cece. You were being honest, and I know you always say exactly what you feel." He pulled at the brim of his Stetson. "That's one of the things I liked most about you."

Cece looked deep into his eyes, hoping to see some sign of the man who had held her on that starry night. But there was no wonder in his eyes today. She pressed her lips together hard.

Ben removed the red kerchief from around his neck. "Now, can I be honest with you?" He pulled her to him and used it to gently wipe away the tears.

"Of course."

He put the bandana around her neck and tied a knot in it. "I've never known anyone like you, Cece. You're smart and funny, and you keep me on my toes."

Ginger's voice cut in. "Ben, we've got Baby hooked up, and Daddy's ready for you to come help."

"Be there in a minute," he called. He turned back to Cece. "My Uncle Fred once told me 'Deep emotions require time. You can't rush into a serious relationship.'" He stepped back. "I think I got out a little ahead of myself. That wasn't fair to you. Or me." He pushed his hands into the pockets of his jeans. "Phil told me you got that invitation to go to Atlanta to audition for *The Taming of the Shrew*. I guess you'll be leaving soon."

Cece dug her fingernails into the palms of her hands to keep from tearing up. "I haven't decided yet."

"Ben!" Ginger's voice was shrill. "The clouds are moving in. It's going to start raining soon."

"Coming," Ben called back. "Look, these new students are real important to me, and Ginger and her dad are going out of their way to help. I need to go." He turned and took a few steps toward the big corral, then he stopped and faced her again. "Good luck with that audition."

Cece watched him jog away from her, his boots kicking up little clouds of dust. After he had rounded the corner of the barn and dropped out of sight, she slid into the driver's seat of her car and sat for a minute. Then she took the kerchief from around her neck, folded it in half, then half again. She put it in her lap and ran her fingers over the cottony surface, a coarse reminder of hope denied. Then she picked it up and buried her face in it.

CHAPTER SIXTY-FIVE

Kate Visits Brad Again

Kate smiled at the guard. Same one as before and same expression. "Good to see you again," she said as he led her down the hall.

"Seat three," he said and pointed to the row of chairs in the visiting room.

Kate thought about making a joke about having a better seat this time, but decided against it. *This probably isn't the best place for humor.* She took a seat and picked up the phone on her side of the partition.

An officer escorted Brad into the room. He looked thinner, but he had shaved and his hair was combed. *That's a start,* she thought.

He lifted the phone. "Hey, Kathryn. Thanks for coming by." A faint smile crossed his face. "Thelma told me how you and Cece took Sara out for an afternoon of fun. I really appreciate that. Thelma said Sara was real happy when she came home."

"It was a pleasure, Brad. Sara is a beautiful little girl, and we had as much fun as she did."

Brad's jaw tightened. "I hate it that she has to go through this. I don't know what all this will do to her."

Kate felt a warm sensation rising in her chest. *So much pain. Surely there's something I can do.* But she had promised Phil she would take a break from the investigation until the doctor released her. Still, it wouldn't hurt to talk to Brad about it. Would it?

"Brad, can I ask you some questions about the night you met with Louis Tinnerman?"

"Sure. Ask anything. I've been over it so many times with the police I can rehash it without even thinking."

"What happened after Louis Tinnerman arrived in the parking lot behind the old terminal? Did he park next to your car or across the lot or what?"

"He pulled up next to my car and got out. He came over to the passenger side of my car."

"Did he get in?"

"No. He opened the door and just leaned in. I think he was surprised to see me instead of Ellie."

"Then what did you do?"

"I told him Ellie was dead and he was a murderer. Kathryn, he didn't even look like it bothered him. He just looked at his watch and said he had another appointment. When he started to back away, I pulled my gun."

"Did he run?"

"No. He laughed. Said there was no way I was going to shoot him. He called me some names and turned his back on me. Then he got in his car and left."

"Did you follow him, Brad?"

"No. I sat there for a minute and then drove around to try to calm down. I went to the firing range and then home. I never saw him again."

"You know they found the body in a field next to Hyde Park. Have you ever been there?"

"I've been to the park before. Ellie and I used to take Sara there for picnics before things went wrong. But they told me the body was in a bushy ravine next to the running trails. I've never been there."

"How about Hyde Park Lake where they found the car? Have you ever been there?"

"Sure. I used to water ski there in high school. They showed me a map where they found the car, but it's a big lake. I don't know if I've ever been to that part of it. I wasn't there that night."

"Do you remember anything else? Anything that might help us know who really killed him?"

"No. I wish I could think of something to help, Kathryn, but that's all I know."

CHAPTER SIXTY-SIX

Juliet

"**I**s Jeremy Dodd in?" The chic woman in the bright green suit, sunglasses, and a broad white hat stood expectantly in front of the receptionist.

"Do you have an appointment?"

"No, sweetie, but I'm sure he'll want to see me." She leaned forward and her voice dropped to a confidential whisper. "I want to discuss a large donation to the Hodges campaign." She removed her dark glasses and replaced them with a pair of tortoise-shell spectacles.

"Wait here, ma'am. I'll see if he's in his office."

The green-clad woman walked over to a mirror and primped the red curls beneath her hat. She adjusted her glasses and admired how well they matched her dark brown eyes. From an angle, she could see Jeremy Dodd talking to the receptionist and looking out toward the waiting room. She offered up a dazzling smile and murmured under her breath, "It's superpower time."

The receptionist returned and pointed toward a side office. "Mr. Dodd will see you now."

The woman breezed into the room with her hand extended. "Mr. Dodd, I'm Juliet Duperie."

Jeremy's face lit up with a broad smile as he walked from behind the desk. "Ms. Duperie, I'm glad to meet you. What can I do for you?"

Cece glanced at the desk. An unorganized mess. *Maybe there's something interesting there.* "I've heard a lot about you, Mr. Dodd. Everyone says you are running the smartest campaign in the history of this state, and I've decided I want to be a part of the winning team."

Jeremy's face virtually glowed as he propped himself on the edge of his desk, looking like a cheap imitation of suave. "Oh, it's nothing. I've been lucky."

Cece smiled like a coquette. *This is going to be easier than I thought.* "Well, that's not what I heard. I understand your genius will win the governor's office for Bob Hodges, and I'm sure you're on your way to the big time in Washington. With your brains, I think wonderful things are in store for you. Now tell me how I can help." She fingered the US flag pin on her lapel.

Jeremy stood upright and his voice took on a deeper, more confident tone. "We can always use financial support."

Cece fought off a smile. "Of course. That's what I was thinking. Do you mind if we close the door? I'd feel more comfortable if we kept this conversation to ourselves." The vending machine in the outside hall would come in handy.

"Certainly." Jeremy strode across the room, chest out, and closed the door firmly. "Now, tell me what you had in mind."

"Maybe you can help me understand the financial rules. I'd like to donate whatever the maximum amount is to the campaign, but I also want to meet Representative Hodges and perhaps have a picture taken with him." She raised her eyebrows as if sharing a secret. "Is there any way to sweeten the pot?"

"Oh, I think we can come up with something." Jeremy reminded her of Wile E. Coyote. He might start drooling over his anticipated conquest at any second.

Juliet Duperie began a fit of coughing. "Oh goodness, my allergies are acting up again." She took a linen handkerchief from her purse and coughed again. "I noticed a vending machine in the hall. Do you think you could get me a bottle of water?"

"Absolutely." Jeremy leaped to the task, rushed out, and closed the door behind him.

Cece jumped up and ran behind the desk. It should take him at least a minute and a half to get to the machine, buy the water and bring it back. She rummaged through the pile of papers on top of the desk. *What a mess. Doesn't he believe in a filing system?* Then she noticed a folder labeled "Hey man." She had heard of Jeremy's habit of labeling people with disparaging nicknames. *Has to be Hadecker.* She opened it and scanned down a list of numbers. It wasn't a typical account listing, just a list of numbers that didn't seem to make much sense. 10, 5, 10. Each number had a date beside it. She pulled her phone out of her purse and took a picture when she heard the door knob turn. *Uh-oh.*

CHAPTER SIXTY-SEVEN

Juliet's Duperie

"I'll get it, Mrs. Goldman," Kate called out when the doorbell rang. A woman, chic in an emerald green suit and white wide-brimmed straw hat, stood primly at the door. Underneath the hat, her hair was light red and wavy. She looked like something from a fifties' fashion magazine.

"Yes?" was all Kate could think to say.

The woman removed her large sunglasses with one gloved hand. "Cece Goldman?"

"No, I'm sorry. Cece isn't here."

"Yes, she is." The woman smiled sweetly.

Weird, thought Kate. *What kind of game is this?* "No, ma'am. I assure you, Cece is not here."

The woman pulled off the glove from her left hand. "I can assure you, she is." She held her hand up so the familiar gold watch was visible. Then she sighed and dropped her hand. "Kathryn, you really should be able to recognize me by now, even with all the makeup."

"Who was that at the door, Kathryn?" Sylvia Goldman appeared from the laundry room with a basket of clean clothes. She glanced at the woman in the green getup as she passed by toward the master bedroom. "Oh hi, Cece," she called out. "You're in time for lunch."

"Never try to fool your mother." Cece stepped into the room.

Kate shook her head. "Cece, I can't believe it's really you. Where did you get that outfit?"

Cece flipped the contacts out of each eye and blinked expressively. "At the local theater. I'm glad you fell for the disguise. Now I know nobody else would have guessed." She took off the white hat and pulled her wig off. "I don't know how anybody ever wore clothes like this. It's like wearing a suit of armor." She ruffled her blonde curls.

"Why are you in disguise? What's up?"

Cece grinned behind her red lips. "I went to see Jeremy Dodd."

"Cece, you didn't!"

"Oh yeah." She pulled off her pumps and shuffled back toward her bedroom. "Come on back. I'll tell you all about it."

* * *

"Jeremy Dodd is one dedicated individual." Cece shrugged out of the green jacket. She rummaged around in a pile of clothes on the bed and pulled out a blue T-shirt. "Oh, that's so much better."

"What do you mean he's dedicated? He seems like a royal jerk to me."

"Yeah, I know. He's totally into himself. It was so easy to fool him, I almost felt bad about it."

"What happened?" Kate sat on the edge of Cece's bed.

Cece found a pair of jeans and pulled them on. "I strolled in and asked to see him. I told him I was interested in contributing to the campaign, but I particularly wanted to talk to him. You should have seen him. He was oozing self-importance out of his fingertips."

"Sounds like Jeremy. Then what?"

"I waltzed into his office in this getup." She waved her hand toward the green dress now lying in the middle of her bed. "I told him I was Juliet Duperie."

"That's a new one."

"Yeah. 'Duperie' is French for deception."

"And Jeremy bought the disguise?"

"Absolutely. You know, there are some people in the world who want to believe something so bad they'll buy anything you're selling them. Jeremy is one of those. He wants to know he's a big shot, and you can feed him baloney as long as it's spiced with adoration, and he'll believe it's prime rib from the grill. It was priceless."

"So what did he say?" Kate leaned back on her elbows.

"He said he'd be happy to take my money and he'd arrange for me to meet Representative Hodges. Blah, blah, blah. Then I hit him with the big one."

"The big one?"

"Yeah. I told him I couldn't contribute unless it was a secret. I had other money situations I couldn't tell him about."

"He must have backed out after that." Kate sat straight up.

"No. He acted like it was just another day at the office. That's when I realized how slimy he really is. So I faked a cough and asked him to get me a bottle of water. That's when I got a picture of a file on his desk."

"You snooped on his desk? Weren't you afraid of getting caught?"

Cece sat on the bed with her eyes open wide. "I almost did get caught. He rushed back with that water so fast, I was still behind his desk when I heard him opening the door."

"Oh no." Kate put her open hands on each side of her face. "What did you do?"

"Old acting trick. I dropped to my knees."

"What?"

"When he came in the room, he asked me what I was doing. I told him my earring had come off and I was searching for it."

"Don't tell me he fell for that line."

"Yes. He even got down on the floor with me to look for it."

"Let me guess. You had it in your hand all along and then did a 'Eureka, I found it' thing."

"Hey, you're good. Maybe I should recruit you for my next excursion."

"No thanks. I'm not into acting."

"Anyway, I put my earring on, hopped up and started coughing like I was caught in an L.A. smog alert. I told him I was having an allergy attack and I would come back another time. He looked so concerned, I almost felt bad. I started to run out of the office when Mike Strickland walked in."

"Oh no! Did Mike recognize you?"

"He looked right at me, but then he told Jeremy that Hodges wanted to see the staff, so he had to go. I rushed out, but I got a picture of that suspicious-looking file. Tell me something, Kathryn. Do you think Jeremy Dodd could be on the take?"

CHAPTER SIXTY-EIGHT

My Kingdom for a Clue

"**S**tan, I met with Brad yesterday. I'm telling you he didn't murder Louis Tinnerman." Kate stood in front of Stan Palmerton's desk with her hands on her hips. "He wouldn't lie to me."

Stan leaned back in his chair and folded his hands together. "Kathryn, we've been through this before. Good people do bad things and then they lie about them. I thought you were right about Brad, but now I'm afraid he's using you because he knows you believe him."

"Look, Stan," Cece said. "I know it seems like a long shot. But Kathryn wants to make sure we've gone through every detail before Brad goes to trial. Who knows, there may be something we haven't found."

Stan sighed and shook his head. "Kathryn, I told Phil I'd look out for you. I can't take the responsibility for you getting hurt."

Kate nodded. "I understand, and I thought about that. Here's the deal—we need you to come so the police will know we didn't plant something there in case we find anything. The only people who will know are Cece, Phil, you, and me. This is our last chance."

Stan opened his hands, fingers splayed wide. "What do you want me to do?"

"I want to go back to the place where we found the body and examine it again. Maybe there's something there."

Stan shook his head again. "The police have been all over that place. If there was anything there, they'd have found it."

"I know they did a thorough job, but I can't sleep if I don't at least try."

Stan sighed, "All right. I'll do this one last thing, but then you have to let this case take its course. Do you agree?"

Kate bit her lip and nodded.

Stan pulled his phone out of his pocket and tapped the screen. "I can get away tomorrow morning. Say around ten?"

"Perfect." Kate gave him a big smile. "Let's meet at the road overlooking the ravine. We'll see you there at ten."

"Okay." Stan walked out from behind his desk and looked down at her. "But, Kathryn, I don't want you to get your hopes up. Chances are it's going to be another dead end, and I don't want you to be disappointed."

"I won't. Thanks, Stan."

CHAPTER SIXTY-NINE

The Final Clue

"There's Stan." Kate pulled the car over to the shoulder of the road behind Stan's Jeep. He was leaning against the back bumper, legs crossed, looking down at his cell phone.

"Been here long?" she asked.

"Nope. Just got here."

"Okay, boss. You're the pro," Cece said. "Tell us what to do."

"Looks like there's a path leading down to where the body was." Stan gestured with his hand toward the bush where the body had been found. "The killer must have dragged or rolled the body down from here to the bush. Let's take our time and turn over everything from the road to the bush and all around."

"What are we looking for?" Cece asked.

"Anything that looks like it doesn't belong. A paper clip, a piece of fabric, anything that might give us a clue." He took several pairs of nitrile gloves out of his pocket. "Wear these. We probably aren't going to find anything, but just in case we do, we don't want to contaminate evidence." He handed them each a pair of gloves and took the lead toward the bush where the body had been found.

They carefully examined the path leading from the road to the bush. Kate and Cece rummaged around the site and scraped the ground in the area. They worked for thirty minutes, but found nothing.

274 • KAY DIBIANCA

Cece sat on the ground and looked up at Kate. "Sister, I know this is important to you, and I know how much you want to prove Brad's innocence, but I think we've run out of options."

"Yeah, I know." Kathryn stood upright and stretched her back. "I think we're coming to the end of the line, but I can't get rid of the feeling that I'm missing something." She did a 360-degree turn. "Something staring me right in the face. I was hoping we'd find it today."

Stan rubbed the back of his neck and walked over to them. "There's a slight depression there." He pointed to an area that was a little lower. "The police said it was raining the night of the murder. Maybe something washed down there."

"Let's have a look," Cece said as she jumped up. "To quote my favorite sister, 'Never give up.'"

Kate laughed, and she and Cece began their examination of the ground down the little slope while Stan continued to check around the path. Ten minutes into the search, Kate pulled a branch back and spotted something half-buried in the dirt. "Here's something," she called out. Stan rushed down and leaned in as Kate brushed dirt off the artifact.

"Careful, Kathryn," he said. "Don't damage it."

Kate gently lifted it out of the dirt. It was a button. A blue button with several threads still attached as if it had been torn from a blue work shirt. "Oh, no."

Stan exhaled a deep breath and held his hand out. "Let me see that." He stood motionless for a few seconds staring at the button she had placed in his hand, then he looked at Kate. "I'm sorry, Kathryn. We have to turn this over to the police." He pulled his phone out of his pocket and took a picture.

"I can't believe it. I thought I'd find something to exonerate him. Maybe it belongs to somebody else." Her voice cracked and she looked at Stan with tears in her eyes. "I don't think I can take this to the police."

"I'll take it in to the station and tell them what you found. The police will probably want a statement from you, but that can wait."

He shook his head. "You need to go home and get some rest. I don't think there's anything you can do for Brad now."

"You're right," she said. "It's over."

CHAPTER SEVENTY

Dead Man's Watch

Kate drove to the car repair shop. Cece had promised Sara to take her to the library in the afternoon, but Kate didn't think she could put on a good face for the little girl.

How could things go so wrong? She had found the final clue that would implicate Brad in the murder. Kate felt she had to see Phil, to be near him. She leaned against Phil's desk and looked down at her watch. A shaft of light from the window reflected off the face of the watch and made her shield her eyes. When Phil came into the office, he closed the door and pulled her to him.

"I'm sorry," he said. "Stan called and told me what happened."

"It's over. I was so sure I could help, but it looks like I made matters worse. Oh, Phil, I feel so bad." She put her hands around his waist and snuggled into him.

"Listen, you did everything you could. More than anyone else would have done. But now you have to face facts. Brad is almost certainly guilty. It's time to move on."

Kate leaned her head against his chest "Yeah, I know, but I really hate this, Phil. I still have a feeling we're missing something obvious, but I can't grab hold of it."

"I'll tell you what we've been missing." Phil sat in his desk chair and drew her onto his lap. "We've been missing time for you and me. Now I want to get that back." He pulled her head down and kissed her.

"Time," she said as she lifted her head. Her eyebrows scrunched together. "That's what Sara said in the ice cream parlor. 'All a watch has to do is tell the time.' Of course!" She jumped up and snapped her fingers. "But a watch can tell more than the time. Phil, that's it! I knew there was something else."

"What else?"

"Louis Tinnerman was wearing a watch the night he was murdered, right?"

"Yes. The police know all about that. The murderer took Tinnerman's watch off and threw it in the trunk of his car with all the other stuff before he drove it in the lake." He shook his head. "I don't see why you're getting so excited about that."

Kathryn pulled at her ponytail. "I can understand why the murderer threw Tinnerman's phone and credit cards in the trunk of the car. Those things could get him in trouble. But why would he take a cheap watch off a dead man's wrist and throw it in with the other stuff?"

"I give up. Why would he do that?"

"He wouldn't. The only reason he would take the dead man's watch is if it was expensive." She smiled at Phil. "That wasn't Tinnerman's watch the police found in the trunk of the car. That was the murderer's watch."

Phil nodded slowly. "Makes sense."

"Do you still have the video of Louis Tinnerman walking across the lot when he brought his car in?"

"Yeah. I saved it on my laptop."

"Show it to me. Please."

Phil swung around and hit a few keys. The video popped up on the screen and he hit the Play icon. Once again they watched Louis Tinnerman walk across the parking lot after he had dropped his car off. Halfway across, he reached up to adjust the lapels on his jacket and his left sleeve pulled back.

Kate pointed to the screen. "There! You can see it."

Phil backed the video up and stopped it at the point where Tinnerman began to adjust his jacket. The frame clearly showed the edge of a watch on his left wrist peeking out from under his shirt sleeve. A silver watch.

"See. The sun reflected off the edge of the watch because it's metal. It couldn't have been that black plastic one they found in the car." Kathryn leaned over to get a better look. "Can you enlarge that frame?"

Phil zoomed in on the watch.

Kate squinted at the grainy image. "It's hard to tell, but that looks like a Galileo watch."

Phil stared at the picture on the screen. "What's so special about a Galileo watch?"

"I met a girl at the race who was wearing one. It's a special GPS timepiece that uploads data to satellites in real time. If the killer took it and the watch was left on, there's an online system that would show where it was every minute."

Now Phil was smiling. "And if we know where the watch went after the murder ..."

"Then we know the killer."

CHAPTER SEVENTY-ONE

Tommy

Kate turned into the parking lot at the grocery store. She wanted to do something to get her mind off Brad, so she had offered to pick up a few groceries for Sylvia. She checked her phone for messages, but nothing. She dropped it in the cupholder and opened the car door.

It had been four days since she and Phil discovered Louis Tinnerman was wearing a metal watch. The police had gotten a search warrant and contacted the Galileo company, but there was no watch registered to Al Hadecker or Louis Tinnerman. Another dead end. Maybe it wasn't a Galileo watch after all. She could only see the edge of it in the video. Earl and Thelma had borrowed money to get Brad out on bail, but the trial was scheduled to start in a week and things looked worse than ever. She sighed as she locked her car and walked into the supermarket.

She rolled a basket up to the produce section and tossed a head of leaf lettuce in. She continued on to the seafood counter and stared blankly at the live lobster tank, mentally working through all the details she knew about the murder. She felt trapped as if she were in a maze and couldn't find her way out. *Imprisoned*, she thought, *just like those lobsters.* No watch. No clues. No escape. The last time things had looked this bad was in Gavin's office at ArcTron Labs when she thought he was going to kill her. There was no way out then, but unexpectedly, her friend Tommy had saved the day. "Tommy!" she said out loud. She abandoned the shopping cart and ran back to her car. She grabbed her phone and hit Tommy's contact.

"Hey, Kathryn." Tommy Abrahams's voice came over.

"Hi, Tommy. How are you? And how's the new job?" She was breathless.

"It's great. Being VP of a tech firm is about the best thing that ever happened to me. And it's all because of your recommendation. I can't thank you enough."

"You don't have to thank me. I always knew you were the best tech guy on the planet, and now everybody else knows it too." She paused and swallowed the lump in her throat remembering how Tommy had stepped in front of her when Gavin had threatened her with a gun. "Besides, you were willing to take a bullet for me. I'll never forget that."

"Okay." Tommy laughed and she could imagine him blushing and pulling on his earlobe. "We'll call it even-steven. Now, what can I do for you?"

"Tommy, I need a favor."

"Sure. Anything for you, Kathryn."

"You might want to hear this first before you agree." Kathryn shifted in her seat and took a deep breath. "I want you to hack into a computer system."

"Whoa. You know I can't do that. It's unethical. And it's probably illegal."

"I think it may help us save a life."

There was a silence and Kate could imagine Tommy shaking his head and remembering the time in third grade when she talked him into helping her save the class gerbil. They had nursed it back to health with vitamin drops and a daily cleaning of its cage. Tommy had never let her forget she was "gerbil messiah."

"Okay." He sighed. "You got my attention. Does this have anything to do with that murder investigation?"

"Yes. You know Brad Lassiter was arrested for the murder of a man named Louis Tinnerman. Tinnerman was wearing a special watch, and if we can find that watch, we may be able to prove

Brad's innocence." Kathryn explained how the Galileo watch might identify the killer if they could trace it.

"So, tell the police. They can get the information you want."

"We did tell the police. They got a warrant and contacted the folks at Galileo, but they didn't find anything registered to the murdered man. Or to Al Hadecker. They say it's a dead end and they dropped it."

"That sounds definitive to me. If it's not registered to either man, there's no use hacking in to the Galileo system. I'd be setting myself up to be arrested for nothing."

"Tommy, I don't know who that watch is registered to, but there must be a way to find it. If anybody can do it, you can."

There was another silence for several seconds. Then Tommy's voice came across with concern. "Kathryn, don't you think you're in this too deep? You sound like you're obsessed with this thing. Now you're willing to do something that could get you and me both in trouble. Are you sure you want to do this?"

Kathryn frowned. *Am I sure?* "Yes. I'm sure."

"If you're that sure, I'll see what I can do."

Kate filled him in on the model of watch he should look for, registered to Louis Tinnerman or Alexander Hadecker.

"Got it. I'll call you."

"Thanks, Tommy. I'm on my way to Stan Palmerton's office. He's a private eye. Maybe he can help."

"Look, don't tell him about me. I'd like to keep this between the two of us."

"You got it. Thanks again, Tommy. You're the best friend a person could have."

"Yeah. Save it for the judge." Tommy chuckled and hung up.

CHAPTER SEVENTY-TWO

Decaf Coffee

"Stan, I think I've got something." Kate had her phone on Bluetooth as she drove toward Stan's office.

"Kathryn? Please don't tell me you're still talking about the Lassiter case."

"No. I mean yes. I figured something out."

A deep sigh came across the phone. "Let's have it."

"Phil's security video of Tinnerman shows him wearing a silver watch. The one the police found in his car must have been the killer's. Maybe the murderer took Tinnerman's watch."

There was a pause on the line. "So what? A stolen watch isn't important." Stan was beginning to sound impatient.

Kate stopped at a red light and took a breath. "It is important, Stan. If I'm right, the watch was a Galileo. That's a GPS brand that uploads data automatically. If we can find the watch, we may find the killer. I'm sure this is the key."

"Did you tell the police?"

"Yes. And they searched the Galileo database, but didn't find anything. They're giving up on it."

"Sounds like a good idea to me, Kathryn. You need to let it go."

"There may be other ways to locate it, though. I have an idea." She couldn't reveal Tommy's involvement. Maybe she could fabricate something about finding the information.

"Okay, why don't you drop by and we'll talk about it."

Kathryn drove to Signal Street, parked, and jogged into the building. She rang the bell at Stan's office and heard the buzz as he released the lock.

"Kathryn." Stan got up from behind his desk and walked around to meet her. "You are one incredible detective. I think I'm going to have to hire you. Have a seat." He pointed to his desk. "There's a cup of coffee I fixed especially for you." He put his hands on his hips. "It's decaf. I don't think you need any more caffeine today."

Kate grinned. "You're right about the caffeine. I haven't had anything to eat yet, but I definitely want to have a cup of your coffee."

Stan took a seat behind his desk. "I'll take you to lunch after we figure out how to handle your latest theory. But first, drink up. Coffee's guaranteed to improve thinking skills, and we're both gonna need that today."

Kate took a long swallow. "Yum. Very good. What is it?"

"My special blend, but I can't reveal all my culinary secrets, now can I?" He took a swig from his cup. "Now finish your coffee and tell me your theory about the watch."

Before Kate could answer, she saw movement in the kitchen area adjacent to the office. A woman walked out.

"Kathryn," Stan said, "this is Mrs. Hadecker."

Kate nodded to the other woman. "Mrs. Hadecker, I was sorry to hear about your husband."

"Nice to meet you, Kathryn. Stan—Mr. Palmerton—has told me a lot about you."

Stan leaned back in his chair. "Mrs. Hadecker hired me to investigate her husband's murder. I'll be working with the police in Curtisville."

"Oh, I see. I hope things work out."

"Mrs. Hadecker," Stan said, "I hope you don't mind if Kathryn and I talk privately for a few minutes. This shouldn't take long."

"No. Not at all. I need to catch up on my email, and I could use another cup of your coffee. I'll wait in the kitchen if that's all right with you." She smiled at Kate. "One of the wonderful things about working with Stan is that he keeps coffee and sweet rolls in the kitchen."

"Sure. Help yourself." Stan watched her go into the other room and close the door. Then he turned his attention to Kathryn. "Okay, let's have this little gem of information."

Kate sat in the straight chair in front of the desk and leaned forward with her arms on her thighs. She could feel her face grow warm with the excitement of telling Stan what she had found. "It's what I was telling you about on the phone. Louis Tinnerman's watch could hold the key to the murder. If I'm right, we may be able to track down the real killer." She took another swallow of coffee, then sat back and hugged her knees.

"Kathryn, you know Phil doesn't want you working on this case. I thought we settled all that."

"No, it's all right. He's okay as long as I'm talking to you."

"Does Phil know you came here?"

Kate blushed and looked at the floor. "Uh, no. I tried to call, but he was with a customer. I'll call him later." She looked at Stan with a slight shrug. "He'll be okay with it. And you'll be amazed at what I found."

Kate's phone beeped and she pulled it out of her purse and tapped on the message icon. "This is from Brad." She smiled. "He's at Reverend Whitefield's home. That's only a few blocks from here." She looked up at Stan. "He's out on bail, you know." She read the message again. "Maybe things are going to work out after all." She handed Stan her phone so he could read the message.

He glanced at the text. "You know, Kathryn, I think you're right. Things are going to work out fine." Stan put the phone on his desk.

Kate took another gulp of coffee and tried to calm down. This was the best coffee she'd ever tasted. Now to tell Stan about her idea. He was going to love this. "Like I said, Louis Tinnerman was wearing a watch. I'm pretty sure it was a Galileo. We discovered it when we looked at the video at Phil's place. Everybody assumed the watch in the trunk of the car was Tinnerman's, but I think the killer took the dead man's watch. Maybe he or she didn't realize the watch uploads data automatically to a satellite."

"So can we access this data?"

"Yes. I gave the police all the information, and they got a warrant to search the Galileo database, but they didn't find any watch belonging to Louis Tinnerman or to Al Hadecker. Commissioner Blake said it's another dead end and dropped it." She took another long swallow of her coffee.

"So it sounds like you should drop it too."

Better not mention Tommy. "Maybe we could find another way."

Stan's eyes seemed to grow brighter. "Another way?"

Kate drained the rest of her coffee and put the cup down. "If I can find a way to get into the Galileo database, I can look around."

"You don't mean you want to hack into a company's computer, do you? You could get arrested for that."

Kate yawned and blinked her eyes. "But it's worth the risk if I find something that will exonerate Brad." She yawned again. "I think all this nervous energy is catching up with me."

"Getting overwrought will really make a difference. Remember, the doctor said you need to take it easy for a while."

Stan's face looked out of focus. Kate rubbed her eyes. "You know, I'm not feeling well. Maybe I should go home. I can call you later and tell y'watt I fund." *That didn't come out right. What's going on?* Kate shook her head and blinked her eyes wide. The room seemed to revolve around her. She sat up straight and tried to concentrate. *Did I really have a concussion after all? Is all this excitement getting to me?*

"Kathryn, are you all right?" Stan's voice sounded far away.

Get a grip. Concentrate. She saw Stan get up and walk around the desk. She felt his hand on her shoulder. She looked hard at a picture behind Stan's desk and tried to focus on the four men standing together in front of several kayaks pulled up on a beach. They were all barefoot. The last thing she saw was the star tattoo on the ankle of one of the men.

Stan Has a Plan

K ate tried to lift her head, but it was too heavy. A bowling
ball would have been easier. *Where am I?* She blinked
hard and tried to focus.

Stan's office. Did I pass out? Where's Stan? She tried to move
but felt like she was glued to the chair. She tried to lift her arms,
but they wouldn't budge. She wanted to call out, but she couldn't
make a noise. Something was in her mouth. A woman's voice,
angry and loud, came from the kitchen.

"First you killed the wrong man. Then you took his watch.
How stupid can you be?"

Kate turned her head to the left, but the door to the kitchen
was barely ajar and she couldn't see into the other room.

Stan's voice was stern. "Keep your voice down. There's no
problem. Just a small glitch in the plan."

"A small glitch?" Larissa Hadecker's voice was shrill and
shaky. "You were supposed to make it look like a robbery. Now
the police are all over it, and that watch is going to blow the entire
thing."

"Listen, honey. I've got this. We're gonna be home free.
Chill."

Honey?

"That girl knows about the watch," Larissa hissed out.

"Yeah, but she's the only one who knows. The police have
already given up on it. The only reason I took it was because that

idiot Hadecker had his user ID and password taped to the back of the watch. I changed all the account information so there's no way they can tie it to me. And I'll make sure Kathryn Frasier doesn't get the chance to dig into that database."

"And how exactly are you going to do that? She won't give up until she's figured it out."

"I can solve that. I just texted Brad Lassiter from Kathryn's phone. Guaranteed he'll come. When he gets here, I shoot him with my gun, then shoot Kathryn with his gun."

An electric shock went through Kate. *He's going to kill me.* The room started to spin again. *Don't pass out. Find a way out of this.* She shook her head hard and forced her eyes open as wide as she could. Her arms felt like water, but still she pulled against the straps that had her pinned to the chair.

"But he won't have a gun." Larissa's voice was brittle with sarcasm. "Remember, he's out on parole."

"I know, but we'll use the stolen gun I keep in the kitchen. After I shoot him, we plant the stolen gun on him and claim he came here looking for Kathryn. He wanted to get even because she found the incriminating evidence against him. It's perfect. We'll be witnesses to the whole thing!"

The sarcasm dropped out of Larissa's voice. "Look, Stan, I'm not going to be a party to murder."

Kate heard feet scuffing.

"Listen, baby. You're in this as deep as I am. I may have pulled the trigger, but you and I planned on killing Al for months. If I go down, believe me, I'm taking you with me. Do you want to spend the rest of your life in jail?"

Larissa's voice went lower, and Kate strained to hear the words. "Al *deserved* to die. He was an abusive monster. Slapping me around, dangling his fortune in front of my face to get me to stay. But these people didn't do anything to us."

"That girl is the only thing between us and the life we want. We've come too far to turn back now. I've been trying to get her to give it up, but she won't quit. Once she's out of the way, we're home free. It's the only way."

Kate heard more movement and what sounded like a muffled sob.

"Good." Stan's voice was calm and controlled. "There's a Colt Mustang in the drawer under the sink. It's loaded. Get it out and bring it here. I'm betting Brad will be here in two seconds and I'm gonna be ready for him."

* * *

Phil and Ben were sitting in Phil's office when his phone played the sound of honking horns. It was Tommy Abrahams.

"Hey, Tommy. How's it going, buddy?"

"I'm great. How about you?"

"Doin' good. What's up?"

"I thought Kathryn might be there with you. I've been trying to call her, but she's not picking up. I guess she let her phone battery run down again. Anyway, I thought I should let her know what I found."

"What you found?"

"Yeah. About the Galileo watch."

Phil sat upright in his chair. "The Galileo watch? She called you about that?" Ben motioned to him, and he put his phone on speaker.

"Yeah. Kathryn asked me to do some digging." Tommy coughed. "Sort of illegal digging. She wanted me to hack into the Galileo site to see if I could find the information on Al Hadecker's watch that the police couldn't find. Don't tell anybody about that."

Phil rolled his eyes. "Kathryn's off on another rabbit trail. Please don't tell me you hacked into the Galileo database."

"Actually, no. I looked up their company and discovered I have a friend who's one of their database administrators. He gave me permission to look through the files."

"What did you find?"

"Nothing. No watch is registered to Louis Tinnerman or to Alexander Hadecker. It looked like a dead end ..."

"Too bad. Well, thanks for trying."

"Wait. I poked around and found a watch that had some geocoordinates around Hyde Park the night of the murder. It wasn't registered to Hadecker or Tinnerman, though. The owner is somebody named Susan V. Neera."

"I'll pass it along to the police. Maybe this Susan Neera was a friend of Tinnerman's. Maybe she was involved in the murder. That might clear Brad Lassiter and it would make Kathryn happy." Phil gave a thumbs-up sign to Ben.

"But there's something else I think you should know. The history of the movement of the watch is all there. I can see where it was the night of the murder and everywhere it's been since then."

"Hey, that's great, Tommy. You may have solved the case." Phil leaned back in his chair, smiling at Ben. "Where has the watch been?"

"Looks like it left Hyde Park the night of the murder and spent a lot of time at 180 North Signal Street. You know anybody there?"

Phil felt the blood drain out of his face. "That's Stan Palmerton's office."

"Palmerton? I think Kathryn mentioned something about being on her way to Palmerton's office when I talked to her."

Phil bolted out of his chair. "Listen, Tommy. I want you to call the police. Tell them to get to Palmerton's office now! Ben, let's go. I'll drive." Phil ran to his car and Ben piled in on the passenger side. "It's a couple of miles. Try calling Kathryn."

Ben punched on his phone and waited. "It rolls over to her voice message."

Phil turned right at Center Street and ran a red light. He floored the Audi and flew down the road until he reached Signal Street. Halfway down the block he saw Kate's car parked in front of the building.

* * *

Kate heard the clacking of Larissa's heels as she walked across the tile floor in the kitchen. She saw Stan's shadow move toward the kitchen door, so she dropped her head down. *What can I do to warn Brad?* She closed her eyes and felt herself sinking into an ocean of blackness. There was no light, only darkness. She pressed her eyelids together tight. *Don't let go.*

In another minute the bell sounded and the door buzzed as Stan unlocked it remotely. Kate pulled herself out of the abyss and raised her head. From where she was sitting, she couldn't see the door. Movement to her left caught her attention. Larissa Hadecker was standing in the doorway to the kitchen, holding a gun and staring at her.

CHAPTER SEVENTY-FOUR

End Game

A gunshot exploded inside the office at 180 North Signal Street just as Commissioner Blake pulled up in front of the building. He jumped out of his unmarked car and started toward the door as a black Audi screeched to a halt beside him. Phil and Ben leaped out.

"Kathryn's in there!" Phil pointed upstairs as he ran toward the building.

Phil, Ben, and Blake raced into the building. As they flew up the stairs, a second shot split the air. Phil got there first, grabbed the door knob and pushed, but the door was locked.

"Move away from the door," Ben said. He backed up a step and ran at it, ramming it with his shoulder. The door flew open and Ben tumbled into the outer office and fell over Earl Weatherspoon, who sprawled on the floor. Earl's gun skidded across the linoleum.

"Put your hands in the air," Commissioner Blake shouted at Earl. "Now."

Earl sat up and raised his arms. Blake picked up the gun and motioned Earl into the inner room.

Phil ran past them into Stan's office. Stan Palmerton was lying facedown on the floor with a woman kneeling by him. Phil leaped over them to get to the man who was standing in front of a chair where Kathryn was tied up. "Get your hands off her," he yelled at the man and shoved him so hard he fell over on the couch.

298 • KAY DIBIANCA

Phil knelt in front of Kathryn, gently untying the gag.

"Ph ... Ph ..." She sputtered and shook her head.

He removed the straps that bound her to the chair. "Don't talk, honey. You're gonna be okay."

* * *

Commissioner Blake knelt and checked Palmerton's pulse while Larissa Hadecker sobbed quietly. "What happened here?"

Larissa Hadecker looked up at him, her eyes wide, then buried her face in her hands.

Blake pulled his phone out of his pocket and hit an icon. "Simon, bring a crew over to Palmerton's office ASAP. We need an ambulance."

He stood and turned to the man who was recovering from Phil's angry shove. "Lassiter, what are you doing here?"

Brad took a deep breath and exhaled. "Earl and I went to see Reverend Whitefield, and we were all praying for healing and reconciliation when I got a text from Kathryn. I couldn't read it because I had tears in my eyes, so I asked Reverend Whitefield to read it to me. It said to come here right away and not tell anybody. But the reverend said he was sure Kathryn didn't write that text. He was afraid she might be in danger. Earl had a gun in his car, so we came over to make sure she was all right. When they let us in, somebody fired a gun and we hit the floor. Then there was a second shot. By the time we recovered, it was over. I came in here and found Kathryn tied up. That's when you came in."

"She okay?" Blake nodded toward Kathryn.

"I'm ... okay." Kate shook her head again and tried to stand but her legs were water. Phil helped her over to the couch. "Stan ... drugged me. I heard them talking when I came to."

"Stan drugged you?" Blake's voice hit a high note.

Kathryn eased down on the couch and rubbed her eyes. "Stan killed Louis Tinnerman. He thought Tinnerman was Hadecker." She nodded toward Larissa. "She was in on it."

Commissioner Blake stood in front of the couch, staring down at Kate. "Are you saying Stan Palmerton and Larissa Hadecker conspired to murder Al Hadecker, but Palmerton killed the wrong man?"

"When I came to, they were arguing. Stan wanted to kill me because I found out about the watch, and he wanted to get Brad here and kill both of us."

"So who shot Palmerton?"

"She did." Kate pointed to Larissa. "She saved my life."

Sirens sounded close by. Two uniformed police officers arrived followed by a team of medics. Commissioner Blake told the EMTs to take Palmerton to the hospital first.

Blake pointed to two handguns lying on the floor. "Dev, retrieve those firearms as evidence." He turned to Larissa Hadecker, who had stood to make room for the medics. "Mrs. Hadecker, we're going to take you to police headquarters for questioning." He nodded to one of the officers. "Simon will read you your rights. You should contact your lawyer."

CHAPTER SEVENTY-FIVE

Tea Party

Phil opened the front door for Kathryn and Cece when they arrived at Ben's ranch for the commissioner's meeting.

Ben was chatting with Mr. and Mrs. Goldman. Commissioner Blake was standing by the fireplace with Earl Weatherspoon. Rabbi Hart and Reverend Whitefield were examining the books on Ben's shelves. Brad Lassiter and Tommy Abrahams were sitting on the couch munching on sweets. Mattie was replacing platters of food on the coffee table, and there was a large map propped on an easel at the front of the room by the fireplace.

"Well, here are the people we've all been waiting for," the commissioner said. Everyone in the room applauded their entrance.

Cece stepped to the side and curtsied to her sister. "Kathryn's the star of this show. I'm just in a supporting role."

Ben walked to the center of the room. "I want you all to feel at home. Sorry, but we're not serving coffee today." There were guffaws all around. "So grab a cup of tea and some of Mattie's cookies. There should be plenty of seats for everybody."

After the group got settled, Commissioner Blake moved to the front of the fireplace. "I sure am grateful to Ben for offering his beautiful home so we could have this meeting." Everyone clapped.

"All the credit goes to Mattie," Ben said. He pulled her to him and put his arm around her. "She's the one who suggested we have the meeting here, and she did all the preparations." More applause.

"In that case,"—Blake bowed in her direction—"thank you, Mattie. I've never wrapped up a case in a prettier room." He took a bite of his lemon cookie. "Or with better food."

Mattie waved him off and toddled back to the kitchen.

Blake put his right foot on the hearth. "I think you're all going to be interested in what we learned from the infamous watch."

Brad pointed to the map on the easel. "I'm guessing that map shows the movement of the watch the night of the murder."

"Yep. Thanks to Tommy and the folks at Galileo, we got this picture of the Hyde Park area with the red line showing the path the watch took between 8:30 and 9:00."

"But I thought Stan had an alibi for the night of the murder," Phil said.

Blake nodded. "When we checked his alibi with the cleaning staff, they said he was in his office the night of the murder. But when we questioned them again, we found out they only heard him talking on the phone in his office. It was undoubtedly a recording he had planted in advance."

"Smart guy," said Ben.

"A little too smart for his own good," Blake said and pointed to the blue circle at the top of the map. "Here's the starting point."

"That's the cabin we saw," Kate said.

"That's right." Blake tapped the map. "That cabin is owned by the county and is inhabited only in the summer months." He shook his head. "Kathryn, you theorized what happened the night of the murder almost perfectly. Stan met Tinnerman at the cabin and killed him there. Then he loaded the body into the trunk of the Jaguar and drove it around to the ravine." His finger traced the red line around to the bottom of the map.

"But why dump the body there?" Cece asked. "Why not leave it in the car?"

"He wanted the body to be found so that Larissa could inherit the estate. If he had left the body in the car and driven it into the lake, it would have been years before Hadecker was declared dead."

"Ah," Ben said. "Now I get it."

"So he drove the car into the lake here." Blake's finger followed the red line to the edge of Hyde Park Lake. "Then he went across the lake back to the cabin."

"But how did he do that?" Kate asked. "It would have been too cold to swim."

"Right. But Stan had stashed his kayak at the edge of the lake. After he drove the car into the water, he paddled across in his kayak." Blake's finger followed the red line back to the cabin.

Kate slapped the side of her head with the heel of her hand. "Of course. Why didn't I think of that?"

Cece raised her hand slightly. "Was Stan really hired by Al Hadecker to follow his wife?"

Blake put his teacup on the coffee table. "Apparently Al Hadecker did hire Palmerton as a private eye to follow his wife around and report back. Hadecker's lawyer told us he wanted to divorce his wife and could get out of their prenuptial agreement if he could prove infidelity. What Hadecker didn't know was that Stan Palmerton would become enamored with Larissa himself. Soon the two of them were carrying on a passionate affair. According to Larissa, it was Stan's idea to murder Al Hadecker so Larissa would inherit the estate and they would live out their lives in luxury."

"So she took a trip to Europe to be out of the picture?" Phil asked.

"Yes. They planned it all out a couple of months before Hadecker was scheduled to come to Bellevue. Stan Palmerton called the hotel and talked to Tinnerman, thinking it was Hadecker, and told him to come to the cabin Friday night to get the report on Larissa Hadecker. Tinnerman probably thought he was going to learn some dirt on Larissa that he could use to blackmail her, so he went.

"Stan was familiar with police procedures, so he figured he could make it look like a robbery. He knew what kind of car Hadecker drove, but he had never met him in person. When Tinnerman showed up claiming to be Hadecker, he had no reason to doubt it."

"Wow. The irony of it all," Cece said. "Since Louis Tinnerman had already killed Hadecker, Stan and Larissa would have gotten what they wanted without doing anything. But in the end, their greed finished them off."

"You're right, Cece. But they still had an excellent chance of getting the money without anybody suspecting them if it hadn't been for Stan Palmerton's pride."

"Yeah." Phil shook his head. "Stan was the one who said criminals like to take souvenirs from their victims. Tinnerman took the watch from Hadecker, and Palmerton took it from Tinnerman. It's unbelievable that he did the very thing that could get him caught."

"He even changed the registration of the watch to someone named Susan V. Neera," Tommy said. "Get it? Sue-V-Neera."

The entire group groaned.

"Classic case of hubris. Stan thought he had outsmarted everybody." Blake nodded toward Kate. "But he hadn't figured on Kathryn Frasier."

Kate felt her face grow warm with embarrassment. "Stan took the one thing that would incriminate him. I was lucky to find it."

"It wasn't luck, Kathryn." Rabbi Hart balanced his teacup on his lap. "It was your commitment to doing the right thing."

"And your determination," added Reverend Whitefield. "That same 'never give up' attitude that gets you through the long races got you to the end of this one."

Phil took her hand. "And it almost got you killed."

"What I want to know is what happened in Stan's office the day he was shot." Earl Weatherspoon turned to look at Ben. "The day Ben flattened me when he broke down the door."

CHAPTER SEVENTY-SIX

What Happened

"**S**orry about that." Ben shrugged and grinned at Earl. "But what were you doing there?"

Brad Lassiter spoke up. "Earl and I were over at Reverend Whitefield's rectory when I got a text message from Kathryn. At least it was from her phone. It's still here on my phone. It says, 'I need u NOW. Found clue. Come to Stan's office. ALONE. Tell no one.' Reverend Whitefield told me Kathryn definitely didn't write that text message."

"How could you know that?" The commissioner turned to Whitefield.

"Because the message didn't have the word 'you' spelled out. It only had the letter 'u.' I've known Kathryn all her life and I remember her telling me she didn't like the way the English language was abbreviated in texts. When I told that to Brad and Earl, they both immediately guessed there was something wrong, so they took off while I called the police."

Brad spoke up. "Earl carries a gun in his car, and he got it out when we went upstairs."

"So who shot Stan Palmerton?" Tommy asked.

"Larissa did," Kate said. "I was watching the whole thing, but I couldn't move and couldn't warn Brad. It turns out I didn't have to. Larissa had gotten the stolen gun out of the kitchen like Stan told her to. When Brad rang the bell at the office door, Stan remotely unlocked it and was aiming at the door when Larissa

308 • KAY DIBIANCA

shot him. She did it to save Brad and me. Then Larissa threw her gun down and it went off. That was the second shot. It's a good thing that bullet didn't hit anybody." Kate looked up at Phil. "We were all fooled by Stan."

"Each of us has a good side and a bad side." Rabbi Hart shook his head and pulled on his beard. "When we allow ourselves to get caught up in our own ambitions, even good people can do terrible things."

"Rabbi Hart and I had a very interesting visit with Stan in the hospital yesterday," Reverend Whitefield said.

The entire group turned to focus on the reverend. "What did he say?" Harry asked.

"Stan asked us to convey his deep regret for his actions and asks you all for forgiveness. Especially you, Kathryn. He knew Brad was innocent, and he kept trying to convince the police it was a robbery and at the same time tried to scare Kathryn into giving it up."

"Do you believe he was sincere?" Phil asked.

"One can never know what's in someone else's heart," the rabbi responded. "But Stan said something that made me believe he is truly repentant." There was silence in the room until the rabbi continued. "He said it was a relief to have it over, and he said his mother used to quote a verse from Proverbs. 'Whoever digs a pit will fall into it, and a stone will come back on him who starts it rolling.' He said he's ashamed, but he's willing to face the consequences of his actions."

"How about Larissa? Let's don't forget her conscience saved my life and Brad's." Kate turned to the commissioner. "I hope it will count in her favor when she goes to trial."

"It's hard to say what will happen to her, but she's cooperating with the authorities. She won't get any of her husband's estate, but she'll probably serve a minimum sentence."

The room fell quiet again, then Cece spoke up. "What about Jeremy Dodd?"

"We did some checking on him too," the commissioner said. "We got an anonymous tip he might have accepted money from Hadecker in exchange for having his candidate endorse the housing development."

Kathryn and Cece exchanged a glance. "Did you find anything?" Cece asked innocently.

"We looked into Jeremy's bank account records and found he had made a few large deposits of cash in the past few months. He's being questioned now, and I understand Representative Hodges has fired him from the campaign."

"Good riddance," Cece announced.

"And Mike Strickland? What about him?" Phil asked.

"I don't know much about him except the Barringer family has agreed to his offer to buy half their acreage. If Jeremy's scandal shuts down the Hodges campaign, Mike Strickland will be free to start his farm. I imagine it will be a far cry from the political arena."

Ben snorted. "I'll sell him a couple of jack—I mean donkeys. That should be an excellent reminder of times past."

EPILOGUE

Cece stood in front of the bathroom mirror, brushing her hair. "So what's all this about a surprise?" she called to Kathryn.

Kathryn peeked around the door. "Don't ask me. Phil said to bring you out to the ranch around ten-thirty this morning. He said Ben has a surprise for you."

"Do you know what it is?"

Kathryn ducked out of the room and called back over her shoulder, "Um. Hey, do you know where my keys are? I seem to have misplaced them."

Cece made a face at herself in the mirror. "That's a definite yes." She took the cowboy hat off the counter, removed the tag, and adjusted it on her head.

Kate returned and leaned against the doorframe. "Well, well. What's this? Cece Goldman wearing a cowboy hat?"

Cece turned to face her sister. "What do you think?"

"You look adorable." Kate stood and positioned her fingers as if she were framing a picture. "The baby blue matches your eyes."

"You're just being nice."

"No! It's perfect for you. And you look so cute in your jeans and sweatshirt."

Cece turned back to the mirror and adjusted the hat, primping her hair as she went along. "I've played a lot of roles in my acting career. Let's see what kind of cowboy I can be." She stuck her thumbs in the waistband of her jeans and posed. "Come on, pardner. Let's go see this surprise."

* * *

"This is about the most beautiful day I've seen since we came to Bellevue." Cece leaned back in the passenger seat of Kate's car as they rode down the quiet lane to Ben's ranch.

As they came to the end of the long driveway and parked in the open area, she could see the Weatherspoons standing next to the corral across from the house.

Phil jogged over to the car and opened the door for Cece. "Good morning, ladies." He gave her his hand. "Glad you could make it."

"Me too." Cece looked at Phil skeptically. What was all this about? Where was Ben?

Kate walked around the car, put her arm around Phil's waist, and smiled up into his face.

"This way," Phil said. "There are some folks over here you might want to see."

Mattie intercepted them as they walked toward the corral. She was wearing her new shawl and carrying a tray of cookies. "Try these butterscotch delights," she said. "They'll get your day started right."

Cece and Kate each grabbed one of the cookies and gave Mattie a big hug. "You're the best," Kate proclaimed and took a bite of cookie.

As they walked toward the corral, Thelma and Earl Weatherspoon met them halfway. "Kathryn, Cece," Thelma said. "I'm so glad you're here. You're not going to believe this." Thelma pointed toward the corral where Brad was leading a small pony around with Sara sitting atop.

Brad walked the pony to the fence while Sara waved and shouted, "Kathryn, Cece, look. I'm riding a horse!"

Kate and Cece leaned against the corral fence and clapped their hands. "Sara! Look at you!" Cece called out while Kate snapped a picture.

Sara's words tumbled out in a deluge. "Ben told me I'm going to be a good rider, and he gave me a hat and everything." She tugged at the red cowboy hat. "He told me I can come out and ride Sport any time I want to." She leaned down and hugged the pony. "He's my most favorite horse in the whole world."

Brad tipped his baseball cap. "I never thought we'd end up here today with Sara riding a pony and declaring it's the best day of her life. I have a lot to thank you two for."

As Brad led the pony back to the middle of the corral, Cece slipped her arm around Kate's waist. "I don't know if you saved the whole world, sister, but you saved the future for one little girl." She swallowed hard. "Seeing Sara on top of that pony is about the best surprise you could have given me."

"Oh, that's not the surprise." Kathryn grinned and glanced at Phil. "Should we tell her?"

"Oh yeah. This one's gonna knock your socks off."

Cece raised her eyebrows. "What?"

"It's behind the barn in the big corral. Why don't you mosey on around there?"

Cece stood still, trying to read the expressions of delight she saw on her sister's face. "Aren't you coming with me?"

"We'll be around in a minute."

Cece left their sides and walked toward the barn. As she rounded the corner, she saw Ben standing at the fence of the large corral with his foot on the lowest rail talking on his phone. He put the phone in his pocket, turned around, and walked toward her.

He stopped several feet away. "Hey there."

"Hi." Her heart thumped hard.

"Hat looks good on you," he said.

"Thanks. I decided to go Western." She pulled at the brim.

He moved closer. "The boots add a nice touch too."

"Yeah." She looked down at her brand-new cowboy boots. "You never know when a horse might wander by and step on your foot."

314 • KAY DIBIANCA

He took another step forward. "So, have you made a decision about Atlanta yet?"

"Yes."

"You're going?" A shadow moved across his face.

"No." Something caught in her throat and she hiccuped.

The crinkles around Ben's eyes deepened. "I thought you said it was your dream. Why aren't you going?"

Cece took a step toward him. "Well, there're things I need to take care of here."

"Like what?"

"My parents have just moved to Bellevue. I need to be here to help them get settled." She moved closer.

"Anything else?" He pushed his Stetson back on his head.

"I only met my sister a few months ago. It doesn't make much sense to leave now."

He put his hands on his hips, fingers spread out, the way she'd seen him do so many times before. "Anything else?"

She gestured toward the corral. "Well, now that I have the outfit, I may as well take a few more riding lessons." She stepped right up to him and looked up into his face. "And I'd like to get reacquainted with that owl."

The grin that had started in his eyes spread over his face. His voice was low and soft. "Maybe I can help with that." He pulled her to him and kissed her. It was a solid kiss, one you could hang your life on. She tasted butterscotch in his mouth and a hint of dust. He must have been out here all morning helping Sara and teaching his riding students. Like her father said, this was a good man.

She held tight to him and felt her body soften as she leaned into his powerful embrace. "I've missed you, Ben."

He released her and took a step back. "Here. I have something for you." He reached in his shirt pocket, took out a small box, and handed it to her.

Cece removed the top. Inside was a gold charm bracelet with a collection of small owl charms. Each owl had eyes made of jewels.

"A whole herd of owls," she murmured as he fastened it on her wrist. She held her hand up and the charms danced and shone in the sunlight. "This is the prettiest bracelet I've ever seen," she said. "Thank you. It's the best surprise ever."

"Oh. that's not the surprise." He took her hand and led her to the fence.

"This is turning out to be the most unsurprising day of my life. If Sara's not the surprise and this bracelet isn't the surprise, then what is?"

"That." He pointed to the far side of the corral where two people were sitting in a buggy behind a dark bay horse. Ben took his hat off and waved to them. The buggy moved forward.

Cece looked carefully. They must be the students he told her about. There was something familiar about them. They both wore red plaid shirts, blue jeans, and white cowboy hats. As the buggy came closer, Cece felt her eyes almost bug out of her head. She climbed onto the lowest slat in the fence to look over. "Mom? Dad?"

Harry pulled the horse up in front of her. "Whoa there, Baby."

"Oh, Cece!" Sylvia's voice embraced her daughter in its delight. "Isn't it wonderful? Ben is teaching your father how to drive a buggy. And Harry is so good at it!" She turned and patted her husband's arm. Harry simply waved to Cece with the buggy whip. Sylvia turned back. "Ben says he's a natural. It's a whole new world for us to explore, and it's more fun than we've ever had."

Cece looked at Ben. "Who are these people? And what have you done with my parents?"

Ben laughed and pulled her closer to him.

Harry poised the whip. "Should I take her around again, Ben?"

316 • KAY DIBIANCA

"Yep. You're on a roll. Keep it going."

Sylvia sang out over her shoulder, "Talk to Ben, Cece. He has wonderful horses. He can teach you things."

Harry made little kissy sounds and flicked the whip above the horse's flank. "Get on, now, Baby." The horse broke into a smart trot, and they began another circle.

"I don't believe this." Cece looked at Ben.

He took her hand. "Come with me, Butterscotch. Let's see if we can find a horse for you." He pulled her toward the barn.

As they got to the door of the barn, he scooped her up in his arms and carried her over the threshold. "Hang on tight, Cece Goldman. Like your mother said, I can teach you things."

"And this heart doth eagerly desire to learn."

Ben stopped. "I don't recognize that. Was it Shakespeare?"

She nestled against him. "No. That was Cece Goldman."

THE END

ABOUT THE AUTHOR

I'm glad to have had the time and opportunity to write *Dead Man's Watch*, and I'm grateful to you, dear reader, for having read it. If you liked it, you may enjoy the first book in the Watch series, *The Watch on the Fencepost*, and it would be especially helpful if you would leave a review on Amazon, Goodreads, or one of the other book sites.

If you want to know a little more about me, here's a short bio: I've had a long and lovely life. I've ridden horses, run marathons, flown airplanes, and written books. My background in computer science provided me with a satisfying career in software development.

I've been blessed with a long marriage to a good man with whom I've shared these interests, and together we raised a wonderful son. Frank and I are deeply thankful for the blessings God has bestowed on our family.

One of my great pleasures in life is problem-solving, and I think that's why I enjoy writing mysteries. Everybody loves a good whodunit, and I like creating a puzzle for readers to solve.

And then there's running. You can often find me at a track, on the treadmill, or at a park near our home. The mantra *Never Give Up* that Kathryn repeats in the running scenes of my books is dear to me.

I'd love to hear from you. You can connect with me on my website at:

kaydibianca.com

or through one of the social media links at the end of this page.

In the meantime, stay safe, enjoy life, and read good books.

Facebook: https://www.facebook.com/authorkaydibianca
Twitter: https://twitter.com/Kdibianca
Instagram: https://www.instagram.com/kdibianca/